CONFESSION

BOOK 1 IN THE DETECTIVE ERIKA KELEMEN SERIES

STEVE DICKINSON

BRIGHTER FUTURES
PUBLISHING

BRIGHTER FUTURES PUBLISHING

Published by Brighter Futures Publishing Ltd.,

Queensgate House, 23 North Park Road, Harrogate, United Kingdom, HG1 5PD

BrighterFuturesPublishing.com

CONTENTS

FOREWORD

In Hungary, names of people are given in what the British and Americans would term as reverse order: Kelemen Erika, rather than Erika Kelemen. In the early days of working with my Hungarian colleagues in Budapest, I did not realise this. Their business cards were written in western order and we tended to use first names only in conversation. Later on they explained it was done that way for the benefit of the head-office and other westerners they dealt with.

For the convenience of most of my readers, I have adopted the western style for the names of characters and, where appropriate, place names. To my Hungarian readers and friends, I hope it doesn't spoil your comprehension and enjoyment too much.

Image Credit: Canva

CHAPTER ONE

HUNGARY, MAY 2020

I f Erika Kelemen had known she would be coming to the police canteen this morning, she may have chosen a more striking outfit. Something that said: here I am and I don't fucking care. As it was, she was wearing a very ordinary pale blue checked jacket, black trousers and a white cotton blouse. She scowled at her reflection in the mirrored glass behind the display counters, which highlighted how short she looked alongside tall, slim Eszter Szabó, the blonde girl in her mid-twenties who wore her hair in a ponytail, a charcoal-grey trouser suit and not one scrap of make-up.

It had taken Erika by surprise when Eszter had asked if the two of them could come here for a private chat. Eszter had appeared at work with bags under her eyes, and Erika, being concerned that something was seriously amiss had agreed to the request, even though she was uneasy about the venue.

Waiting alongside Eszter in the queue for coffee, Erika's green-grey eyes flicked from side to side, always on the lookout. She adjusted her face mask and patted her shoulder-length auburn hair into place.

Ever since Erika's sudden and painful departure from Homicide in 2015, she had tried to minimise her contact with the dicks from the tenth floor. Consequently, that meant steering clear of places where they were known to congregate. She wanted to put the whole sorry episode behind her, and nowadays was proud to head a small group of talented women which formed part of the Financial Criminal Investigation Division CID team, based on the second floor. Her seniority meant they had given her the title of departmental supervisor, but Eszter and at least two other members of her team could do their jobs blindfolded. Erika gave them the freedom to shine. Perhaps they had grouped the women together for a reason.

The Police Headquarters on Teve Street marks the intersection of two of Budapest's main arteries, Váci Street and Róbert Károly Avenue. Known to the locals as Police Palace, its shining cylindrical tower of sapphire-blue glass rises twenty-storeys high and is crowned with a communications mast half as tall as the building itself. The ground floor canteen is light and airy, with ceiling to floor windows. Erika led the way to a table by one of the windows. She removed her face mask and pouted her matt-red lips. *Not too bad for a woman approaching her fiftieth birthday.* It was a milestone she was dreading and was kept a closely guarded secret, known only to herself and her lover Marcel. No one at work had a clue, and that was precisely the way she would keep it.

They sat. Erika steepled her fingers and waited.

Eszter cleared her throat. "I tested positive. I wanted you to be the first to know."

Erika's jaw dropped. "Then what the fuck are you doing here? You should go straight home and isolate for ten days."

From across the table came an ear to ear grin. Eszter's eyes sparkled. "I don't have Covid. I'm pregnant."

Her smile was infectious and Erika beamed in return. She reached out and placed her right hand on top of Eszter's, giving it a squeeze. "Congratulations, to you both."

"Ferenc is over the moon, too. We just moved into our new apartment. The timing couldn't be better."

"I couldn't be more thrilled."

Eszter looked up, beyond Erika. Her smile evaporated.

Something had caught her attention, but what? Erika's nose twitched. She was picking up an odour at the polar-opposite end of the scale from a good Burgundy; she inhaled the all-too-familiar cheap cologne with undertones of stale sweat.

From behind her back, a nasal voice said, "Well, well, Kelemen. I haven't seen you down here for a very long time."

A rising tide of nausea welled up inside her. After all this time it just had to be him, didn't it? She swivelled in her seat and looked him up and down disdainfully. In five years he had aged ten; and in a crumpled brown suit, creased yellow shirt, with a stained tie at half-mast, he looked as bad as he smelt.

Her throat felt as rough and dry as sandpaper. "What do you want, Rigo?"

He sneered and had the audacity to move a step closer. When he opened his mouth to speak, she caught the whiff of his halitosis. But before he could utter a word, his phone rang. He pulled it from his frayed trouser pocket and stepped back.

Despite this, Erika heard a raised voice at the other end of the call. A familiar voice, barking out orders.

Rigo's face blanched. "Yes, Commander Rácz. I'm on my way." He pocketed his phone and the sneer returned. "We must do this again soon," he said before making his way towards the exit on the far side of the canteen, looking more like a tramp than a policeman.

Erika waited until he was out of sight before dabbing her brow with a serviette.

Eszter said, "I've seen that creep around the place from time to time. He's no friend of yours, is he?"

Relieved the cloud had passed, Erika said, "That's one way of putting it. Still, if it wasn't for him, I would never have joined the FCI and found myself working with you and our amazing team."

Eszter was no fool and furthermore, had recently passed her detective's exams. She raised her eyebrow, inviting a fuller explanation.

Erika had never been one to pour her heart out, certainly not to a junior colleague. Even though her departure from homicide was a matter of record, she had never discussed the details of the events with those she now worked with. It was all in the past, and she had no desire to provide them with ammunition to gossip behind her back. Nevertheless, Eszter had confided in her this morning, and she felt she owed her at least a partial explanation of what had just taken place. Anyway, Rigo's version of today's encounter would no doubt soon be doing the rounds of Police Palace. Even if Erika stayed clear of the canteen for another five years, Rigo would surely prey on Eszter the next time they crossed paths. It was only fair to forewarn her.

Erika sipped her coffee and leaned forward, elbows on the table, eyes locked on Eszter's. She whispered, "You know I used to work in Homicide?"

It was common knowledge. Eszter nodded.

Erika continued, "I had never expected to be working there. But eleven years ago there was pressure from above to employ more women in high-profile, frontline roles. I'd been working behind the scenes for almost twenty years in the National Economic Crime Unit, although I did pass my detective exams and got involved in some serious investigations. Then my chief told me to apply for a detective's role that was coming up in Homicide. I was more amazed than anyone when I got the job."

She placed her mug on the table and toyed with it. "Rigo was my partner in the Murder Squad for six years. He liked to tell everyone I worked under him." She shivered at the thought. "Five years ago, I filed a formal complaint against him, for sexual harassment. The idiot pulled his cock out in an elevator full of people. The thing was, all the others were his cronies. He did it to humiliate me in front of them. When I filed the complaint, not one of them remembered seeing anything. Commander Rácz, tried to hush things up too. He told me the instruction had come from the top. I either withdrew my complaint, or I was out."

"That's awful," said Eszter. "Do you really think the order came from the top floor?"

Erika's voice descended to an almost inaudible level. "Rigo's brother-in-law was the Deputy High Commissioner." She clenched her right fist and cracked her knuckles. "But don't worry. As they say, revenge is a dish best served cold."

CHAPTER TWO

Axel Rácz edged his black Audi A6 through the traffic, crossed the Chain Bridge onto the Buda side, and headed south on Lánchíd Street. The piercing wail of the two-tone siren wasn't helping with the stress headache that had been building all morning. During the fifteen years he had been head of the homicide department, it had never once been this close to breaking point. His scarce resources had been stretched to the limit, and now every new murder investigation created a major staffing problem for him.

It was almost midday when he parked alongside other police and emergency vehicles on Bertalan Lajos Street, before slipping into a pair of overalls. He weighed one hundred and thirty kilos and stood almost two metres tall. His SOCO overalls were the largest in the force, yet they were still tight.

A uniformed police officer on sentry duty outside the apartment lifted the crime scene tape and saluted. "Commander Rácz, sir!"

Two hours earlier, he had ordered one of his few remaining detectives to come to the scene and prepare a status report. He needed answers and he needed them now. "Where's Detective Rigo?"

"Inside, sir."

He nodded before pulling on a facemask, latex gloves and overshoes.

The place smelt of old books and disinfectant. In the living room, he caught sight of the oldest detective in his dwindling squad, idly leaning against a wall and watching the SOCO team at work. Perhaps the recent organisational changes meant he would finally be allowed to offload him, when the present crisis was over.

When Rigo realised he was being watched, he straightened himself and mumbled an apology.

Rácz was impatient and snapped back. "What's the situation?"

"Klára Menges. Eighty-eight-year-old spinster. Lived alone. Discovered by her cleaner, Hanna Balogh, at nine-thirty this morning. She's in the kitchen, if you want a word."

Rácz heard wailing. "Is that her?"

Rigo nodded.

Rácz grimaced. He would get to her in due course. "And the victim?"

Rigo gestured to an open door on the other side of the room. "In there."

The walls of the small bedroom were decorated with flock wallpaper. The ceiling had browned with tobacco staining. On the floor was a worn Persian rug. The room seemed claustrophobic and was stuffed full of heavy mahogany furniture. Upon the large sleigh bed lay the naked body of an old woman. She was laying face down, with her head to one side. Her cheek rested in a pool of vomit. She was small, frail, and had been badly mutilated.

Leaning over the body was the wiry figure of the forensic pathologist, Professor József Baldi. He was dressed from head to toe in SOCO gear, but was instantly recognisable to Rácz. The two of them went back many years and had worked together on hundreds of homicides.

Rácz said, "What do we have here?"

For a moment, Baldi's gaze was averted to the new person in the room. Above his face mask, his eyebrows raised in unison. "My word, Axel. It's rare we see you in the field these days."

"Needs must. Short staffed, and a new Deputy High Commissioner who likes senior officers to be more hands on."

Baldi said, "We are also down to the bare bones – no pun intended. As you can see, the victim is an elderly female. Her clothes are in situ at the end of the bed. There are no obvious signs of a struggle. Her neck, shoulders, back and legs are covered by multiple wounds. The murderer probably used a sharp, finely pointed instrument. These wounds are unlikely to have caused the death and may even have happened post-mortem. My theory is, she was poisoned before these wounds were inflicted. We shall have to wait for the blood tests to confirm the time of death, but my initial observations lead me to believe the victim has been dead for approximately eighteen hours."

"So that would mean she died somewhere around six o'clock yesterday afternoon."

"Correct."

Rácz glanced at his phone. Fourteen message alerts! There was no time to waste, but he wanted to question the cleaner before he left the scene. "Send me your report. Shall we say, by six this evening?"

Rácz turned away, not waiting for a response. He made his way to the kitchen, where he found a stout, middle-aged woman with bottle-blonde hair, seated on a wooden chair and chattering to a young female police officer.

The woman's eyes were red and she dabbed them with a tissue. "I need to make a living, but I still fear for many of my older clients. They've been shielding, and some won't let me back into their homes. Not as though Klára was a problem. I phoned her a week ago, on the thirteenth, and told her I'd be here this morning. She told me her heart complaint had been playing up, and was having trouble getting hold of her medication. I called her again, yesterday lunchtime to ask if she needed me to pick anything up for her. She said she had everything she needed and was looking forward to being cleansed again."

Mrs Balogh, who wore no face mask, blew her nose into a tissue, loudly and extensively.

The wave of COVID-19 that had spread so viciously throughout his department made Rácz consciously paranoid. He had seen others of his age and heavy build taken down by the virus, each ending up in intensive care. Mrs Balogh sneezed again, this time not into a tissue. It was time to delegate.

"Rigo, take Mrs Balogh's statement, check through the victim's belongings and keep me posted. I have other urgent matters to attend to."

He ignored the belligerent mutterings from behind him, and was quickly out the door.

The body bag was carried out on a stretcher, down four flights of stairs to the waiting ambulance. Waiting on the pavement was the media, in the form of a TV crew and several reporters and photographers. Alongside them were local residents. During the last three months they had witnessed several elderly neighbours carried out, normally en route to the hospital. Word spread quickly, that someone had murdered Klára Menges in her own bed. Sexual assault and robbery stories were quickly doing the rounds. Someone who claimed to know Klára's sister said this was more than likely a revenge killing.

Back in the apartment, even after several hours of painstaking work, the only fingerprints and footprints found belonged either to the victim or to her cleaner. SOCO concluded, whoever had killed Klára wore gloves and overshoes, and had carefully wiped away their presence from the bedroom. Mrs Balogh had seemingly swept and mopped away anything the killer had left behind in the other rooms. There were no signs of forced entry. This investigation was going to take longer than previously expected.

The Honvéd kórház — the Hungarian Defence Forces Military Hospital – sprawls along Róbert Károly Avenue, and lying in its bowels is the morgue. Professor Baldi entered the examination room at 4.00 p.m., wearing a green mortuary gown, latex gloves, black-rubber apron and black wellington boots. Klára Menges' body bag lay on the massive marble slab of Autopsy Table One. His burly assistant, Vilmos, was already checking the tools.

Baldi picked up his clipboard.

"Let's make a start. Commander Rácz wants us to perform miracles yet again."

Vilmos unzipped the bag and slid it away. He checked the label tied around the foot. The small, wrinkled corpse gazed blindly at the overhead banks of fluorescent tubes.

Time pressures imposed by Rácz had forced Baldi to conduct only the most limited inspection at the crime scene. But now, under the lights, the full extent of her mutilation became obvious. Fine rivulets of blood had crisscrossed and scabbed over the body from head to toe.

He spoke into an ear mounted microphone. "There are several hundred small wounds; each penetrating the cutaneous surface by only a few millimetres. It appears similar to the work of a tattooist, yet there appears to be no discernible pattern."

Under his direction, Vilmos swabbed some of the dried blood and dropped the sample into an evidence bag.

Baldi spread the discarded clothes on the adjacent table. He examined the calf-length, grey woollen skirt. On the front of it was a small red stain. There was also a patch pocket, from which something poked out. Using tweezers, he extracted a laminated card, measuring approximately ten centimetres high and five centimetres wide. He held it aloft with the tweezers and Vilmos snapped a photograph: an iconic image of Jesus and the Sacred Heart.

"We'll check for prints. Lights, please," said Baldi. He used ultraviolet to examine the card and the body, before using a magnifying glass to focus on the hem of the victim's skirt. "There are some small fibres here."

Vilmos used tweezers and bagged the fibres.

With the lights up again, Baldi examined Klára's hands. "No signs of ligatures or cuffs around the wrists, and no signs of blood or skin residues under the fingernails. Nothing to suggest a struggle or any resistance."

The victim's stone grey hair was worn in a tight bun, which looked remarkably tidy, given the circumstances. Baldi plucked a hair and placed it into a fresh bag. He used separate bags for fingernail clippings and nasal swabs.

Vilmos pulled out a measuring tape and ran it the full length of the body.

"One hundred and fifty-seven centimetres," he called out.

He read from the weighing scale readout. "Fifty-one kilograms."

Baldi examined the victim's genital area with his magnifying glass. There were no external signs of sexual assault, but to be certain, he took internal swabs. It pained him to think this poor woman had been the same age as his own mother. His stomach churned when he imagined the horrific events during her last moments. It was almost too much to bear; even for someone who had seen so much death and depravity over the years.

The public reception area on the ground floor of Police Palace in Teve Street was buzzing. It was early Wednesday evening, but for the tall, uniformed duty officer at the desk, this looked and felt like a Saturday night. There were no signs of social distancing, and few face masks.

The officer raised himself to his full height and looked across the boisterous crowd, estimating it to be over fifty strong. Hardly able to hear himself think, he slammed his fist on the desk and called for silence. It had the desired effect for a moment, until the raucous clamour for attention resumed. He sank back into his seat, head in hands. After two months of lockdown, people were back on the streets in force. He was in for a busy night.

Péter Rigo had missed his lunch, and his stomach growled. After an afternoon of taking statements from the cleaner, and some of the neighbours, he peeled off his grubby overalls and flung them onto the floor.

"We've pulled together the woman's belongings," said one of the SOCO team, handing him a box.

Rigo yawned. "Anything interesting?"

Her purse is in there, with over forty thousand forint in cash, plus credit cards. There are some gold and silver necklaces from the bedroom. Her mobile phone is there too, and an address book. It doesn't look like robbery was the motive."

Rigo browsed through the bags, but saw nothing to excite him. "I'll drop them off at Teve Street. One of the girls can go through them in the morning. You going to be here much longer?"

"Just a few more things to do. Will you be in charge of this one, Pete?"

He shrugged. "Knowing Rácz, he'll probably throw the file in my direction, when something more interesting comes his way."

Ever since the lockdown forced tourists to stay at home, river traffic had been much quieter. Cruise ships and tourist boats no longer ploughed along the Danube. And for the last eight weeks, road traffic had also reduced by ninety percent. Today, however, the streets looked busier. Looking from his tenth-floor office, Axel Rácz felt cocooned from the city. Down below, where the people looked like scuttling ants, he knew the criminal fraternity continued to wreak havoc.

From the statistics on his screen, it was clear. Homicide was the hardest hit of all the departments in the Criminal Investigation Division. Yet, in this morning's weekly meeting, the new Deputy High Commissioner had urged all departmental heads to be flexible and solution-oriented, emphasising there would be no excuses for poor performance. That had been followed up by an email, containing a few 'helpful suggestions.'

Rácz sat at his desk in shirtsleeves, his navy blue suit jacket hanging on the coat stand in the corner of his office. Despite the air-conditioning, the back of his shirt was damp. His head was still pounding. He swallowed some pills and bellowed for his assistant.

"Dora!"

He'd trained his gatekeeper, and now she was nearing the level he expected and needed. Dora was efficient, polite and always well turned out in a twin-set and pearls way. She had hazel eyes and short brown hair, cut in a bob. In her forties, married with no children. She knocked before entering and sat, legs crossed, notepad and pen poised.

He jabbed his finger at the email on the screen.

"We need to fill the gaps until the rest of the team is fit for active duty. I need a file from Human Resources."

"Will tomorrow morning do, sir? My husband was wondering if I could be home early this evening."

Rácz raised his left eyebrow. "For how many years have you worked for me?"

She blushed. "Eleven, sir. I'll get straight onto it."

Even after Rigo's departure, the SOCO team continued their inspection of the apartment. By late afternoon they had revealed little in the way of evidence. Frustratingly, the sharp instrument used to inflict the myriad wounds on Klára Menges' body remained elusive. One of the floorboards was discovered to be loose and two of the team heaved aside a heavy sofa and removed a Persian rug, while another prised away a section of the loose board. There, in a void, they found a small metal box. The box was found to be unlocked, and its contents quickly examined by the senior officer.

"Seems like a bundle of old letters," he said.

Rácz groaned. The intercom crackled and broke his train of thought. He was in the middle of writing his departmental report.

It was a task he loathed, but knew he must finish before he could head home to the wedding anniversary dinner his wife was preparing.

"What is it?"

"Sir, it's SOCO on line one. You asked them to contact you directly, with any developments concerning the Klára Menges case."

He jabbed a button.

"Commander, apologies for the interruption. We gave Detective Rigo the victim's belongings before he left for the evening, but we've also found some letters which could be of interest."

Rácz sighed, louder than he thought. He knew this was not the level of detail he should concern himself with. *There must be someone I can delegate this to. But to whom?*

He growled, "Right. Bring them here."

The blood and urine samples had already been sent to the toxicology laboratory, with instructions to fast track the tests.

"Pass her skirt, Vilmos," Baldi said.

The assistant picked up the grey woollen skirt and handed it to the professor.

Baldi took a magnifying glass and studied the stain soaked into the weave. He held the knitwear to his nose.

"An interesting bouquet. Call the lab again. I need those bloods back within the hour."

The diamond-white, Hungarian made Audi A3 with RENDŐRSÉG emblazoned on its doors and bonnet roared along Dob Street, the narrow, one-way road that cuts through

Budapest's Jewish quarter. With the city already easing into its second phase of COVID-19 defence, some shops and businesses could officially open. But with bars, restaurants and clubs still closed, and no foreign tourists and marauding stag parties allowed, life on Dob Street was much quieter than normal.

Not for long.

Flashing blue lights and a piercing siren wail echoed off the tall, narrow buildings. Everyone up ahead dived onto the pavements and wondered what the hell the emergency was all about.

Erika felt pride in the dedication of her team and trusted them. Unlike the murder squad, there were no overt office politics. She wouldn't allow it, and her colleagues seemed to thrive. She picked up her handbag and slung her pale blue jacket over her arm.

"I'll see you girls tomorrow."

"Before you go, boss, have you seen this?" Eszter leaned back in her seat and pointed at her screen.

Erika pulled her half-moon spectacles from her bag, perched them on her nose, and moved closer. It was a Hungarian daily news website, and she read the article aloud, *'The Hungarian parliament has rejected the ratification of a treaty to combat violence against women, which the Council of Europe had spearheaded. The Istanbul Convention Treaty was the world's first binding instrument to prevent and combat violence against women, from marital rape to female genital mutilation. Yet, the Hungarian parliament, which has one of the lowest proportions of female members in Europe, has stalled on ratifying it.'*

Erika yelled at the screen, "Fucking morons! What kind of message does that send out to the victims, never mind to the perpetrators? Is this country still in the Dark Ages?"

One of Marcel's favourite dishes was chilli con carne: easy to prepare and always with a satisfactory outcome. He added the red kidney beans and green peppers before sliding the casserole dish back into the oven.

He poured a glass of red wine and smiled when he read Erika's message to say she was on her way home. How his life had changed since moving in with her in February. For most of the three months that had followed, the country had been in lockdown. It had forced him to run his accountancy business on his laptop from her apartment. He insisted on contributing to the rent and also did most of the cooking and housework while Erika was at work.

The truth was, he was happier now than he'd been in a long time. Who would have seen that coming? After cancer had taken Mia, his life had fallen apart. His business crumbled, and the bank called in the personal guarantee on their house. It had taken two long years to rebuild his client base and to make ends meet while living in a rented studio flat on the Pest side of the river.

Just before Christmas, some well-meaning friends had invited him to dinner. It was the first invitation he'd accepted, and he found his hosts had strategically positioned him next to a woman called Erika. From the very beginning, he had almost blown his chances by making some asinine joke about the police. He remembered seeing Erika raise her dark brown eyebrows and tilt her impish face with the exasperated look of a teacher to a naughty child. Fortunately, from that point on, things had improved. They had a lot in common, and he had been amazed to find out she too had an accountancy degree. Hers had been earned in London, where she had lived with an aunt in the early nineties. She now worked for something called the Financial Criminal Investigation Division, where she investigated a wide range of white-collar crimes, including fraud, embezzlement, Ponzi schemes, money counterfeiting and insider trading. It was all work he could easily relate to and found fascinating. She also knew a lot about wine tasting and had a good nose for it. By the end of the evening, after drinking more alcohol than he normally consumed in a month, he had asked for her number. Somewhere he still had that business card.

At just after seven, he heard her key in the lock.

"Hey, gorgeous, come here." He threw his arms around her.

They kissed passionately. It was more than a minute before they drew breath.

She sighed contentedly. "I need a shower before dinner, love. It's been one of those days."

Every day in Erika's life seemed to be *one of those days.*

While she was showering, Marcel lit the scented candles, played soft music, and opened another bottle of wine. He was seriously hooked on this formidable pocket rocket of a policewoman, with her unruly, shoulder-length auburn hair, her cheeky smile and twinkling green-grey eyes. Eyes that could drill deep and draw him out of himself.

Rácz looked over the final draft of his report.

Dora knocked and hovered. "The file you asked for. And something SOCO dropped off from the Klára Menges scene. Some letters. I logged them into the evidence room but brought them for you to see."

"Just leave them there," he said, hardly raising his eyes from the text.

"Will there be anything else?"

"No. You go. Have a good evening, with your husband."

"You too, sir. Happy anniversary to you and Mrs Rácz."

He looked up and raised his eyebrows. His phone chirped. He waved her away and answered the call. "Is there a problem?"

"Axel, you need to come back to the morgue. There's something you should see." The pathologist sounded anxious.

Rácz looked at his watch. He reckoned he could meet Baldi and still be home by eight. On his way out, he slipped the file from HR into his briefcase.

On his way to the morgue, Rácz called his wife, Lili. She was far from happy that he would be home late for their wedding anniversary dinner. By the time he arrived, his blood pressure was soaring and he felt a sharp pain in his chest, which he put down to indigestion.

"You seem out of breath, old man," said Baldi, puffing on a cigar in the otherwise deserted corridor.

"You wanted to see me?" Rácz said flatly.

"Come this way." He stubbed out his smoke in an ashtray and led the way back into the examination room where Klára Menges' naked corpse remained uncovered on the slab.

Previously, Rácz had seen only her rear-view. The sight of her now, face up, her entire body perforated with hundreds of tiny stab wounds, made him nauseous. He covered his mouth.

"Was she bound and gagged, while they tortured her?" he asked.

There's the thing," said Baldi. "There's a high probability that whoever did this, they carried it out post-mortem."

"You're saying she wasn't conscious?"

"Try to keep up, Axel. She wasn't conscious because she was dead." Baldi held up a piece of grey woollen fabric. "The red stain on her skirt shows some spillage. Smell it."

Rácz sniffed. "Bitter almond?"

Precisely. I believe the blood tests will confirm, the cause of death of our victim was cyanide poisoning."

Rácz scratched his head. "So, the killer poisoned her and, once she was dead or dying, played out this bizarre *game*? None of this makes any sense. Was she raped? What about the weapon?"

"We found no signs of sexual abuse, although we're waiting for the test results on the swabs. Have your boys found any signs of the tool or weapon used? My guess is, they should look for a long, sharp pin, or perhaps a sewing needle."

Rácz glanced at his wristwatch, convinced he could still be home at a respectable time and salvage something from the evening. Racing from the bowels of the hospital, he reached the exit and strode across the car park. His car was in sight when his phone vibrated. It was Dominik Kemény, an old friend and counterpart in the Rendőrség. He considered letting it go to voicemail, but that wasn't his style.

"Dominik. What's up?"

Axel, we've got a multiple homicide. Corner of Dob Street and Kertész Street. The Hotel Queen Mary was closed throughout the lockdown. A neighbour heard gunshots, just over an hour ago. Looks like it's gang-related. Four Romanian males, probably in their twenties, blown away with multiple head wounds."

Rácz groaned. His day wasn't getting any easier, and a quadruple murder was not something he could hand off to one of his juniors.

"Thanks for nothing," he said.

If the Klára Menges' case had been almost the last straw, this latest reported killing felt like someone had just landed ten bales of hay onto his back. The consequences for his department would be dire, as were all prospects of dinner and reconciliation with Lili.

The shooting in Dob Street drew everything into sharp focus. Now, more urgently than ever, he needed to delegate the Klára Menges' investigation. Yet he needed someone with sufficient experience and motivation. Someone who could hit the ground running. He opened his briefcase, pulled out the HR file, and found the phone number he was looking for.

One of Erika's self-indulgences was to spend an extraordinarily long time in the shower before dinner. It was a daily ritual she used to rid herself of the physical and mental grime that accumulated on the job. Stepping out of the shower, she wrapped herself in a fluffy, white dressing gown and wiped condensation from the mirror with her towel. Running a brush through her wet hair, she frowned. Too much of it remained tangled around the bristles.

There was a gentle knock. "Dinner and a glass of Cabernet Sauvignon awaits you, madame," Marcel said in a playful tone.

"Pour the wine. Let it breathe. I'll be straight out."

Her phone vibrated. She looked twice at the screen, hardly believing Axel Rácz had the nerve to call her.

"I'm dishing up now." Marcel called. He sounded impatient.

Okay, I'll be right with you," she said. She paused for a moment, but accepted the call and snapped, "Now isn't a good time."

"Something has come up. Something that may interest you. An enormous opportunity…"

Erika peered into the steamy vanity mirror. She wiped it with her towel and caught the reflection of her furrowed forehead.

"And why would you be calling me about an opportunity? Don't you remember? It was you who fucked me off."

Rácz pressed on. "I know you. I know the cases you like. This one is just up your street. But let me be upfront with you. I *need you* to accept."

"You need *me* to accept? That is a surprise."

"See you in my office, in thirty minutes? You won't regret it."

Erika opened the bathroom door. Steam billowed out. She had some explaining to do.

Axel Rácz parked the A6 in the underground car park at Teve Street and took the lift to the tenth floor. When the stainless steel doors slid open, his phone rang.

"The tests confirm my preliminary diagnosis. A lethal dose of potassium cyanide caused the death of Klára Menges," Baldi said.

Rácz paused, processing the information. "I'll be in touch."

The lights were still on in his office, and the cleaners were doing their rounds. Rácz slumped dejectedly into his executive chair to make his second call of the evening to Lili.

The evening traffic along Váci Street was light, meaning an expected journey time of less than ten minutes. Erika used the time to make her regular evening call to the Daybreak Nursing Home: the daily call that her mother, Nora, depended upon. After her father died, and the family apartment became too much for Nora to handle, the sales pitch from the nursing home had been perfect. 'Removal of loneliness and vulnerability; removal of daily woes; a peaceful old age.'

Everything had worked well for over a year. Unfortunately, the onset of Nora's dementia in 2019 had made the situation far more challenging. Then came COVID-19. After an early spate of deaths, the Budapest care and nursing homes had banned visitors from entering to see their loved ones. As a result, it had been eight weeks since she had seen her mother in person.

Erika made the call on her hands-free. She was already approaching Teve Street and was short on time. She was always short on time.

She tried to sound upbeat and cheery. "Hello, Mum. How's your day been?"

"You have to get me out of here. The staff wear masks and make me stay in my room all day. It's like a prison."

Erika sighed, but held her nerve. "We talked about this so many times. It's all for your own good. They wear the masks and protective clothing to prevent the virus from spreading. And they keep you in your rooms to protect you and the other residents. Just hold on for a while longer. The city is coming out of the lockdown. It won't be long before I'll be able to come and see you again. Then we can go out. I'll take you to the park. Won't that be lovely? Listen, Mum, I'm still at work. So I need to say goodnight now. Is that okay?"

"Work? It's time for bed. You should be at home, with that nice man you told me about."

Chance would be a fine thing. Straight ahead, the low, late evening sunlight reflected brilliantly off the blue-glazed façade of her office block.

"I have to go, Mum. Take care of yourself and sleep well. I love you."

Erika ended the call, even before her mother could respond. She turned down the ramp and parked as close to the pedestrian staff exit as possible. She switched off the engine and contemplated the 'groundhog day' nature of the daily calls with her mother: the same issues raised; the same placatory explanations offered. She wondered for how much longer this dialogue would continue?

Right now she needed to compartmentalise, to focus on the meeting with Rácz. What could she expect from meeting a giant of a man whom she could no longer trust as far as she could throw him? Inside the lift, she hit the button marked 10.

The doors slid open, and Erika strode towards the corner office. She had dressed casually, in blue denim jeans, a white cotton blouse and black pumps. He can take me as he finds me, she told herself. Initially she saw no one other than a cleaning crew, but closer to Rácz's open door she spotted a young man working at a desk. Then it came to her: Gábor Márkos. The last time she had stepped onto this floor, he had just completed his detective exams and was still wet behind the ears.

She had no intention of entering into conversation with one of Rigo's cronies. Instead she marched up to Rácz's office, tapped upon the glass partition and entered, not waiting for an invitation, before closing the door and sitting down.

Axel Rácz swivelled in his chair and strummed his fingers on his desktop. His eyes narrowed. "Come in, why don't you?"

She was pleased to see that she had already irritated him. *One nil to me.* His trimmed beard had greyed considerably since she had last seen him.

The last time she had been in his office was the day he had axed her for filing the complaint against Rigo. So angry had she been then, that she had pushed back her metal-framed chair with force, and shattered one of the glass partitions. "I'm pleased to see they repaired your wall," she jibed. Two nil.

He sneered in return. "How's life down on the second floor?"

"Busy. White-collar crime is booming during the lockdown."

"I'm sure it's important work you're doing, but how would you like to get your teeth stuck into another murder investigation? A fascinating case, a woman in her eighties…"

He had come straight to the point, but Erika cut across him. "Spare me the details. I know about your staffing levels. You must be *desperate* to have called me. If only you'd thought about what you'd be missing before you fired me."

"I didn't fire you. You put in for a transfer."

"Only after you made it clear that it was Rigo or me."

The conversation was turning out to be as acrimonious and futile as she had expected. Yet she wanted to find out what was on offer, and how far he would go to accommodate her. She felt her cheeks burning. She folded her arms tightly across her chest and glared across the desk.

Rácz stood. He was head and shoulders taller than her and more than twice her weight. She had watched him use his size to intimidate others, especially during interrogations. If he intended to loom over her, she'd tell him to fuck off.

Instead, he walked to this teak drinks cabinet. "Can I offer you something?"

"Mineral water will be fine."

He opened the mini-refrigerator, shook his head and said, "Dora should have some outside."

She exhaled and rubbed the back of her neck. The tension was giving her a headache. He returned, carrying water bottles. He pushed at the door with his broad shoulder, leaving it slightly ajar, before handing her one of the bottles and a glass.

Her mouth was dry and the chilled, sparkling water was a godsend.

He said, "Just let me walk you through the case. You're an experienced homicide detective. I'd like to hear your opinion. If you're still not interested, we'll say no more about it. Okay?"

She took another sip and nodded.

Rácz explained the basic facts about yesterday evening's murder of an eighty-eight-year-old woman in her apartment. Blood tests had shown the cause of death to be cyanide poisoning. Possibly after she had breathed her last, the killer had stripped the woman naked, and punctured her body hundreds of times with a sharp implement.

The story was intriguing. There were aspects of it that elevated the case above the level of a humdrum, domestic killing. Yet it was not clear what role he was asking her to play.

"If you just need another detective, to support the senior investigating officer…"

"Don't jump to conclusions. I'm not asking you to support or assist. I want you to be the SIO. It's all yours, if you'll accept it. Just find the murderer and keep me posted along the way."

She was being drawn in, and she knew it. Yet there were complications to consider.

"Even if I was prepared to take this off your hands, I have other cases and a department to run. I'd need to speak to my boss."

"The new Deputy High Commissioner is on board with this, and thinks it's an elegant and flexible solution to our current problem. We'll be back up to strength in a week or two. Surely you could delegate your existing cases until then? What do you say?"

Rácz was clearly doing his utmost to remove obstacles as quickly as she could raise them.

The prospect of running her own murder investigation was certainly appealing. Yet she already knew what the reaction of the men in the murder squad would be like. They would marginalise her, slow everything down, doom her to failure. She simply could not accept that fate. To succeed, she would need genuine support.

"I'll accept on one condition," she said firmly.

"What's that?"

"I bring Eszter Szabó with me, as my second in command. She's got the makings of a good detective and I'll need a bag carrier."

"You need someone with experience for that role. Péter Rigo was already at the crime scene."

She snorted. "You must be joking! I'd rather stick my head up a dead bear's arse than have him on the case." She rose and pushed back her chair, careful to keep it some distance away from the glass partitions. "When you reach a decision, you know where to find me."

Rácz rose too, walked around the table and held out his loaf-sized fist.

"Rigo is no longer a protected species. I thought I'd kill two birds with one stone. If he gives you any problems, we'll move him onto something else. You have the final say on him. Do we have a deal?"

She wished she could resist. What if things went badly? On the other hand, it was a golden opportunity to show Rigo and the others she was better than them. "We have a deal."

The virus meant handshakes were out of the question. Instead, she extended her clenched fist and awkwardly bumped his.

"And when do you plan to announce this?" she asked.

"Incident Room, 8.30 a.m. tomorrow."

She nodded. "We'll be there."

Through the half-open door, Gábor Márkos had heard every word of the conversation between his commander and the hard-nosed bitch from the FCI. Her departure from the murder squad five years ago had caused quite a stir, but none of the men had shed any tears.

When she walked past his desk on her way out, they exchanged forced smiles.

Moments later, he headed for the washroom and made a call.

CHAPTER THREE

The Incident Room was buzzing, but when Axel Rácz entered, a nervous hush fell. Most of the men sat looking sombre, arms folded. From the front of the room, he spotted Erika Kelemen standing at the back. She was wearing a navy blue trouser suit, with a white, open-necked blouse. Next to her was a taller, younger woman in a dark-grey trouser suit. She had blonde hair in a ponytail, and he assumed she was Detective Szabó, the bag carrier Kelemen had insisted on bringing with her. He imagined the stir those two must have caused on arrival.

He cleared his throat. "Today is the funeral of Bálint Dudás."

There were heavy sighs, slumped shoulders and shaking of heads all around the room. Dudás had been a popular member of the team. Aged only forty-one years old and with fifteen years of service, he'd left behind a wife and three children. Prior to catching the virus, he had played sports regularly and often, and had no underlying health issues.

Rácz continued, "Under lockdown rules, only limited numbers may attend the funeral. His family has asked for privacy. We will pay our respects, when it's possible to hold a proper memorial service."

There were nods and some murmurs of approval.

With the terrible news out of the way, he pushed ahead. "On a more positive note, Gyula Horvát, Izsák Ormán and Szilveszter Petri are out of hospital and expected to return in the coming weeks. Once they are back on duty, our situation should look rosier."

He shuffled from side to side and tugged at his beard. "In the meantime, two new investigations landed yesterday. The first, an elderly woman, Klára Menges. She was poisoned and mutilated. The second, a quadruple murder, believed to be part of a gangland turf war. I realise these new investigations will stretch our resources even further."

"Let's hope the crims go on holiday until the three lads get back, sir," quipped Gábor Márkos.

Laughter rippled around the room.

Rácz remained stern-faced. "We need experienced detectives to handle the two latest cases. For that reason, I have appointed Erika Kelemen to take charge of the Klára Menges investigation." He had anticipated some resistance, but was surprised by the volume of groans, all of which he ignored. "Detective Kelemen learned her craft in this department, before transferring to another unit. Assisting her will be Detective Eszter Szabó. I'm also assigning Detectives Rigo, Márkos and Dolman to the investigation. I will make a further announcement concerning the team for the four Romanian murders but, in the meantime, I shall take charge of that investigation myself."

Chairs grated along the tiled floor, and the grumbling was vociferous.

He raised his hands. "Calm down, gentlemen. I expected better from this team."

Rigo stood up, like a shop-steward, and addressed Rácz. "If I could speak up for a moment, sir, on behalf of the lads. We *are* a team. We've taken losses on the front line and we can deal with that. Like you said, Horvát, Ormán and Petri will soon be back with us. Until that time, I'm certain we could cope, without the need to bring in… outsiders."

Rácz felt hot under the collar of his crisp white shirt. Even if he was having second thoughts about the wisdom of bringing Erika and her buddy in, there was no way he would now back down in front of the men.

"My decision is final. I expect maximum cooperation. I'll be down on any laggards like a tonne of bricks. That's all. Carry on."

On the way out, he caught Kelemen's eye and gestured for her to meet him by the exit. He intercepted her by the door and said, "Follow me. I'll provide you with some tips on how to handle the men."

"Should Detective Szabó join us?" she asked.

"Just you," he said. He marched away with Dora in his wake.

Eszter was doing her best to imitate a chameleon. She sat at the back of the Incident Room, hoping she could quietly observe her new colleagues while they let off steam.

Some hope.

Being a stranger and the only woman left in the room, it came as no surprise when Rigo made a beeline for her. His hair was greasy and his suit looked like he'd slept in it. He appeared to be wearing the same ensemble since they had briefly met yesterday morning in the canteen.

Eszter stood as he approached. She was several centimetres taller than him. Having the wall behind her was also an advantage. One of the freestyle fight tactics she had learned at her karate classes was not to let the enemy encircle you.

With her most earnest smile in place, she said, "Detective Rigo. You guys have certainly got your work cut out. Glad to support the team."

"Don't make yourself comfortable on the tenth floor, darling. You and the bitch won't be staying long."

Some others approached them, and Eszter saw the odds stacking up in their favour. Then, in a more conciliatory tone than she expected, one of them said, "Come on, Péter, give the girl a break."

Rigo turned on his mate, his eyes wild and his mottled complexion flushed. "You don't know what Kelemen, is capable of. Mark my words, Lajos, she'll have you dancing a merry tune if we don't send them packing. Are you with me, or against me?"

Rácz poured two glasses of water from a jug and handed one to Erika.

He seemed hyper-tense, and she watched him swallow some pills and gulp his drink. It was impossible to miss the large, damp stains that radiated from under his arms, or the sheen on his forehead. He seemed different from the large, domineering man she used to work for. The pressure was clearly getting to him.

"It will be alright. You've made the right decision, under the circumstances," she said.

"I'm not so sure. They are a close-knit team. Perhaps it would be better after all, if I took direct control of the Klára Menges case and directed Rigo and the others during the investigation?"

His apparent U-turn was bemusing.

She said, "Do you think that going back on your decision will help you get out of the mess you're in? You've lost one of your key men to the virus and his funeral is today. You're short staffed. You suddenly have more murder cases than you can shake a stick at. God knows what Lili, is making of all this. You're far too young for her to be collecting a police widow's pension. By the way, has she fully recovered?"

"You always knew how to call a spade a spade, Erika. And yes, Lili is doing well, thank you."

Her full, red lips formed a smile. "That's half my charm, isn't it? I have to admit, I was sceptical when you called me in last night. But these are extraordinary times. If I can help out, it's my duty to do so. Don't you fret about me and the team. I've been working with the likes of them for thirty years, and I know how to get results."

Rácz strummed his fingers on his desktop. "You reckon you can handle them?"

She stood and winked at him. "No worries."

He nodded and she left.

On her way out, Erika had a spring in her step. She found Dora working at her desk and wondered what the assistant thought about her appointment. For a fleeting moment, their eyes met.

Dora smiled. "I've found you an office. Do you have time for me to show you?"

Unlike Rácz's spacious corner office, the tiny room had no windows to the outside world. The furniture comprised a battered, gun-metal-grey desk, a cheap swivel seat complete with frayed arm rests, one dented filing cabinet and two unpadded steel visitor chairs.

It appeared that Dora was going out of her way to be helpful. Erika had no ego when it came to office real estate. This place was better than the desk by the toilets she had previously occupied five years ago. Best of all, there was a door that closed and provided some degree of privacy when she needed it.

"It's good to have you back in the department. Let me know if you need anything."

Erika expressed her gratitude. But as soon as Dora had left, she tapped her speed-dial for Eszter. "Still alive?"

"Only just. Where are you?"

"If you're still in the Incident Room, step outside."

When she saw Eszter appear, she beckoned her over and ushered her into the office, closing the door behind them.

"You need to learn how to stay calm under pressure, if you are going to work in homicide. What's the word?"

"Your name is currently mud, and Rigo is the one you need to shoot first. You could win the rest around."

"No surprises there. I told Rácz I want you as my second in command on the case."

Eszter's eyes widened. "I don't know what to say."

"You passed your detective exams with flying colours and have done outstanding work in the FCI Division. Opportunities for women don't come up too often in homicide. Stick close to me; learn and do. If you're lucky, you'll get another bite of the cherry before you reach my age. Understood?"

"Absolutely. What do you want me to do?"

"The others can stew for a while," said Erika. "Right now, I don't trust any of them to give me the time of day. The first thing we're going to do is get ourselves up to speed."

The property room was a secure area on the tenth floor, kept under the watchful eye of Antal Eger, a semi-invalided officer, shot on active duty in 2010. All evidence taken in or out passed through his hands.

"Hey, look who it is!" Eger said, a warm smile spreading across his face.

"What you doing up here, Ms Kelemen?"

Erika regarded Eger as one of the most reliable people working in the homicide department. She doubted he had joined in the mass backstabbing that had reportedly taken place after her departure five years hence. She smiled back. "I'm the new SIO on the Klára Menges case. This is my partner, Detective Eszter Szabó. What's been logged in?"

Eger lifted a plastic tub off the shelves and placed it on the counter. "Detective Rigo brought these in yesterday afternoon. Everything we've got is here, apart from some letters which were booked out by Dora for Commander Rácz to look over."

Erika picked out the bagged items one at a time: a purse, jewellery items and a phone. Perhaps the identity of the murderer was there in front of her? Had Rigo bothered to examine any of these items? She knew him of old, and doubted he had troubled himself. "May we take these?"

"You sign the book, I'll scan them out for you," Eger said.

Eszter carried the tub to a trestle table, while Erika slipped on a pair of disposable latex gloves. Erika removed the purse from the evidence bag, examining its contents carefully: a few thousand forints in cash, a bank card, receipts for groceries, postage stamps, nothing untoward. She slipped the purse back into its bag and resealed it. Then she pulled a black nylon backpack from her handbag and stuffed the entire contents of the tub into it.

She said to Eszter, "We'll need the address of the crime scene, a copy of Hanna Balogh's statement and those letters. You could ask Dora for all those items."

"Who's Hanna Balogh? And who's Dora?"

"The cleaner who found Klára's body, and the commander's PA. Meet me downstairs in the car park in ten minutes. And bring your car keys."

The journey from police headquarters to the drab-looking, five-storey apartment block in Bertalan Lajos Street took twenty-five minutes. At the entrance to Klára Menges' fourth-floor apartment, a bored-looking male uniformed officer checked their ID before lifting the tape.

"Is anybody in there?" asked Erika.

"The last of the SOCO team left a few minutes ago. He told me they've done everything they can do and left me with this," the officer replied, handing over the key.

"We'll take it from here. I'm expecting a Mrs Balogh. Let me know when she arrives," said Erika, beckoning Eszter to follow her.

The uniformed officer nodded and removed the crime scene tape, but before Erika had stepped across the threshold he said, "Looks like she is already here."

She turned and saw a stocky, middle-aged woman wearing brown overalls approaching them along the gloomy corridor.

The woman announced herself loudly, "Are you the detectives they said were coming? I am Hanna Balogh. I've just finished one of my other clients, on the second floor."

"Thank you, for coming so promptly. I'm Detective Kelemen and this is my colleague, Detective Szabó. We have a few questions. Let's step inside."

"I told that other detective everything. Told him all I know,"

Erika held in her hand a copy of Mrs Balogh's statement to Rigo. "Let's go inside, anyway. I'd like to retrace your footsteps. Just give us a running commentary of what you did, what you saw. My colleague will take notes."

The cleaner led the way into the hallway of the apartment. "I can't spend long chatting. I have another client at midday."

Erika's hackles were already rising. The woman had only just arrived and was trying to dictate the terms of their interview. Erika was having none of it. She replied brusquely. "What time did you arrive here yesterday?"

"Nine a.m., sharp. She was my first client, on the first day after the lockdown."

Erika led the cleaner through to the living room and said, "Did you speak with Mrs Menges before you came to clean the apartment?"

"Yes. Last week, and at lunchtime yesterday."

"Do you remember what she said?"

Hanna Balogh paused for a moment, then replied, "I remember exactly what she said. She told me she was looking forward to being cleansed."

"Didn't that strike you as a little odd?"

"Mrs Menges could sometimes be very odd."

Eszter made a note and Erika changed tack. "How did you get into the apartment?"

"I let myself in. She trusted me with keys, like most of my clients do."

"Does anyone else have her keys?"

"Not that she ever mentioned. Like I told the other detective, she was a solitary person. I never saw signs of visitors, nor did she ever mention anyone coming around to see her."

"This time, did anything seem unusual?"

Hanna Balogh dug into her overall pocket, pulled out a wad of tissues, and wiped her nose. "This place was in darkness, and there was no kávé on the stove. Also, that's new, I swear I never saw it before yesterday." She nodded at the religious statuette on the sideboard.

It was a mini version of the Christ Redeemer statue that stands at the summit of Mount Corcovado in Rio de Janeiro. This one was plain white and stood about thirty centimetres tall.

Erika pulled on a pair of latex gloves and inspected it. There was a label underneath the base: HOLY ART. "Why is this unusual?"

The cleaner said, "She told me she was a non-believer. Look around, there are no other religious objects in this apartment."

Eszter took note.

There had been no mention of this in the witness statement that Rigo had taken.

Erika continued, "So, you saw the statue. What happened next?"

"I noticed the light on under her bedroom door, but decided not to go in until the kávé had brewed. I just thought she was sleeping in late. I never dreamed…" Hanna covered her face with her hands. "I mean, what kind of freak does that to an old woman?"

Erika handed the cleaner her business card. "That is precisely what we intend to find out. Call me, if you remember anything else."

Back in the squad car, Erika delved into her holdall. She re-examined each evidence bag, slowly and tried to imagine the type of character Klára had been. *It was hardly unusual for people to return to God as they approached later life, but had there been a specific catalyst? And if so, what?* She stuffed the evidence bags back into the holdall, called the hospital morgue and left a message, saying she was on her way and wanted to inspect the body of Klára Menges on arrival.

It was just after one o'clock when they made their way through the subterranean depths of the military hospital. For Erika, this was familiar territory, but it was Eszter's first time. Next to the autopsy suite, they found three men seated around a table in a small office, eating and chatting. Erika recognised József Baldi, although he had aged since their last encounter over five years ago. There was so sign of reciprocal recognition, and the men ignored the arrival of their visitors.

Erika cleared her throat. "Sorry to interrupt. I was wondering how long you're likely to be, professor?"

Baldi peered over his spectacles. "It's been a busy morning, ladies. We sat down for our break barely ten minutes ago. Commander Rácz has asked for urgent reports on the four males shot yesterday evening. I'm surprised you're not aware of his priorities, Detective Kelemen."

"I heard about the case, Professor, but my concern is Klára Menges. I am now in charge of that investigation. I called ahead and requested an inspection of the body."

"It's the first I heard of it. I would urge you to be patient."

Patience was not Erika's strong suit. She turned on her heels and led Eszter by the elbow until she thought they were out of earshot. She said, "They should have put him out to pasture years ago. He's rude, cantankerous, and his treatment of women…"

"My treatment of women? Don't you listen to anything she says, my dear?" The professor had followed them and was now standing close by. "Before you dig yourself into a bigger hole, I can offer you fifteen minutes. Come this way."

He led the way to the anteroom where they gowned up. The autopsy room, reeked of formalin, disinfectant and open bowels.

Erika handed Eszter a piece of chewing gum and popped a piece into her own mouth.

Centre stage there were five autopsy stations encased in stainless steel, spaced approximately two metres apart, each topped with a massive marble slab, with grooves for a wheeled trestle table to run along the long sides.

Baldi pointed to the station furthest away from the door. "She's over there, on table one."

They had to walk past four corpses, each of which were in the process of their own post-mortem examinations. The ones with open intestines were particularly gut-wrenching.

The assistant pulled back the sheet to reveal a small female corpse laying on its back. Hundreds of tiny wounds were visible on what they could see of her naked body.

Baldi said, "Because of yesterday evening's mass shooting, we have yet to complete her autopsy. What we know so far, is she was murdered on Tuesday evening, probably around five p.m. Blood tests have shown an overdose of potassium cyanide caused her death. With the dosage we found in her blood, it's likely she died painfully, within fifteen to twenty minutes. Within a short time of ingesting it she would have shown symptoms such as dizziness, gasping for breath, headache, nausea, vomiting, and a drop in blood pressure."

Eszter was trying to take notes, but her complexion had turned a pale shade of green.

Erika said, "If you're going to poison someone with cyanide, why go to the trouble of repeatedly stabbing them?"

"That's for you to find out, detective," Baldi said.

Erika snorted at the man's impudence. "No signs of sexual abuse?"

"None," he said. "Neither were there signs of restraint. I believe the stabbings occurred after the victim had lost consciousness, or perhaps even after her death. We also found this, in the victim's skirt pocket."

He handed over an evidence bag containing the laminated picture of the Sacred Heart.

She looked at the picture. Klára was more religious than anyone knew.

"I'll take that, thanks." Turning next to the autopsy assistant she said, "Please spread her legs and raise her arms."

Baldi nodded, and the assistant did as instructed, although the rigour-mortis required him to exert some force.

"Do you have a magnifying glass?" Erika said.

The assistant produced one.

She chewed harder on her gum and leant in closer, peering at the flesh between the victim's thighs before tracking slowly up her belly, across the chest and along the raised arms. The pattern of the tiny stab wounds seemed random, although the spacings between them varied, and in some places seemed clustered closer than in others. She was about to ask for the corpse to be rotated into a prone position when she spotted something.

"Spotlight!" she demanded.

Eszter produced the flashlight from her phone. There, in Klára's right armpit, the stab wounds formed what looked like a three letter word, spelt out in capital letters, each about one inch tall.

Erika turned to the pathologist. "Was this in your report?"

Baldi spluttered, "We haven't finished with her. I'm sure I'd have spotted it, during the full post-mortem." His gaunt cheeks flushed pink.

She had scored a direct hit, and Baldi knew it too.

It was Eszter who broke the silence. "Excuse me, but what exactly does that mean?"

Axel Rácz loosened his tie, ran a finger around the inside of his shirt collar, and bellowed.

Dora came, pen and pad in hand, peering over her spectacles.

"Get Baldi on the phone. I need his status report on the Hotel Queen Mary autopsies."

She shot him one of her looks and disappeared.

Thirty seconds later she called out, "He's on line one."

He stabbed the speakerphone button. "How's it going with the four Romanian victims?"

"My God, man! Give me time. I've only just got rid of that awful woman. She turned up unannounced with her sidekick, demanding to inspect Klára Menges. She's still the know-it-all I remembered her to be. What the hell are you doing bringing her back into Homicide? I thought you had enough problems to deal with." The professor hardly came up for breath.

Rácz groaned. The pathologist continued his rant, oblivious to the dull ache in the back of his neck, which was increasing in magnitude by the minute. He looked up. Dora was standing by his desk, with a glass of iced water on a tray.

"Thank you," he mouthed to her.

On and on went the professor's rant.

In his rush to bring an extra pair of hands on board, Rácz had downplayed in his own mind just how antagonistic Kelemen could be. She certainly had a knack of rubbing colleagues up the wrong way. But right now, he just needed Baldi and the others to suck it up, like he had done. He spoke over the top of the irate pathologist to make himself heard. "I can assure you; she won't be here for long. Now, could we get back to those shootings at the hotel?"

Marcel liked to take his daily run in the early afternoon. Throughout the lockdown, many of the clients of his accountancy company were no longer open for business. Work had been thin on the ground, and he normally dealt with his clients' needs in the morning, leaving the afternoon free for his run and a shower.

The weather was exceptionally warm and humid for May. He set his sports watch and filled a water bottle before leaving Erika's apartment in Victor Hugo Street on his seven-kilometre circuit.

The roads were much busier today, reflecting the end of the lockdown. People and traffic were out in far greater numbers. On reaching Alkotmány Street, he turned right and loped into Kossuth Lajos square. The main entrance to the parliament building came into view, but a small group of protestors partly blocked his usual path. He was curious, and instead of giving them a wide berth, he ran close enough to read the slogans on their banners. The most popular messages seemed to be, "No One is Above the Law" and "We Cannot Build the Future on Hatred."

Marcel paused for a moment to sip some water. He was jogging on the spot, about to move on. One protestor – a fresh-faced girl, in denim jeans and a yellow t-shirt who looked to be in her mid-twenties - stepped out and said, "Hey, Mister, why don't you join us?"

Marcel stopped jogging. "I don't even know what you're protesting about," he said.

"Romanian rights," she replied, "We're protesting against the government's refusal to pay compensation to Romanian kids, unlawfully segregated in a school in eastern Hungary. The government is blocking justice for the victims of segregation and is stirring up hatred against the Romanians."

"Why would they do that?"

He was really looking for the first opportunity to bypass the girl and get on his way.

"Because they want the votes of the far-right in the next elections."

The commotion of wailing sirens abruptly truncated their conversation. Marcel watched with growing interest as a fleet of black Volkswagen T5 Transporters sped towards them across the pedestrianised square. When the vans drew closer, the bold, yellow markings on the doors showed these were no ordinary police vehicles. The TEK -the Counter Terrorism Centre -had arrived in force. The vans screeched to a halt, doors slid open, and dozens of heavily armed men in black paramilitary uniforms piled out and surrounded them. Marcel found himself trapped among the protestors. He tried to extricate himself before the net tightened.

One of the armed officers blocked Marcel's exit and flung him forcefully to the ground.

"Get back in there, you scum!" the officer yelled

Marcel looked up. The officer was wearing full anti-terrorism gear and was brandishing a semi-automatic rifle.

He scrambled to his knees; his hands raised in the surrender position. A growing sense of panic was rising inside.

"Look at me!" he said. "I'm a runner, not a protestor. I've got nothing to do with this lot. You can see that, surely?"

The eyes behind the black balaclava hardened. Then a black boot swung in his direction. It connected, and something inside him snapped. He gasped. Behind him, a hard object crashed into his kidneys. A boot or a baton? Either way, he was in agony. The next thing he knew, four gloved hands tightly gripped his limbs and dragged him face down. The ground rushed by, and his bare knees scraped across the hard granite tiles. They flung him into the back of a van. His head collided with something hard and metallic. For a moment he felt dizzy. A sharp pain shot down his spine.

From the open doorway at the back of the van, one of the masked officers said, "He's a Román sympathiser."

Another officer decked out in full paramilitary gear pushed Marcel onto one of the benched seats and handcuffed him to a post. Sitting opposite was the girl in the yellow t-shirt. Tears were streaming down her cheeks and a wound on her forehead dripped blood onto her nose. Before long the van was full of protestors, and the doors were slammed shut. Marcel's head and ribs ached, as they took off at speed, siren wailing.

By mid-afternoon, Péter Rigo, Lajos Dolman and Gábor Márkos had been hanging around the office for the best part of six hours, looking busy, but achieving nothing. Rigo had spent much of the time bad-mouthing Kelemen. Even if she now returned to HQ with the killer in handcuffs and a six-month bonus for the entire team, he would still have been intent on making her life miserable until she was sent back to her white-collar crime job with her tail between her legs.

At just after three, Dora found them and made an announcement.

"Detective Kelemen wants to see you all, in the Incident Room at 16.00. Don't be late."

Rigo called after her, "Tell her she can shove her meeting. Better still, I'll tell her myself!"

After leaving the basement of the military hospital, Erika and Eszter returned to Police HQ on foot. The ten-minute walk along

Róbert Károly Boulevard helped clear their heads, although the smell of the autopsy suite clung stubbornly to their clothes.

"Another suit for the dry cleaners," said Erika.

They bought sandwiches and coffee from a street vendor, then sat for a few minutes in the shadow of their own office block and chatted while watching reflections of the passing traffic in its blue glass façade.

They were back in the Incident Room by three thirty but no one else had showed up early. Erika wasted no time in going to the whiteboards. She drew up a timeline and a mind-map, and sent Eszter back and forth, retrieving photographs from the printer. She pinned these images — the ones she had snapped at the crime scene and in the morgue — to the boards and labelled them. Step by step, she displayed the known facts, also highlighting the many gaps in their current knowledge.

"What time is it?" she asked.

"Five past four," replied Eszter.

Just then, the door swung open. In marched the three musketeers. Rigo led from the front, and all three took their seats and folded their arms. It was the most remarkable display of juvenile petulance she had ever seen. The tension in the room was palpable.

With the whiteboards as her backdrop, she faced them and cleared her throat.

"As you are all aware, Commander Rácz brought me and Detective Szabó in, to provide backup to the Murder Squad. Specifically, he asked me to lead the investigation into the murder of Klára Menges. He's given me an outline of the case, but let's go around the room and see what we know."

"If you're in charge, you tell us," said Rigo.

Erika met his gaze and stared him out, stepped forward a pace, and drew herself up to her full height. The three men remained slouching in their seats glaring up at her.

"Let's make it very clear from the start, gentlemen, it was the commander's decision, a decision supported by the *new* Deputy High Commissioner. Anyone here who doesn't support their actions is free to put in for a transfer. Just be man enough to fuck off now and not impede those intent on catching the killer of a defenceless old woman. Is that clear and understood?"

Her eyes scanned the scene in front of her. The two younger detectives shuffled into a more upright position and, although Rigo continued to slouch like an insolent teenager, there was no sign of him leaving. Seated behind the men, Eszter covered her mouth with a hand, evidently trying to prevent herself from laughing out loud.

Erika's last five years in the FCI had honed her skills in team-building. Whether this particular team would ever make the grade was a moot point, but so early in the new team's formation she offered them an olive branch. "Shall we start again?"

The question was rhetorical, and no responses were forthcoming. She turned to the whiteboards and pointed out the photograph of Klára Menges, taken while she lay prone on her bed, displaying the random pattern of myriad tiny wounds all over her naked body. "Detective Rigo, was this how you found the victim?"

"The cleaner found her, but the body wasn't moved. I took the cleaner's statement and brought the victim's personal possessions: phone, address book. They're sitting in the evidence room." He spoke in his usual nasal monotone, although his body language did not improve.

At least for now, Rigo was playing ball. She'd tolerate him while he did that, but if he stepped out of line, she'd have him out. She nodded towards the trestle table next to her, where she had laid out the evidence bags.

"Everything you've collected so far is there. But first, let's discuss the timeline." She turned to the whiteboard, on which she'd written a horizontal line with five arrowed comments. "On Wednesday May thirteenth, Hanna Balogh called Klára Menges. She called her again at lunchtime on Tuesday the nineteenth, and Klára said she was 'looking forward to being cleansed,'"

Rigo's nose wrinkled, and his eyes narrowed into rodent-like slits. "Balogh didn't say that to me."

"There are several things which didn't appear in that statement," said Erika, turning to face the group. "Perhaps her memory was a little clearer when Detective Szabó and I spoke with her this afternoon."

Rigo shuffled in his seat and rolled his eyes towards the ceiling.

Erika returned to the whiteboards and said, "The next point on our timeline is later the same day, around five p.m. on the nineteenth. That was when Professor Baldi believes the killing occurred. Baldi confirms that the cause of death was a lethal dose of potassium cyanide which, once administered, would have taken around twenty minutes to finish her."

Erika pointed at a blown up image of the stab wounds. "The absence of any signs of struggle or restraints on the victim suggests the process of repeatedly stabbing her, with a small, sharp implement, carried out *after* Klára had either lost consciousness or had died. It must have taken quite some time to inflict this number of wounds. All of this took time and I doubt the killer left the apartment before six-thirty p.m. Before he departed, he also wrote us a message."

She moved to one of the close-up images she had pinned to the whiteboards. The three men leaned forward in their seats, peering to make out what they were looking at. "Under her right armpit," said Erika, "The letters, AVH. Any ideas?"

Márkos said, "The killer's initials?"

Rigo sniggered.

Erika wrote Márkos' suggestion on the whiteboard. She would not allow Rigo's negativity to knock the meeting off course.

"Any other thoughts?" When there was no further response, she continued. "The following morning, Hanna Balogh arrived at nine. She used a spare set of keys to let herself in. She has been cleaning this apartment fortnightly for the last two years. She says she noticed nothing unusual on this occasion, with one exception." Erika pointed towards the whiteboard, to a photograph she had taken this morning. "A statuette of Christ the Redeemer. Apparently a recent acquisition. The cleaner thought it odd because Mrs Menges was known not to be religious." Erika walked over to the evidence table, picked up the bag containing the small laminated card found in Klára's skirt pocket, and held it up.

"The Sacred Heart. So what?" Rigo shrugged.

Erika nodded. "Our victim seems to have recently found God. Detective Dolman, I want you to get forensics to look at the statuette and the card. Perhaps our killer left some traces on them?"

She handed the bag to Dolman. Moving back to the evidence table, she picked up the bag containing the bundle of letters. "The killer took great care to remove all signs of his presence. SOCO found these, hidden under the floor in the apartment. Detective Márkos, I want you to read every one. Who knows what secrets Klára was hiding? Perhaps the killer was searching for these letters?"

"Sure thing," said Márkos.

"Detective Szabó, you take her phone and the address book. Check her call records and contacts. Let's see who she has been talking to, and when. And check her online usage too."

"Will do, boss," said Eszter.

Erika finally switched her attention to Rigo. "I want you to check out everything you can find concerning cyanide poisonings: where to source potassium cyanide; how to administer it; how to treat it."

She watched closely for signs of rebellion, but Rigo simply shrugged. At this stage, it was enough. Strong doubts remained whether this team would ever get to the 'norming' and 'performing' stages of classic team-building, but she had issued her orders and it was now up to each of them to do their job.

Marcel had lost track of his whereabouts. All he knew was the van he had been thrown into had been driven at speed for approximately twenty minutes. He could not be more accurate, because his mobile phone had been confiscated along with his keys, as soon as he was seated on the bench seat in the back of the vehicle. Once they stopped, he and his fellow detainees were bundled out and corralled in an indoor processing area the size of a small warehouse. They were forced to stand in line, while personal details were demanded and recorded, then mugshots, fingerprints and nasal swabs taken. Then the men and women in the group were segregated. He and the other men were pushed into a crowded, sweaty holding pen. There he stood, as distanced from the next man as he could manage. His hand cradled his side, trying to protect his ribcage from further damage. He found it incredible that a law-abiding person such as himself could ever be in this situation. The whole episode was so degrading.

After a while, an officer wearing black fatigues and a now all-too-familiar black balaclava approached the gate. He pointed at Marcel, the only detainee wearing Lycra gear, and shouted over the din.

"Hey you, runner, come here."

The pen gate was opened, and Marcel was hauled out and led along a corridor to an interview room which contained a table and two chairs.

He was pushed towards the chair on the far side of the table and ordered to sit.

He did not have to wait long. A slim man, slightly taller than himself entered. He was wearing a black suit with a white, open-necked shirt and had black hair and a moustache. He sat opposite Marcel and placed a folder on the table.

Marcel was desperate to explain the circumstances of his arrest to the first unmasked person in authority he had come across. *It was all a big misunderstanding. Surely he could make him see that.* He opened his mouth to speak, but the man raised his hand, signalling silence.

The man produced a form from his folder and said, "You gave a home address on Victor Hugo Street. It is an address that our records show is the home address of a serving police detective. How can this be?"

At last, Marcel was getting somewhere. He had been biding his time before revealing his relationship with Erika. He didn't want to involve her unnecessarily, but as this man seemed to know they lived together, there was no need to hold back. "Not much gets past you, does it? My girlfriend is Detective Erika Kelemen. We've been living together for the last few months. That's the address I began my run from today. I bumped into the protestors, or rather one bumped into me. You can call Erika, Detective Kelemen, if you need someone to vouch for me."

"I see," the man said, making notes. He picked up his folder and stood, gesturing to the door. "You can go now, but you are on our file, and we know where you live. Make sure you stay out of trouble."

Marcel felt a wave of relief come over him. "Thank you, Mr…"

"Kudár, Rudolf Kudár."

After Rigo, Márkos and Dolman had gone, Erika felt a wave of tiredness sweep over her. She rubbed her tired eyes with her fingertips, massaging them in a circular motion. When she finished, Eszter handed her a compact, and she looked at herself in the mirror. She had spread mascara around her eyes and cheeks, making herself look like a panda bear. She let out a deep, throaty laugh, fished out some make-up-remover from her handbag and cleaned herself up.

Her phone vibrated, and seeing it was her mother she asked Eszter to step outside.

Erika was about to offer her normal cheerful greeting, but all she could hear from the other end were heaving, gut-wrenching sobs. She felt helpless, and blind to what was going on. A sinking feeling gripped hold of her, but it was important she didn't panic. "Have you fallen? What's happened?"

The wailing continued unabated. Some crisis was occurring, and if her mother could not describe what was happening she needed to speak to someone who could.

"Mum, I'm going to hang up now. I'll call the manager and get them to come to your room straight away. Hold on!"

The Daybreak Nursing Home was busy, so she hit the redial button, again and again and again. With each busy tone, she became more desperate, both for a response, and for a solution to the long-term problem of her mother in care. How long could this situation continue? Erika scrolled in her address book until she found the contact she was looking for. It was time *he* stepped up to the mark. She was his mother too; in case he'd forgotten.

After three rings, her brother answered with a jaunty, "Hey, sis, what's happening?"

"Don't fucking 'hey, sis' me, David. Mum is in some kind of a meltdown at the home. I've tried to get through, but they're not answering. Right now I'm in charge of a brutal murder case, and the commander wants me in his office ten minutes ago. You need to call the Daybreak straight away, speak to the duty manager, get them to find out why our mother is wailing down the phone. Ask them to call you straight away with an answer. Then you need to message me and put my mind at rest. Is everything clear? Do it now, before you forget. Bye." Erika ended the call and stared anxiously at her phone. Her chest was heaving as adrenaline coursed through her body. She exhaled deeply, puffing out her cheeks. Axel Rácz wasn't the only heart attack waiting to happen.

On the way to the commander's office, Erika stopped off in the ladies' washroom and splashed cold water onto her face. The last thing she wanted, was to show up looking like the case was already too much for her to handle.

Her phone rang once again. This time the caller display showed it was Marcel. Her forefinger hovered before accepting the call. How many times had she told him not to call her at work, unless in an emergency?

"Marcel, I'm just about to step into a meeting. Can I get back to you?"

"I had a close encounter with the TEK today," he said. "I'm okay, but a bit shaken up. What time will you be home?"

Erika's phone vibrated. There was another call waiting, and she was sure it would be Rácz chasing her up. She was certain Marcel was attempting to dramatise some minor episode or piece of news. His news certainly didn't sound like an emergency. Not compared with the life and death matters she was dealing with. He could explain over dinner, when she had more time.

"Look, I have to go. Tell me later, when I see you. Bye."

"Go straight in," said Dora. "Anything to drink?"

Without a hint of irony Erika said, "A large vodka tonic would be good. Go easy on the tonic."

Axel Rácz was on the phone in his office, but gestured for her to take a seat. Dora soon appeared with a tray of cold, non-alcoholic drinks and placed it on the conference table. Rácz continued to shout orders down the phone to somebody. Erika was pleased she wasn't on the receiving end. She composed herself, sipped her mineral water, and re-focused her mind back on the case.

Rácz finished his call. He rested his elbows on his desktop and put his head in his hands. She poured a glass of water and placed it in front of him. "Try the vodka."

He took the glass and downed its contents. Droplets of water glistened on his beard. He wiped his mouth with the back of his hand and said, "That was another tremendous disappointment, in a day of disappointments. I hear you've been making yourself popular down at the morgue."

She slid the photograph of Klára's armpit onto his desk. "I can't believe Baldi didn't spot it.".

He placed his wire-rimmed spectacles on the end of his nose and studied the photograph. "What is this?"

"Among the random pattern of stab wounds, the killer left us a message: three letters, AVH. He poisoned an old woman and wrote a message on her flesh."

"You think he'll strike again?"

"Perhaps his motive relates only to Klára Menges. Only time will tell. We're reviewing all the evidence we have to date. Rigo is investigating the cyanide poisoning, and Márkos is looking at the letters discovered by SOCO. Meanwhile Szabó is checking out Klára's call records and Dolman is taking a few interesting artefacts from the apartment to forensics."

"At this rate, you'll soon have a suspect in your sights, won't you?" There was optimism in his voice.

She needed to manage his expectations, and there was no point in mincing her words. "We're at first base here, dealing with a complex case. I don't want you calling me, day and night, asking for updates. That just will not happen. Am I making myself clear?"

He scowled and waved her away dismissively. "Just find out who did this."

The IT department at Police Palace lies in a distant corner of the ground floor. Few people, other than the smart geeks who work there, know its precise location, and even fewer have ever visited. The place resembles a cave, full of screens, servers, cables and mountains of spare parts and accessories. The multitude of IT systems used by the Hungarian police requires a team of smart, young minds to keep everything running. Eszter knew the cave better than most. It was where Ferenc worked.

Eszter made a call, switching on her most persuasive voice. "Hey, babe, I need a favour. My boss is in charge of a murder investigation, and they've assigned me to the case. I need help, and I need it in a hurry."

"It's after six. I'm just packing up for the evening," he said.

"I have the victim's phone. It's locked and I need to see her calls and internet usage. You know I'll make it worth your while. Just wait until we get home."

"Will first thing in the morning do?"

"Couldn't you look before you leave?"

"There really is no peace for the wicked."

Eszter smiled to herself. The thought of rewarding him later made her tingle. "You can be as wicked as you like," she purred.

With Ferenc onboard, she packed Klára's phone and address book into her holdall and slung it over her shoulder. At the lift, Péter Rigo approached and stood uncomfortably close to her. He was the last person she would want to invade her personal space.

"On your way home, dear?" he said.

He had something of the night about him, and his presence made her shudder.

Right on cue, the doors slid open, and she stepped inside. So did he. She pressed the ground floor button. The doors took an age to close. She looked straight ahead, determined not to engage more than necessary.

"She's an evil influence. You'll get burned if you get too close," he said.

"I can look after myself."

"Think you're tough, do you, darling?"

"Not really. Being a second dan black belt in Shotokan karate has taught me to run away from a fight, and only use force in self-defence."

"That bullshit won't stop you getting knifed in the back."

The ping heralded their arrival on the ground floor, and the doors slid open. She turned and looked at the odious man, meeting his hooded grey eyes.

"She's been a good boss to me. Don't waste your breath trying to turn me against her."

She set off but he called after her, "You'll find out."

David Kelemen had been in the middle of an important video-conference business meeting. At forty-five years old, he was an experienced steel importer, but his business had suffered terribly these last few months, and the crucial meeting had been with a potential client. An hour and a quarter passed before he wrapped the meeting up and finally made the call to the care home. He was glad to finally remove his pale grey suit jacket, and he paced around his office in shirtsleeves with no tie, phone pinned to his ear.

His older sister, Erika, could be such a drama queen, and when she wanted something doing, nothing could stand in her way. He was several centimetres taller than her, but for as long as he could recall, she always managed to bully him into doing things her way. It had been that way since they were kids.

He was almost on the point of hanging up when someone answered.

"Daybreak Nursing Home. How may I help you?"

"David Kelemen here. My mother, Nora, is one of your residents."

"Hello, Miszter Kelemen. This is Jazmin. We have met previously."

He scratched his head. He had no recollection of meeting anyone at the home, but he had obviously left an impression on her.

"Jazmin, yes, I remember. I received a message from my sister, saying that mother is distressed. I'm calling to find out what's happening."

"I was just on her corridor. She was a little upset earlier, but she's calm and sleeping now."

The news was reassuring. He stopped pacing and took a seat in the swivel chair behind his desk. "Was there anything specific?"

"It's so difficult for all our residents, Mr Kelemen, but especially for the dementia patients, like Nora. They see themselves trapped. The social activities we offer have not been possible. Some of them get spooked by our PPE. Your mother is calm again and there's nothing specific for you to worry about."

"That's a relief. Tell her I called."

"I'll do that, Miszter Kelemen. You have yourself a good evening and try not to worry."

He raged inside. This was yet another example of Erika going over the top. He'd have words with her when they next spoke.

When Eszter returned to the tenth floor, it was with relief she found Rigo was nowhere to be seen. Gábor Márkos and Lajos Dolman were still at their desks, and both appeared to be hard at work.

Dolman looked up at her. "How are you getting on with her phone records?"

"Making progress," she replied. "I've got the lock off her phone and can see her recent calls. I'm going to match them to her contacts list, and with the address book from the apartment. How's it going with you guys?"

Dolman said, "I handed over that religious stuff to forensics, and now we're sifting through the letters SOCO found."

Márkos chipped in, "They all seem to be from her sister, Lotti. Written in the sixties and seventies. Clearly no love lost between the two of them!"

"Interesting," said Eszter. "Give me a few minutes with her calls, and then we can compare notes."

Dolman nodded. "Pull up a chair."

She noted the first sign of a thaw in relations. "Thanks," she said, dropping her holdall and parking herself on one of the empty chairs. For the next ten minutes she searched through Klára's call log, contacts list, and address book. Meanwhile, the two men pored over the letters. Each person had their task and each was getting on with it.

It was almost seven o'clock when Kelemen arrived.

"Fuck me," she said. "Am I dreaming, or does this look like teamwork?"

She dropped two large pizza boxes on Dolman's desk and said, "Didn't anyone tell you, an army marches on its stomach? Dig in."

This was Erika's well practised tactic of *management by pizza*. Dolman and Márkos instantly stopped what they were doing and tucked in enthusiastically.

After the first slices were devoured, Erika said, "So, what have we got so far?"

Dolman was still chewing but replied, "These letters are from Klára's sister, Lotti. It seems like she blamed Klára for destroying their family." He ran his finger along one of the letters written on gossamer-thin blue airmail paper. "Listen to this. It was written on the fourteenth of December 1966, with the sender's address in Toronto, Canada."

Dear Klára,

After ten long years, we were astonished to receive your letter, which was forwarded by one of the Hungarian consulate staff.

There were always rumours of AVH spies amongst the refugees. Given your position in that cursed organisation, it should come as no surprise that you had ways to track our movements. You will know, therefore, after we fled across the Austrian border, we were fortunate enough to be airlifted by the Canadians.

We have created new lives for ourselves here, and I cannot say that receiving your letter has rekindled anything other than the most painful of memories for Mother, Uncle Lajos and I.

Your betrayal cost us everything we owned, and so nearly cost all three of us our lives. The last we ever saw of Father was the day your thugs arrested and sent him to the camp at Recsk. Uncle Lajos still suffers from the nightmare of being tortured at 60 Stalin Street. My pain will never go away. Please be clear, you are no longer a sister of mine.

I write this letter only to urge you to never again attempt any further contact with us.

Lotti

"AVH!" exclaimed Eszter. "The same initials you found under Klára's arm."

Erika nodded and said, "She is referring to the *Államvédelmi Hatóság.*"

Márkos said, "What is that?"

Dolman took another slice of pizza and said, "Didn't they teach you history at school? It's the State Security Authority, our secret police in the fifties."

Eszter held up her hand to attract attention. She had evidently found something important and was eager to share it. "Hold on. According to Klára's address book, there's an entry for Lotti Menges, and there's a postal address, not in Toronto, but in Esztergom. Also, Lotti's telephone number, listed here in Klára's recent calls. The two of them were in contact, just days before Klára's murder."

"Let me see that," Erika said.

She reached across the desk and took the page from Eszter's outstretched hand.

"Yes, it's a thirty-three area code. If Lotti is in Esztergom, let's see what she can tell us." Without hesitation, she dialled the number and put the call on loudspeaker.

After three rings, a female voice answered and said, "Hello? Who is this?"

"This is Detective Erika Kelemen from the Budapest police. I'd like to speak with Mrs Lotti Menges."

"I am she. How can I help you?"

"I'm calling concerning your sister, Klára. I have some important information to discuss with you, in person."

"In person. I see. I rarely travel to Budapest."

Erika checked the time. "Don't worry. We'll come to you. It's 7.15 p.m. It should take an hour. We'll be with you by 8.30, if that's okay?"

Lotti sounded unperturbed. "I shall put the kettle on. Now, let me give you the address…"

Few of the city's pubs and bars were open, so soon after the lockdown. Yet, for Péter Rigo and his pals, there had never been a problem in getting served with a few beers, either on or off-duty. On this occasion, Rigo was picking the brains of Balázs Gellér, his buddy from the Organised Crime Division.

"Ready for another one, Balázs?"

"It would be rude not to if you are buying, Péter."

"They're on the house, my friend. The landlord owes me. Fancy a shot too?"

"Why not? So, back to business. Are you saying, the killer is using potassium cyanide, with some kinky torture in the mix, to spice things up?"

"I've seen nothing like it before. And that bitch, Kelemen, wants me to educate her on cyanide killings. I mean, how the fuck should I know? Have your lads in the Drug Squad ever had to deal with it?"

Gellér emptied his beer glass. "It's not something we come across often. I've read studies and reports about cases from around the world. Its most common use is for suicides, but there have been some high-profile cases where it's been used to get rid of family members. There's an ongoing case in India, where they arrested a woman last year. She confessed to using cyanide to kill six people over a fourteen-year period. Even a pinch of the stuff is lethal, and once the victim ingests it, death is virtually guaranteed."

"Isn't there a tell-tale almond smell?"

"There can be a distinctive odour of burnt almond, but it's not detectable by everyone and it can be so subtle that by the time the victim recognises it, the poison is already at work."

"What makes it so lethal?"

"It kills by preventing oxygen from getting to the body's red blood cells. The heart and brain use a lot of oxygen, so cyanide is deadly to those organs. Your murderer probably watched his victim becoming dizzy, then gasping for breath and vomiting before she expired."

"Before he perforated her a few hundred times. At least we know suicide wasn't at play."

"That's true." Gellér drained his glass.

Rigo caught the eye of the barman. "Two more beers down here, and leave that bottle of Unicum."

Even though traffic was light along Route 10 for the hour-long journey northeast of Budapest, Erika had ample opportunity to curse the driving of almost every other road user. Eszter sat tight-lipped, eyes on the road ahead, with both hands clamped to the steering wheel of their squad car.

Finally, they arrived at the outskirts of Esztergom and a bumpy, patchwork-quilt of tarmac and potholes called Zsigmond Moricz Street. There they discovered a scruffy piece of grass and a handful of trees which divided two rows of ugly, five-story apartment blocks.

Lotti Menges lived on the second floor of one block. She answered the door. Erika made her introductions, and she and

Eszter both presented their ID.

Despite her slightly hunched posture, Lotti looked elegant and seemed in good health for a woman in her eighties. She had a stylish cut of short grey hair, swept back off her face, and wore red lipstick, an elegant blue woollen dress with matching blue pumps. Her greeting seemed genuinely warm and friendly.

"You must be thirsty after your long journey. The kettle is on. Tea, kávé, or something stronger?"

"We're on duty, but tea would be lovely," Erika said.

While Lotti made herself busy in the kitchen, Erika browsed around the living room. The place had been decorated in a contemporary style. There were several maple leaf mementos of Canada and photographs of a younger, smiling Lotti at Niagara Falls, and another at the CN Tower in Toronto. Placed upon a coffee table between the two comfy sofas were elegant china cups and saucers.

There was a call from the kitchen.

"Could one of you young women help me carry things through?"

Eszter jumped up. Moments later, she reappeared with a tray of tea things and a plate of sweet pastries.

Even with experience and years of practice behind her, whenever Erika had bad news to deliver, she always felt queasy. She imagined how it must feel to be on the receiving end. In the past, Axel Rácz had repeatedly told her to toughen up and grow a pair, but that had made no difference to her empathy levels.

When Lotti joined them, Erika said, "Mrs Menges, please come and take a seat. I'm afraid we have bad news concerning Klára."

Lotti sat on the sofa and reached for the tea-tray. "Shall I be mother? How do you take your tea?"

Erika placed her hand on Lotti's, uncertain whether she was trying to steady the old women or herself. "Could we leave the tea for a moment, please? We found your sister dead in her apartment, yesterday morning. Someone murdered her."

Lotti freed her hand. She picked up the teapot and began pouring. "Better have this before it goes cold. Help yourself to milk and sugar."

Erika spoke louder, in case it was a hearing problem, "Mrs Menges, did you hear what I said? We found your sister murdered in her apartment."

"There's no need to shout, dear. You may think it a little strange that I am not beside myself with grief. However, my sister and I were not close."

"She kept your letters all these years. We found them in her apartment."

"Then you'll know why we were not close." Lotti poured milk into her own teacup.

Erika sat on the edge of the sofa. She tried to weigh up the lack of reaction. and glanced across at Eszter, prompting her to take notes. "It's important you tell us everything you can about her."

Lotti took a sip from her cup. Her hand was steady when she placed the cup back onto its saucer. She gave out a long sigh.

"We did everything together when we were young. There were just two of us girls. She is, I mean was, three years older than me, and was always the leader. The war years were hard, especially under the Arrow Cross, but somehow we survived."

Lotti's eyes met Erika's. "Our parents brought us up as Catholics, and the community was strong. Things changed after the war, when Klára fell in love. It turned out her beau was an officer from the State Security Authority. She became obsessed with him, and he inducted her into that foul organisation"

Her voice remained steady. "He found her a job at their headquarters in Andrássy Street, or Stalin Street, as they called it back then. She told us she worked in administration. But we learned the truth from a neighbour who survived imprisonment there. They actually used Klára in what they called 'softening up' of prisoners. She did unspeakable things. I was so naïve and still refused to believe the stories, right up to when she eventually admitted to her heinous crimes.

"Having a member of the family in the AVH, made us outcasts. After the uprising, we made a dash for the border. One would think that forcing her family to flee the country would be enough, but not for Klára. During the uprising, the people disbanded the AVH. But once the communists regained control, many former AVH members turned up in other government jobs. My sister was one such person. She made a career in the intelligence service. We only learned this later, because she used her contacts to track us down in Ontario. If you have seen the letters, you will know my feelings towards her never changed. She was a despicable traitor, to her family and country!"

Eszter was filling page after page of her notebook.

Lotti's eyes were granite-like, hard and unyielding.

"What about you?" said Erika. "How was your life, on a different continent?"

"It was hard at first. We had little money and few possessions. Mother cleaned and Uncle Lajos took what work he could find. I was twenty-one when we arrived and, through the Canadian government's aid programme, could finally study at the university in Toronto, alongside my three part-time jobs."

Although sixty years seemed like a very long time to carry a grudge, Erika admired Lotti's fortitude. She reminded her of her own Aunt Sofia, who had also fled Budapest with her family after the uprising, ending up in London. "What was your subject?" she asked.

"Chemistry," said Lotti. "I became a science teacher. Married to the job for forty years. But ever since the end of the Cold War, I yearned to return here to my homeland. Budapest had too many unhappy memories, so I settled here in the old capital. Life is slower in Esztergom. I do volunteer work at the Basilica as a communicant, delivering the sacrament to the sick and needy."

"Did you tell Klára you were back in Hungary?" Eszter asked.

"I had no intention of informing her. But, once again, her contacts within the immigration service alerted her to my arrival. She wrote to me again and again, begging forgiveness, and I told her repeatedly and in no uncertain terms, that I wanted nothing to do with her."

"When were you last in contact with her?" Erika said, exchanging a knowing look with Eszter.

Lotti smoothed the lap of her dress with her hands.

"She called me here at home, last Saturday afternoon."

A five-minute call at 17.34 on Saturday, the sixteenth of May, had shown up on Klára's call record, so that much was true. "What did she want?" said Erika, leaning in closer.

Lotti arched away, maintaining her distance. "It was so strange," Lotti said wistfully. "She told me God was back in her life. She wanted to make a fresh beginning, and she was calling to tell me she prayed for my soul."

"How did you respond?" asked Erika.

"I told her to enjoy it while she could, because she was surely going to spend the rest of eternity in hell." Her jaw muscles twitched and her lips pursed tightly.

"Lotti, I have to ask you this. Where were you, in the afternoon and evening of Tuesday, nineteenth of May?"

"You mean at the time someone murdered my sister?"

Lotti's mind appeared razor sharp for someone her age. She seemed not in the least perturbed by the questioning.

"I'm sorry, but we have to ask. Just in order to eliminate you from our enquiries," Erika said.

"I was here, alone." Lotti's hands were clasped tightly together, but her voice remained calm.

"Did you see anyone? A neighbour, perhaps?"

"Not a soul."

Erika closely watched her body language.

"I want you to come to Budapest, to identify the body formally. At midday, on Monday if that's possible. Do you drive?"

"I'll take the train."

"Perfect," Erika said, placing her business card on the coffee table. "Let me know which one you plan to take; we'll collect you at the station. For now, thank you for the hospitality, but we need to make tracks."

Lotti pushed herself up from the sofa, needing no help.

Five years older than my mother, yet far more nimble. Erika's eyes focused on a delicately patterned porcelain object, sitting on top of a small chest of drawers by the front door. The vintage hat pin holder stood approximately three inches tall. "You like hats?"

Lotti made her way to the front door. On the way, she plucked a hatpin from its holder. "I'm from a generation of Catholic women who would not be seen dead in church without a hat. These come in handy. Thank you for coming all this way. I'll pray for my sister's soul tonight, and also for yours."

It was already after ten o'clock when Erika adjusted the rake of the passenger seat, settled back, and wearily closed her eyes.

"What do you think?" she asked.

Their headlamps pierced the darkness of the leaden night sky.

"She's as sharp as one of those hatpins, and I wouldn't like to get on the wrong side of her," Eszter replied. "Do you think she knows more than she is letting on?"

There was no reply.

Eszter focused on the road ahead and mild snoring soon reverberated.

She caught the road signs to Route 11 and Budapest in her headlamps, and smiled contentedly. It had been a long day, but if the traffic was light, she should be in bed with Ferenc by 11.30, repaying him for unlocking Klára's phone earlier this evening. The snoring was rhythmical. Best of all, there was no manic passenger seat driving. Life was good.

"I can't believe I slept all the way," said Erika, rubbing her eyes and realising they had arrived in the car park outside her apartment. She rummaged in the passenger footwell until she found her handbag.

"My car's still at HQ. Could you pick me up on your way in tomorrow morning? Say, at six forty-five."

Eszter was holding back a yawn. "No problem, boss. See you then."

As she stepped out of the car, Erika's phone rang. She mouthed for Eszter to stay put while she accepted the call and leaned against the side of the car.

After several glasses of wine, Marcel was feeling morose. The dinner he had prepared hours ago was no longer worth eating, and by eleven o'clock he was beyond caring about Erika's thoughtlessness. He still felt shaken by this afternoon's episode outside the parliament building, and by his traumatic time in custody.

He mumbled to himself, "The bloody woman could have called, or sent a text. Just a word, to say she'd be late."

Erika's number one house rule was no smoking in the apartment under any circumstances, but ignoring that, he lit one up on the balcony. The evening was balmy, and three floors below him, Victor Hugo Street appeared calm. Yet, no sooner had he lit up his cigarette than he noticed a squad car pull up. Erika got out. Even from this distance, he could hear her voice.

Marcel quickly stubbed out his smoke, using a saucer as an ashtray. He watched and waited while she spoke on her phone and leaned against the car. Several minutes later, she jumped back into the passenger seat and slammed the door. The car set off again, tyres screeching as it turned the corner and disappeared from view.

Frustration, anger and bewilderment filled his mind. Marcel lit another cigarette on the balcony and took a long drag. He shouted, loud enough for the neighbours to hear, "I'm just the lodger. Don't mind me!"

They turned the corner into Visegrádi Street, and Erika suddenly felt re-energised and wide awake. "Rácz is about to blow a gasket. Another body has been found. This one is on Hős Street. Apparently there are similarities to the MO used on Klára Menges. You want me to drive?"

"I'm fine." Eszter yawned. The dashboard clock showed it was already 23.25.

With blue lights flashing and two-tone siren wailing, Eszter weaved her way through the traffic. Ten minutes later she turned left, into a neighbourhood the tourists did not visit: poor, rough and often dangerous.

Outside a decaying, four-storey tenement block was a line of police vehicles. Inside one van sat a police driver who directed them to the top floor of the tenement.

They took the stairwell. The acrid stench of urine-impregnated concrete was enough to turn Erika's stomach, and on every landing she saw discarded needles.

They showed their ID to the uniform standing guard outside. He lifted the tape and waved them through. Several men from the SOCO team were already at work in the tiny apartment.

Erika's nose wrinkled. A rancid smell hung in the air, and its cause was soon apparent. The body of an obese old man was sprawled over a faded, red-velvet sofa. Protruding from the middle of his forehead, about an inch above the bridge of his nose, was what appeared to be the blunt end of a red pencil. A stream of blood and brains had coursed down the victim's nose and flowed in rivulets across his fat, bloated cheeks. The stream had merged with a pool of vomit from his half-open mouth.

One of the white suited men was kneeling close to the body. For the second time today, Erika recognised the slim physique of József Baldi.

"Good evening, professor."

He was using a small brush to sweep debris from the victim's forehead into an evidence bag. He glanced up.

"Good evening, ladies. This was a brutal way to go, even by the standards of this neighbourhood. Bone dust, I believe. My theory is, they drilled the hole before inserting a pencil. Whether he was conscious when the drilling began is still unclear."

Erika's stomach heaved at the thought. "Time of death?"

"My current estimate is twelve to fourteen hours ago. As always, we'll know more after the autopsy."

Eszter held a hand across her mouth. She looked like she may faint at any moment.

The uniformed officer at the front door coughed. "Ahem. Detective Kelemen, the victim's name is Ervin Nagy. His next door neighbours, Mr and Mrs Juhász, found him, at around ten this evening. They've been told to wait up and make a statement. Shall I send them in?"

Erika pondered for a moment. It was now after midnight. She had wondered how she would spend her fiftieth birthday. Now she knew. "Tell them we'll be back in the morning to take their statements." She nudged Eszter's elbow. "There are too many people in here. We're in danger of contaminating the evidence, and we'll see more when it's daylight."

After showering, Erika crashed down in her spare room so she wouldn't wake Marcel. These last few months, with a man to keep her warm in bed, she had grown accustomed to sleeping naked. It felt strange, without him there to cuddle.

This tiny room felt hot and stuffy. She threw back the duvet and lay on her back, gazing at the open window, listening to the dawn chorus and watching the skies slowly lighten.

Klára Menges, poisoned with cyanide, her torso mutilated by hundreds of tiny stab wounds. Ervin Nagy, possibly also poisoned, his forehead drilled, and a pencil planted into his brain like a flagpole. The pencil was surely intended to be a statement, but what did it mean?

The gruesome images went round and round in her head until finally she dozed off at around five o'clock.

CHAPTER FOUR

S tartled by the alarm, Erika shuffled into the kitchen to switch the kettle on. Sitting on the breakfast bar was a white envelope with her name handwritten on it. Had it been there when she arrived home? She didn't think so. She tore it open and pulled out a birthday card. The message inside said,

Happy 50th Birthday Erika, with love from Marcel xx.

She scowled and thought how little he really knew her.

The master bedroom door creaked open. Marcel appeared, wearing only a pair of boxer shorts. His grey hair was uncombed and his beard was unshaven.

She felt obliged to say something nice. "Thanks for the card." It was all she could manage. "You couldn't make the coffee, could you? I've got a hell of a day ahead, and Eszter's picking me up in half an hour."

He grunted. "Late night?"

She nodded.

As she cleaned her teeth in the bathroom, she could hear him slamming cupboard doors.

Eszter followed instructions, and was waiting in the car park outside the apartment block at 6.45 a.m. She'd only grabbed four hours of sleep since dropping Kelemen off and needed several more. In between the time she and Ferenc had woken, made love and showered together, they had spoken again about work. She asked him to check out a phone number that had appeared on Klára's recent calls, but for whom she had no other contact details.

While she waited in the parking bay for Kelemen, she listened to the radio news and current affairs show. Her ears pricked up when the presenter introduced Sándor Farkas, Lieutenant Colonel of the Hungarian Police Force. Farkas droned on about winning the fight against Covid, reminding everyone it was still compulsory to wear masks in shops and on public transport.

When Kelemen arrived, her face looked like thunder. She flung open the door, threw her handbag into the footwell and slumped into her seat, slamming the door.

"Sorry, I'm late. That bloody man! I don't know why I bother."

Dora smiled kindly and handed Erika a black coffee and a chocolate muffin with a single lit candle. There was never any gushing from Dora.

"Happy birthday!" she said.

Erika didn't know whether to laugh or cry. For a moment, she covered her eyes with her hands. "How did you know?"

"I just did. Hope it's a good one for you."

The intercom buzzed. "Send her in." Rácz sounded grumpy.

Erika raised her eyebrows and took a deep breath before stepping into his office and taking a seat at the conference table.

Dora followed her in. She placed the coffee and cake on the table, then left.

Rácz took one look at the cake and smirked.

"Twenty-one again?"

The cake and all the fuss from Dora made her cross. That woman just didn't know when to take a hint. The thought that news of her fiftieth could soon spread around the tenth floor was too appalling to contemplate.

She replied brusquely. "Don't ask. Move on."

His smirk evaporated. "The situation in Hős Street?"

"It's too early to say whether there's a connection with the Klára Menges case, but this time the killer drilled the victim's forehead and left the sharp end of a pencil in his grey matter. However, as with Klára, there were no signs of a struggle, nor any evidence of restraint being used. Baldi was there when we arrived. He thinks the victim may have been poisoned, which could also link the two cases."

Rácz ran his hands through his dyed coal-black hair and rubbed his temples.

"My God! Every old person in Budapest will soon be demanding police protection! Don't waste my time, Kelemen. Get out there. Find the psycho who did this."

The glass partition walls of his office reverberated when she slammed the door on her way out.

It was almost ten a.m. when Eszter parked the Audi outside the Hős Street tenement next to a SOCO van. This time, however, there was no police officer guarding the vehicles. Instead, a couple of scruffy, feral-looking kids were taking a keen interest in their presence.

One of them called over, "Look after your car, ladies?"

Erika tried bluffing. "No, thanks. We've got a police dog in the back,"

"Put fires out, can it?" said the cheeky boy. "The SOCO guys gave us 500 Forint, and the van still has wheels, don't it? C'mon, ladies, you know it makes sense."

She turned to Eszter, who pulled a banknote out of her purse. The boy ran over and grabbed it before she could change her mind.

Erika wagged a finger at him. "Not a scratch, or else!"

She was glad it wasn't her own car.

Mr and Mrs Juhász, a married couple in their sixties, sat side by side on their sofa. He held a box of tissues on his lap. She used them to dab her eyes and blow her nose. Erika sat on the edge of the armchair opposite, and Eszter stood by the front door taking notes.

Erika said, "It must have been very upsetting for both of you. Had you known him for long?"

Mr Juhász scratched his chin. "We moved here in 2011. He was already living next door. He mainly kept himself to himself, but we always got on well. He was another cat lover."

Erika's nose twitched, and she readied herself to sneeze. "Who discovered the body?"

Mrs Juhász's eyes were red and puffy. She said, "I'd been knocking, ever since we got back from the supermarket. We bought some fish for the cats. I mean for his and for ours. I kept the fish in my fridge, but I knew Ervin was running low. During the evening I kept knocking on his door. We could hear his TV, but he didn't answer. A few years ago, he gave us a spare key, just in case. I said to Ed, maybe this is one of those 'just in case' times. And it was. It was both of us who found him. I didn't want to go in on my own." She plucked another tissue from the box and dabbed her eyes.

Mr Juhász nodded ruefully. "Who would do such a thing to an old man?"

"Did you see anyone come or go?" said Erika.

"We were here all afternoon, from about two o'clock onwards. We heard nothing, but the sound of his TV. The walls are thin. None of us have much privacy."

A ginger cat sauntered out from behind the sofa, tail up. It brushed past Erika, leaving hairs on her black trousers, before disappearing into the kitchen. She tucked her feet in, trying hard not to show her discomfort.

"Did Mr Nagy have family or friends, or anyone who called on him?"

"He was a very solitary man," said Mr Juhász. He turned and looked at his wife. They shrugged at one another. "No one comes to mind. Nobody at all."

"What about the other neighbours? Did he have any enemies around here?"

"If he did, he kept it quiet," said Mr Juhász. "This place has a terrible reputation. But some good folks live here too. We keep ourselves to ourselves. Ervin did the same."

For the time being, Erika had heard enough. She placed her business card on the coffee table and stood to leave, brushing hairs off her jacket.

She said, "Thank you. If anything comes to mind, you can call me on this number. Just one more thing. Did Mr Nagy ever say what line of work he was in before he retired?"

"Only that he used to work for the government. He never told us more than that, did he, love?"

Mrs Juhász shook her head and blew her nose once more. "How much longer will the police officers be next door?" she asked.

How long is a piece of string? Erika replied with a smile. "Difficult to say. It depends on what they find."

Outside in the corridor, Erika said, "Let's hope SOCO finds something useful, because other than knowing he owned a bloody cat, he appears to have been a closed book to his neighbours."

Eszter's phone rang. "It's Ferenc, shall I...?"

Erika nodded and turned to speak with the uniformed officer at the taped-off entrance to the Nagy apartment.

Eszter kept her voice low. "I'm in Hős Street with the boss. What's up?"

"I've got some information for you, about that number you asked me to check out," he said.

"Thanks, babe. I'll see you when I get back. I owe you one."

She ended the call before he could respond with any embarrassing remarks. A warm glow tingled deep inside her.

For the next hour, they knocked on doors around the crime scene. None of the neighbours had a nasty word to say about Ervin Nagy. Nobody seemed to know much about him, other than he was overweight, had mobility problems, and owned a cat. No one had seen a visitor yesterday afternoon, nor could they shed much light on his background. For those who knew him, the consensus seemed to be: he had once been a civil servant.

By mid-morning, Erika's headache had worsened. There had been not one hint of a breakthrough. She temporarily paused the door-to-door enquiries, but before returning to Teve Street, she called in at the victim's apartment and collected his belongings from the SOCO team. They were already waiting in a cardboard box, bagged and labelled.

She handed the box to Eszter and eased her way under the crime scene tape.

Voices came from the direction of the stairwell. Then, from around the corner came a woman carrying a microphone, followed by a man with a video camera, and another man carrying other equipment. Erika recognised the black-haired woman leading the pack as Viktoria Gindl, a pushy reporter from a local TV News Channel. Gindl was probably in her mid-thirties, was tall and thin, and reminded Erika of a preying-mantis. Erika presumed a neighbour had called the channel with word of the ongoing police presence in Hős Street and a body bag carried out in the middle of the night.

Erika was not anti-media, but she hated being door-stepped. She whispered to Eszter, "Look out, here's trouble. Tell the uniform on the door to make sure he keeps this lot away from the crime scene."

"Ahem! Excuse me. Viktoria Gindl, M1-TV."

Gindl thrust her microphone towards Erika's face. Meanwhile, the video camera swung in her direction.

"Are you with the police? We have received reports of the suspicious death of a resident. I understand the victim was a man in his eighties. I urgently need to speak with the senior investigating officer."

Erika bristled. "I am the SIO on this case, Senior Detective Erika Kelemen. I can confirm we are gathering the facts and attempting to speak to the next of kin. We will issue a press statement as soon as possible."

"You are the SIO? Really?" Sarcasm dripped from Gindl's mouth.

Having to deal with discriminatory and derogatory remarks from a man was one thing. There was no way she was putting up with barbed comments from another woman. She beckoned for Eszter to follow her, and they carefully manoeuvred their way past the TV crew.

"No further comment," said Erika, conscious of the rolling camera, and unwilling to provide them with any sound-bite ammunition.

Leaving Gindl's protestations and questions in her wake, she marched towards the stairwell, her jaws clenched tightly. The foul smell perfectly matched her mood. The next time I cross paths with that bitch, it will be on my terms, she told herself.

Throughout their drive back to HQ, Eszter listened patiently to Kelemen bemoaning what she described as the ambush, and barking her orders into the phone. The boss demanded to see Rigo, Márkos and Dolman in the Incident Room at twelve-thirty, sharp.

Once back at Teve Street, Eszter logged the victim's belongings with Antal Eger and made her way to the IT department where Ferenc was waiting for her.

"What did you find out?" she said, still slightly out of breath.

"It's good to see you too, babe," he replied. Seeing that they were alone, he put his arms around her and squeezed.

Eszter wriggled from his embrace; cheeks flushed. "Not here," she chided.

He dropped his boyish grin and said, "The unidentified number that called Klára, it came from a pre-paid burner phone."

She raised her eyebrows. "I need to know everything you can tell me about the burner. And while you're at it, look at this." She handed him the evidence bag containing the phone belonging to Ervin Nagy.

"This phone belonged to our second victim. I'll need access to his call records too. Just as soon as you manage it."

He smiled in his familiar, lopsided way. "You don't ask for much, do you?"

Eszter checked the coast was clear before landing a kiss on his lips. "Must run," she said. "Call me when you have something."

Erika retreated to her tiny office and slumped into the chair, her head still pounding. From the depths of her handbag she found paracetamol and a half-empty bottle of warm water. She swallowed the pills then made a call.

"I'm busy. What is it?" said Rácz.

The bloody man had asked to be kept informed. She gritted her teeth and did her best to keep her cool. "The media have already got hold of the Nagy story. A TV crew ambushed us outside the crime scene."

"Welcome back to the Murder Squad. These days, everyone has a camera in their pocket and privacy no longer exists. Talk to the Press Office. Get them to issue a statement."

That was it. The call was terminated. While she silently cursed him, the name of *David* appeared on her screen.

Her brother *never* called her at work. "To what do I owe the honour?" she said.

David launched into a tirade. "You can't just dump all of this care home shit on me, Erika. Mum's not going anywhere. It's scary for her in the home, but it's scary for us on the outside. My business has taken a whack during the lockdown. The phones aren't ringing, and customers aren't paying their bills. If things don't improve, I'll be out of business in a fortnight."

Her twelve-thirty briefing was due to begin in two minutes. *She dare not be late herself, having kicked up such a fuss to get*

everyone there. Not that she lacked empathy about her brother's
predicament, but he needed to remember the facts. She had
single-handedly shouldered the burden of her mother's care for
so long. David had been absent when she had chosen the home.
He had been absent when Mum had moved in. He had been
absent again when she struggled to deal with such massive life
changes. For now, he needed to step up. It would be character
building for him.

"It's been a long time since you have had to fit Mum into your
busy schedule, David. Sorry, but I need to go. Talk again soon.
Bye."

She had trained herself to compartmentalise, and for most of
the time that worked well for her. Although right now, she felt
pangs of guilt for not keeping on top of Mum's problems.

Erika raced across the open-plan office and burst into the
Incident Room. There she found Rigo slouched on a chair,
reading a newspaper. Dolman and Márkos were laughing and
larking about, while Eszter was on her phone.

She strode to the front and turned on her heels to address
them.

"Right, listen up. Our investigation is now dealing with two
homicides. What I need to know is, are the two crimes related?"

She took a marker pen and wrote on the whiteboards while
she spoke. "We know someone murdered Klára Menges at
approximately five p.m., on Tuesday 19 May, just hours after she
spoke on the phone with her cleaner. There were no signs of
forced entry into the apartment, meaning she freely allowed the
killer into her home. The cause of death was potassium cyanide
poisoning, which is likely to have finished her within twenty
minutes. There were no signs of ligatures or restraints, so the

stripping of her body and the subsequent multiple stab wounds appear to have carried out after she lost consciousness."

Erika turned to face them and saw she had their attention. "As we also know, the killer used the same sharp instrument to inscribe the letters AVH under Klára's right arm. It's pretty clear, from the letters found in her apartment that Klára was once a member of the State Security Service. Her sister, Lotti, told us that Klára worked at the AVH headquarters in Andrássy Street, and tortured prisoners for a living."

Márkos quipped, "Revenge, for something that happened sixty-five years ago? We're looking for an ancient killer, with the memory of an elephant."

The suggestion wasn't completely outrageous, but she wanted to keep an open mind. "Don't jump to conclusions. Not until we have more pieces of the jigsaw in place."

Then, switching to a second whiteboard, she continued to write. "The second victim, Ervin Nagy, murdered in his apartment, around midday yesterday. Detective Szabó, have you arranged the video call with the pathologist?"

Eszter aimed the remote and pressed the button. Within seconds, Professor Baldi appeared on the screen.

"Good afternoon, professor," Erika said. "Good of you to join us. Do you have any news concerning our second victim?"

"I can confirm his blood tests of Ervin Nagy confirm potassium cyanide as his cause of death. You have a serial killer on your hands, detective." He paused, perhaps for dramatic effect, perhaps allowing them to absorb his conclusions. The professor's face shrank to a small image in the screen's corner. The primary screen switched to a photograph of the victim's head with the blunt end of a pencil protruding from between his eyes. There were gasps in the room; hardly surprising given the three men had not previously seen the image.

Erika said, "That sounds too general. A serial killer implies someone with an indiscriminate approach to finding his victims. It looks to me like we are dealing with someone who seeks his predetermined targets and customises their end. Wouldn't a more apt description be we're dealing with an assassin?"

Baldi continued, "Perhaps your definition could be correct, detective. As I suspected, prior to inserting the pencil, the killer bored the skull with an electric drill. We found residues from a steel drill bit with the bone dust on his forehead."

"What about the time of death?" she said.

"I would say, between midday and 1.00 p.m. yesterday. That's all I have for now. I'll send my full report over once we've completed the post-mortem."

The video call was over. The screen went blank.

"We've got a fucking psycho on our hands," said Rigo.

Erika added the cause and time of death to her whiteboard.

She turned to face the group. "These are not just examples of gratuitous violence. The killer has found a way of being allowed to enter the homes of two old people. In their own homes he poisoned them, then played out some grotesque scene that means something to him, perhaps also to the victim. A signature, or even a message. Also, he or she, because I discount nothing until we have evidence, struck twice in two days. This is a person in a hurry."

Dolman was staring at the whiteboards, his elbows resting on his knees and chin cupped by his hands. "Was Nagy also connected to the AVH?"

"Perhaps, but there's no evidence to confirm that yet," she said. "Let's stick to the known facts for now. Come on, people. What else do we know?"

Eszter raised her hand like a schoolgirl at the back of the classroom. She was straining once again to get noticed.

Erika pointed at the outstretched hand.

"Just speak up when you have something to say, Detective Szabó."

Eszter's index finger tracked down the report she was clutching hold of. "I've matched most of Klára's incoming and outgoing calls, either with contacts in her phone, or from her address book. All except one, which I now know belongs to a burner phone. What's more, I just received a message from Ferenc. A different burner phone appears to have been used to make calls to Nagy's phone."

Erika paced in front of the whiteboards. "Has he pinpointed the location of these burners?"

"He's working on it, boss," Eszter replied.

"What about the rest of Nagy's belongings?" Erika said.

"I booked them into the property room," Eszter said.

The second killing had ratcheted up the stakes. Whoever was responsible had developed a system, and had the potential to strike as many times as he wanted. There was no time to waste. Erika clapped her hands. "Okay. Rigo. You, Dolman and Márkos, go through his stuff. See what else you can find. Szabó, keep on the phone tracking. All of you, be aware: the press has already got hold of the Nagy story. When the media finds out about the link between the two cases, things are going to get crazy. I'll get the Press Office to put out a release. In the meantime, don't discuss this with anyone outside the team."

The door to Erika's office was open when she arrived. Seated in her visitor chair was a young man with the mop of blond hair and a smoothly-shaved, fresh complexion. He wore a khaki suit, with a brightly coloured shirt which made him look more of an advertising or media type than a homicide detective.

"You must be the Press Officer," she said. "Don't mind if I don't shake your hand."

His smile was warm and friendly. "I'm Levente Barna from the Press Office. I'm your one o'clock appointment. The only information I've been given is that your case is attracting media interest and you need some support. Perhaps you could start from the beginning?" He leant back, crossed his long legs, and opened his iPad.

She marshalled her thoughts before replying. "A situation which began on Wednesday, with the murder of an old woman, has now become far more complex. We found a second victim last night: a male, also in his eighties. It now appears the same person committed both murders."

He grinned. "A serial killer case. How exciting!"

She stiffened. "That's precisely the reaction we don't want from the media. I need you to help me close this down until we have some idea concerning the direction we're heading in."

He turned the screen of his iPad to face her.

The midday TV news was playing. She saw her own startled face in the closeup, a microphone pressed close to her mouth. Her only words were, "No further comment." The scene pivoted to where TV reporter Viktoria Gindl spoke to the camera. Her tone well-modulated, and her words well-articulated. "Residents are in shock, since yesterday evening, when a brutal murder took place in their community. Those we spoke to, are angry. They complained about poor communication from the police and a lack of information. This is Viktoria Gindl, M1 TV, Hős Street."

"Have you done much media work?" he asked.

She shook her head in disbelief at the travesty she had just watched, too shocked to speak.

"Don't worry about it. It's too late to try to 'close this down.' Better we get a simple message out there and use the media to help us achieve our objectives. Does that make sense?"

Levente Barna had an easy-going confidence about him, yet without the brashness of youth. She found him reassuring, even though she was old enough to be his mother.

"Why don't you fill me in with the details, then we can talk strategy," he said, settling back in his chair, iPad on his lap and stylus in hand.

Erika ran through the key points: the cyanide poisonings; a killer who had entered his victim's homes without force; the bizarre forms of post-mortem torture inflicted; Klára's alleged connection with the State Protection Authority, whose AVH initials the killer had spelt out on her corpse. Then there was Klára's sister, Lotti, who openly harboured a sixty-year-old grudge. Then there were the burner phones used to communicate with both victims in the days leading up to their deaths.

"Erika, this is one hell of a story. The AVH was a brutal organisation. For sure, there will still be former members alive today. Did the second victim have links with them?"

"We don't know. We're still searching his apartment and belongings, but you seem to know more about the AVH than some others your age."

"I studied Hungarian twentieth-century history at the university. My professor was one of the most well-informed people you will ever meet. He's now the curator of the House of Terror Museum at 60 Andrássy Street."

"The place where Klára worked. What's his name?"

"Professor Turay. Give me your number and I'll send you his details. Have you ever visited the museum?"

"No, I've never been. It's not a place I would visit, even out of historical interest. Now, regarding our media strategy, what do you think?"

"I advise openness. Never try to hide things the media can find out easily for themselves. You've had two murders land on your desk in less than forty-eight hours. Even if we feed them to the media as two separate cases, it's only a matter of time before someone connects the dots. If we have a serial killer, who knows where and when he will strike again? My advice is: run a media conference on Monday. I'll issue the invitations, and you prepare a brief presentation. Outline what you can legally make public. Then set up a hotline and invite the public to call in with any relevant information. Chances are you'll get plenty of crackpots, but you may strike lucky. In the meantime, press on with your regular investigations. Does that make sense?"

Erika nodded. She loathed being the centre of attention, and a press conference was way outside her comfort zone. Yet, everything this young man had said so far made perfect sense.

Marcel's client work had been quieter than normal today, which meant he had too much time on his hands, much of which he'd spent brooding about their row. In the months he'd known Erika, it was abundantly clear she loved her job. There was a time, at the beginning of their relationship, when she'd kept him informed about working late. Nowadays, it seemed she preferred to keep him in the dark.

Something major had happened to her at work this week. That much was obvious. Not as though she had bothered to explain. All he wanted was information. He needed to be part of the solution to whatever problems she was facing. Instead, he felt he was part of the problem.

Damn it! It's still her birthday today, and a significant one at that.

From experience, he knew she was unlikely to reach out. 'Never apologise and never explain,' seemed to be her motto. So, if something was to be rescued from this car crash of a day, he would have to make the running.

He made the call, expecting to be greeted by her all-too-familiar voicemail message. When she answered in person, he was surprised and stumbled through his words.

"Look, I know your birthday didn't get off to the best of starts. How about I prepare a celebration meal for us this evening? We've got those good sirloins in the fridge and a bottle of Tokaji. Come on, darling, it's Friday, the weekend. Have an early night and let's enjoy ourselves."

After a pause, she said, "That sounds great. I can't promise, but I will try to be home by seven. I'll message later with an ETA. Must go. Bye."

It was hardly the result he had hoped for, but it was something. Yet that was Erika, in a nutshell. What else could he expect? It was one-thirty. Time for his daily run and a chance to let off some steam. Only this time, he would stay well clear of the parliament building.

The call from Marcel had put Erika off her stride. For several seconds she sat alone in her office, trying to re-focus. The most daunting task ahead of her was the media conference on Monday. She truly hated to be in the limelight, and would have to compensate for her nerves by leaving nothing to chance in her presentation. One enormous gap in her knowledge was around the former Hungarian secret police organisation, and if Klára's involvement in the organisation was a link to her murder, she needed to know more. Speaking to an expert on the subject sounded like a good idea. She found Levente's message on her phone, saved the contact, and tried her luck.

"Professor Turay?"

"Yes, who is this?"

"Detective Erika Kelemen from the Budapest Homicide Department. My colleague, Levente Barna, recommended I call you. I need some advice concerning the AVH. Levente says you are an expert in the field."

"That's kind of him. Also, your timing is impeccable, Detective. I shall be out of town from this evening, until our public reopening next month. But, if you think I can help, you are welcome to come this afternoon. We can meet here at the museum. The lockdown means we are still closed, but the security guard will expect you."

"We're on our way," she said.

Eszter parked the car in Csengery Street, just fifty metres walk from the tree-lined boulevard that connects downtown Budapest to Heroes' Square. When they approached the museum entrance, Erika paused and read the brass plaque mounted on a concrete plinth:

A MEMORIAL OF POLITICAL TERROR
WHERE PEOPLE WERE DETAINED,
TORTURED AND MURDERED DURING
THE ARROW CROSS AND COMMUNIST
DICTATORSHIPS FROM THE LATE 1930S.
THE BUILDING WAS USED AS A MEETING
PLACE BY THE ARROW CROSS AND
LATER AS THEIR PARTY HEADQUARTERS,
DUBBED THE HOUSE OF LOYALTY.
IT WAS THEN TAKEN OVER BY THE COMMUNIST
SECRET POLICE IN 1945 AND LATER
SERVED AS HEADQUARTERS FOR HUN-
GARY'S SECRET SERVICE ORGANISATION
THE STATE PROTECTION AUTHORITY.

She considered how she had been past this place hundreds of times, yet never felt the urge to enter. The entire concept of the museum harked back to such an awful period in the country's history. It was a period hardly ever spoken about during her school days. Anyway, who would want to dwell on such terrible times?

The matt-grey paintwork on the double entrance door and fluted stone columns looked like it had all seen better days. Erika wondered whether the museum was short on maintenance budget or whether it was all part of the communist-era retro look. She tried the door and found it locked. Then, peering through the wrought-iron latticework that protected the arched half lights, she saw a security guard smoking in the foyer. She knocked. He looked startled, and brusquely waved them away. But when she held out her ID, he responded by stubbing out his cigarette. As he opened the door, he tucked in his shirt and straightened his tie.

Erika raised her right eyebrow. "Here to see Professor Turay."

The guard made a call, using the old-fashioned telephone mounted on the wall.

Once inside the foyer, Erika stared ahead at the imposing black granite staircase, flanked with grey neo-classical stone columns. They had illuminated the staircase from above by backlighting the vaulted ceiling. At the top of the stairs were two matching and symmetrically placed granite obelisks: one black, one red. On the left they had inscribed the black granite in gold leaf with a large Arrow Cross motif and the words *In Memory of the Arrow Cross Terror Victims*. To its right, the red obelisk was similarly adorned with a large gold star and the words *In memory of the Communist Terror Victims*.

A short, plump, grey-haired man appeared at the top of the stairs. He wore baggy brown corduroy trousers, a grey flannel shirt, and a blue V-necked, sleeveless pullover. He was jocular and called to them.

"You two are young. Come along."

They walked quickly up the steps and were soon exchanging rueful elbow bumps with him.

"Thank you, Professor, for seeing us at such short notice. I am Detective Kelemen. This is my colleague, Detective Szabó. Like I said on the phone, we are investigating the murder of two victims. One female, one male, both in their eighties. We have information that the female victim had connections to the AVH. It is said she once worked in this building. I am hoping to find out about what precisely went on here, and specifically about the role of the guards."

His welcoming smile turned into a concerned frown. "Then let's walk as we talk. Follow me."

They passed through the security barriers on the ground floor and walked into an atrium housing a full-sized Soviet battle tank. Behind the tank, stretching to the full, four-storey height of the building, was a wall of black-and-white photographs. Erika estimated there to be at least a thousand head and shoulders portraits and, at the top of the wall, were the words, ÁLDOZATOK VICTIMS.

"Let's take the stairs," said the professor, leading them into a stairwell and up several flights of stone steps. By the time they reached the second floor, he already seemed out of breath.

They entered a room dominated by a large central display, housing screens showing moving images. He spoke in a reverential, hushed tone.

"Welcome to room 201, which we call Double Occupation. The architects designed this building in 1880, but it first reached notoriety in 1937 when the Arrow Cross party took it as its headquarters. During the war, our country came into the crossfire of the Nazi and Communist dictatorships. Hundreds of thousands of Hungarian soldiers fought on the eastern front, and in 1943 suffered heavy losses inflicted by the Red Army. Then on March nineteenth, 1944, Hitler ordered the invasion of Hungary and the Nazis installed a puppet government. They forced our Jewish citizens to wear the Yellow Star. They rounded many up, then deported them to the German death camps. The Arrow Cross ironically called this building the 'House of Loyalty' and Arrow Cross people tortured and killed hundreds of Hungarians down below us, in the basement."

The professor guided them around to the other side of the display.

"And then came the communists," he said. His voice sounded heavy, and even sadder. "On August 27th, 1944, Soviet troops crossed the Hungarian border. Our country became the theatre of war in the clash between two superpowers. Soviet rule followed the short, but disastrous Nazi occupation. We lost our sovereignty on March nineteenth, 1944, and occupying forces remained on our soil for over four decades. In fact, the last Soviet soldier, Viktor Silov, only left us on June nineteenth, 1991.

"When the Hungarian communists arrived in Budapest on Soviet tanks, one of their first tasks was to take over this building. First, they called themselves the Department for Political Police. Later on they transformed into the State Security Office, or the AVO. Then finally they became the State Security Authority, or AVH, which you are now familiar with.

"A gentleman called Gábor Péter was head of all three organisations. He was a former tailor's apprentice, and the country learned to fear him and his terror network. Péter and his cronies attempted to reduce our people to insignificant objects: thousands feared them, and they feared each other. If ordered to do so, they killed without hesitation, or on the strength of confessions extorted during brutal interrogations, they sent their victims to the gallows, to prisons and to labour camps. Come, we have more to see."

The professor marched them on, through a myriad of rooms and exhibits. Erika wished they could have paused in each room, but knew their guide was watching the clock. They took more stairs and dropped a level to the first floor, eventually coming to a corner office, with beige walls, wooden parquet flooring and a mahogany desk and chair in one corner.

"This," said the professor, "is the office of Gábor Péter. We reconstructed it, based on original photographs. Under his leadership, a vast network of spies infiltrated the general population. These informers received full backing, and ideological and practical guidance from the Soviet occupiers. Nothing and no one could feel safe from them. It was with their support that the communists kept their grip on the country – a tyrannical regime which seized, mistreated or crippled one person from every third family."

Erika focused on the far corner of the room, trying to imagine Gábor Péter seated at his desk, using the black telephone, giving orders, signing away the lives of so many.

"Is it possible that Gábor Péter would have kept a file on each AVH member who worked here?" she asked.

"Not only personnel records, but evaluations, informer's reports, anything that could coerce and control the officers, guards and their families," said the professor.

Eszter noted his reply, "Do you know what happened to those files?"

"Many were lost. Though they still store some at the Ministry of the Interior. Here at the museum, the documents we hold are on display. But during the uprising in October 1956, the freedom fighters entered the building and ransacked it. Many things went missing. Now, if you've seen enough here, let's go to the basement."

Once again the professor led the way and they passed through first-floor rooms and exhibits bearing names such as Justice, Propaganda, Everyday Life, Treasury, Churches and Cardinal Mindszenty. Finally, they came to an elevator and entered.

His finger hovered over the button marked *Basement*. "Are you ready for this?"

Erika didn't know what to expect. She simply nodded in silence. Whereas Eszter looked as pale-faced as she had in the autopsy room.

The doors closed, and they descended.

The professor said solemnly, "There was an AVH slogan in the fifties: Don't only guard them, hate them!"

When the doors slid open they stepped out into a passage and turned left. He spoke as he led the way. "When the communist political police took over the building in January 1945, as a warning they changed the name from *House of Loyalty* to the *House of Terror*. Interrogations took place in upstairs rooms, usually at night, in line with Soviet practice. Suspects were prevented from sleeping for several nights, and most times held without food or water. Eventually they were brought down here, where every method of physical and psychological pressure was used. Beatings with truncheons were everyday affairs. They forced some prisoners to face the wall with the sharp end of a pencil pressed to their forehead, arms stretched out horizontally, sometimes for ten to twelve hours."

Erika caught Eszter's eye.

The professor continued, "What you see in these reconstructed cells will help you understand the hatred these barbarians felt for their fellow countrymen and women. Detainees were not allowed to change their underwear, nor take a bath. They were kept in these cells with a lightbulb shining all day and night. They had to lie on wet plank beds, or even on the bare floor. Sadistic warders beat them at every opportunity with rifle butts and truncheons, and fed them only once a day, with their ration of a cupful of bean soup and one hundred and fifty grams of bread."

The professor's description of life in the basement shook Erika. Such was the realisation that all he had described had taken place on the very spot where they now stood.

"The guards who committed these atrocities, were they all men?" she asked.

"Mostly, but not all. There are survivor reports that tell of unspeakable torture carried out by some female guards, using electric current, burning cigarettes, pliers and hatpins."

"Hatpins?" Her voice shot up an octave, and Eszter scribbled furiously.

The professor checked his watch. "I hope that's been useful, but I have a flight to catch, if you'll excuse me."

Erika handed him her card and said, "Professor, thank you for your time. It's been most informative."

He led them up a flight of worn stone steps. Erika imagined them worn away by the bare, bleeding feet of political prisoners, and the heavy boots of their oppressors. *Don't only guard them, hate them!* A shiver ran up her spine.

Once they were out on the street, Eszter said, "How could I grow up in this city all these years and not know what truly went on here? At high school I learned about the Nazis and the communists, and about the people's uprising in fifty-six. That doesn't even scratch the surface of what really took place here. Extremists maimed and tortured thousands of their own neighbours. When the tables are turned, what could happen to the people who committed those crimes?"

Erika said, "Especially the ones who used pencils and hatpins as weapons of torture. It's all a black box for me too. The uprising wasn't even mentioned in school in my day."

Eszter noticed Kelemen's pensive mood and said nothing until they reached the car. It was four thirty on a sunny Friday afternoon, the start of the weekend. She and Ferenc had planned to chill out together this evening, conditional on whether they could both get away at a reasonable time. For her, that depended on what Kelemen had in mind.

"Back to Teve Street?" Eszter asked tentatively.

Kelemen seemed to ignore the question. "Didn't the professor say, some records are archived at the Ministry of Interior?"

Eszter had no choice but to go with the flow. "Yes, although he also said, many were destroyed when the House of Terror was ransacked during the uprising."

Kelemen was clearly in no mood to be deterred. "The ministry is only five minutes away. I have a contact there who may help. We'll call in, on our way back to HQ. I need to pick my car up, and I told Marcel that I'd be home by seven. He's trying to make up for being a dick, by cooking me a birthday dinner this evening."

The planned dinner was positive news for Eszter. Perhaps she would get away in time. "You kept your birthday to yourself, boss."

"Don't tell a soul, or else you're in trouble. Now, let's go. You can park next to the Gresham Palace."

The Ministry of Interior has a look of faded grandeur. Standing on Széchenyi István Square, with commanding views across the Danube to Buda Hill, the ornate, once-grand building had never benefited from a multi-billion forint renovation programme like that provided to its next door neighbour. With its grimy limestone walls, pitted bronze entrance doors and corroded steel windows, the ministry remains as the perennial poor relation, standing next to the resplendent Four Seasons Gresham Palace Hotel.

Erika led the way in, but it took a full ten minutes before they were both scanned, searched and allowed through the lobby into the grand foyer.

At the receptionist's desk, she said, "We are with the Budapest Homicide Department and would like to see Tibor Dali."

The receptionist was a middle-aged woman wearing a black uniform. Her raven-black hair was scraped back into a bun. She was po-faced. "Do you have an appointment?"

"No, but this is official business. I'm sure he'll see me."

She asked for their ID and instructed them to wait.

With the humourless woman away from her desk, Erika whispered, "Tibor is an old boyfriend."

After several minutes, the receptionist returned their credentials. She led them into a large oak-panelled waiting room, closing the door when she exited. There were floor-to-ceiling bookcases on two walls and sofas with faded upholstery. Sunlight flooded into the room through the large, sealed windows, making it unbearably hot and stuffy.

Erika paced up and down, smiling to herself as she recalled the wild times she and Tibor had enjoyed together.

Eszter browsed through a pile of Hungarian governmental journals and picked one out. She turned the pages in quick succession, scowling at the dense text until she said, "Perhaps we should make an appointment, and come back another time?"

It was Erika's turn to frown. "You're not rushing to get away, are you?"

The door to the waiting room opened. Erika's expectant smile froze when she saw it was not Tibor.

Instead, a young woman wearing a white silk blouse, navy blue pencil skirt and matching heels marched into the centre of the room and addressed them. "Mr Dali has left for the day. May I help you?"

Erika tried not to show her annoyance and frustration. She had secretly been looking forward to seeing Tibor's roguish smile once again. It was obvious she should not have turned up without an appointment, but with Szabó watching on, she could hardly leave empty-handed. "We are investigating the murders of two victims we believe worked for the State Protection Authority in the nineteen fifties. We believe the ministry may keep personnel records of former AVH employees in its archives. I hoped Mr Dali could allow us access to those records."

"I see," said the assistant curtly. "Would you mind waiting here, while I ask the responsible person?"

It was already after five, but there was still plenty of time for Erika to pick up her car at Teve Street and return to the apartment for whatever Marcel had planned for this evening. "Thank you," she said sourly.

The assistant exited and left them sweltering for what seemed an eternity. By six o'clock Erika was pacing incessantly and swearing.

Eszter had long since given up on reading journals. She slumped on a sofa, scrolling through her phone with a sullen expression.

Finally, the door opened, and the assistant returned. "My apologies. That department head has already left for the weekend. Could you call again on Monday, or submit your request by email?"

Rudolf Kudár leaned forward on his desk, his chin resting on his fists. On his PC screen at TEK Headquarters, he watched the two women in the waiting room at the Ministry. He smiled at the foul language and invective of the older woman with auburn hair, while the younger girl — taller and prettier with blonde hair — looked miserable and said little. The facial recognition scan on his screen showed him the older woman was Erika Kelemen of the Financial Crime Investigation Division; it also provided him with her date of birth, home address, marital status, and curriculum vitae. What was she doing, investigating a murder case, especially one that touched on such sensitive issues? From the audio, he listened to their conversation. He continued to watch them, even as the CCTV camera in the entrance hall showed the pair leaving the building. The external cameras captured their vehicle registration plate.

Kudár had his own plans for the evening. But first, there was something he had to take care of.

After being dropped off outside the Police headquarters entrance on Teve Street, Erika resisted the temptation to return to her desk, electing instead to set off directly for home. She made good time, and it was just after seven when she pulled into the underground car park of her apartment block. She gathered her things off the passenger seat, stepped out of the car, and locked it. Her punctuality would surely put her in Marcel's good books.

"Not so fast, Erika." The unfamiliar male voice came from behind her.

She turned but at first saw no one. "Who's there?" she said cautiously, trying to control her emotions.

A figure emerged from behind one of the concrete columns. He was slim, swarthy, around six feet tall, with black hair and a black moustache. He wore a black suit with an open-necked white shirt.

"I am an old friend of Axel Rácz. You've been sticking your nose into things that don't concern you. My advice is rein things in."

Who was he? And what objections could he possibly have to the investigation? Whoever he was, he knew where she lived.

"Who are you?" she demanded, with as confident a tone as she could muster.

He produced credentials and held them close to her face. Instantly she recognised the yellow double-headed eagle on the black background. The ID said 'TEK Counter Terrorism Centre. Rudolf Kudár, Special Agent.'

"This doesn't have to be difficult. Marcel is waiting for you, with your birthday dinner. By the way, tell him to stay away from trouble from now on."

She felt numb. How could he know so much about her private life? What did he mean about Marcel staying away from trouble?

Kudár looked her straight in the eyes.

"Enjoy yourself, have a few drinks, take the weekend off. Find a different angle to explore. Or I'll be back…"

Chapter Five

Erika's heart slammed like a piston against her chest. She closed her eyes for a moment, but when she reopened them, Kudár was nowhere to be seen. Seizing her chance, she ran to the stairwell, raced up all six flights of stairs, and dashed along the corridor. She fumbled for her keys, only to find her apartment door unlocked. Slamming it shut, she dead-locked and chained it. Panting, she sucked air into her lungs.

Marcel's cheerful voice came from the kitchen.

"Erika, is that you? You've made good time."

She staggered to the bathroom, tears streaming down her cheeks. He mustn't see her like this.

She called out to him, "I'm going to grab a shower before dinner. Won't be long."

In the mirror she saw the face of a morbidly sad circus clown. Mascara was in free-flow. Her eyes were red and puffy and her bottom lip trembled.

She undressed. The shower drenched her from head to toe. She soaped, shampooed, and scrubbed. Billowing steam filled the room, obscuring her reflections. That was what she wanted; to be invisible, no longer in a world of murders, criticism, and painful decisions.

Everything in the kitchen was going to plan. The salad was prepared, two juicy sirloins were sizzling on the grill, and Marcel was already into his second large glass of red wine. He had set the table for dinner. Candles were lit, and Miles Davis was cranking out *Stella by Starlight*.

He transferred the steaks onto a warm plate and slid them into the oven to rest. Erika liked her steak medium-rare, nothing more, nothing less. In the days before the lockdown, he'd seen her send steak back at a restaurant, twice over, until it came back the way she liked it.

He was just about to issue a five-minute warning when the bathroom door opened. Erika emerged, wearing her fluffy, white bathrobe; her wet hair tied up in a towel. He was wearing chinos and a pale blue open-necked shirt. Suddenly he felt over-dressed.

"Do you mind? I've had a lousy day," she said.

"Of course, no problem." He stepped closer, but she picked up a glass and blocked him from hugging her. She half filled it with Tokaji, downed it in one, then reached again for the bottle. This was an excellent and pricey wine; one she had selected herself. *What was she thinking of?*

He said, "Sit down, love. You look exhausted. The steaks are ready."

Erika flopped into her chair at the dining table, taking another deep draught from her glass.

"There you are, madame. Medium-rare, the way you like it. Salad is coming."

He finished serving them both and sat opposite her. She helped herself to salad and toyed with her meat. Her mind was clearly elsewhere.

"You want to talk about it, love?"

"Oh, you know, just your typical fiftieth birthday. They are short on numbers right now, so they drafted me back into homicide. What looked like a straightforward case has become complicated. We're looking for a sophisticated killer who poisons his victims, then tortures their bodies."

No wonder she had been preoccupied.

He leaned forward and placed his hand on hers. "You're supporting on this case?"

She pulled her hand away and picked up her glass. "Leading the investigation. It's all on me now."

This explained everything. But why had she kept it from him? "Shit, Erika! Why didn't you tell me?"

"I've only been on the case since yesterday. You and I haven't exactly been on speaking terms, have we?"

He felt ashamed at how self-absorbed he'd been. "You making any progress? I mean with the case."

"At least one of our victims has links to the former secret police, the AVH. The torture MO used by the killer imitates what the State Protection Authority did to soften up prisoners in the nineteen fifties."

"You mean like they did in the House of Terror?"

Erika chewed on a piece of steak, swallowed, and washed it down with Tokaji. She gave a single nod of her head. "I had a guided tour around the museum today. It wouldn't take long for someone to pick up some tips and tricks of a psychopathic terror organisation."

She placed her cutlery down, the steak half-finished, the salad untouched.

He looked at her plate.

"Sorry," she said. "The steak is just how I like it but I'm not hungry."

He cleared away the dishes. Erika clutched her glass with both hands. He had intended this birthday dinner to be a romantic celebration. It felt more like a wake.

"Anything else on your mind?" he asked, more in hope than expectation of a meaningful response.

She closed her eyes and pursed her lips tightly.

There was no way in for him.

Péter Rigo ordered another round from the barman. It was the first time in days he had felt relaxed.

"It's eight o'clock and I really ought to be on my way," said Gábor Márkos.

Lajos Dolman drained his glass and slammed it down onto the heavy pine tabletop. "Stay for another beer, mate. It's Friday, and the night is still young."

"Okay, one for the road, but then I've really gotta go. My wife's been looking after the baby all week. She gets stir crazy, especially since lockdown. No kids' club, or nothing."

Rigo scoffed at the notion. "Teach 'em well, Gábor. Otherwise they can turn out to be like that bitch."

"Hey, steady on," said Márkos. "Are you saying my Zoe is like Kelemen?"

The barman arrived and placed a full tray in front of them.

Rigo slid two large beers down to the others. "I'm saying nothing of the sort. But you and Zoe are newlyweds and the magic hasn't worn off yet. But if you don't train her right, you'll always be under her thumb. She needs to understand, you deserve a few beers, ol' buddy. These are on me. Well, they're courtesy of the house. The owner of this establishment owes me, big time. So drink up! Here's a toast: To the gentlemen detectives of the Budapest Murder Squad. Long may we keep the fucking streets free of scum. Egészégédre!"

"Egészégédre!" said Dolman, clinking his glass with Rigo's.

Márkos raised his glass, but did not clink with the others. "Egészégédre."

Ferenc stroked a strand of blonde hair away from Eszter's cheek. They were stretched out on their blue leather sofa, listening to music after a busy and challenging week. It was their first weekend of living together. Even though they had moved in on Monday, most of their possessions remained packed in cardboard boxes, piled up around them.

Eszter snuggled in closer and yawned. "You think we should unpack now?"

He yawned too. "Tomorrow we paint the walls, Sunday we unpack, but tonight we chill. Deal?"

She needed no further persuasion. "It's a deal. I've had enough of chasing around after Kelemen. She forgets that the rest of us have a life outside the force."

"Is she as bad as they say?"

"Bad, no. She's bloody good. The trouble is, she doesn't know when to stop."

He stretched, reaching for the beer perched on top of the nearest cardboard box. "You want a drink?" He tipped the can above her face. Some of its contents found her open mouth, the rest dribbled down her chin.

"Hey, watch out!" She shrieked with laughter.

There were no clothes to stain.

To the strains of Miles' rendition of *Autumn Leaves*, Marcel cleared away the dessert dishes in silence. Despite his prompting, and repeated attempts to lighten the mood, Erika's revelations regarding the serial killer investigation had been the last words she had spoken.

He tried once again to open up the conversation. "It's a lovely evening. Why don't we take a walk?"

"Not now. I'd have to get dressed."

"Okay. Let's sit on the balcony for a few minutes. You look exhausted. I reckon you'll be in bed before nine."

She nodded and picked up her glass. "Bring the second bottle."

There was talk of a storm passing through that would freshen things up, but out on the balcony, there was a balmy stillness to the evening. Erika had spent her fiftieth birthday in pursuit of a sadistic killer. Truthfully, she was nowhere nearer to finding the perpetrator. For now, it was a game of cat and mouse, trying to catch the scent, chasing imagined motives, hoping to narrow down the needle search to just a single haystack. The line of enquiry she had been following looked promising. Klára Menges' former role within the State Protection Authority, and the killer's use of known AVH torture methods, suggested she was on the right track.

Everything had been going well until Kudár had confronted her at home. In her mind she played back his words, 'Sticking your nose into things that don't concern you', and 'My advice would be to rein things in.'

He had known where she lived, he had shown up on her doorstep. He knew it was her birthday. He knew Marcel was cooking dinner. And what kind of trouble was Marcel meant to stay away from? Was her apartment bugged, or was it a colleague spying on her? Rácz, Dora, or even Szabó? Such irony. It was how the communists had ruled so effectively. Divide and conquer. Paranoia created by a culture of informers.

Marcel pressed something into her hands. "Your phone. It's ringing," he said.

Melancholy hung around Erika like a dark cloud. She had tried alcohol to numb her senses, but that only made the depression worse. Somewhere in the background Marcel was chattering, but she did not want to engage in conversation. She shook her head, as if waking from a bad dream. Her phone *was* ringing. She saw it was Mum calling and answered it. "Are you okay?"

"You've got to get me out of here…" Sobs punctuated her mother's words. "You need to come now and take me away from here. It's like a prison. The staff all hate me, and the residents are dying from the virus. I can't take it anymore."

A sudden sharp pain struck between her eyebrows, causing Erika to wince. "Mum, how many times have we had this conversation? Daybreak is an excellent nursing home. They've handled the virus well. I doubt we'd find a better place."

"Let me come and live with you."

Erika sighed. "It's a small apartment, Mum, with stairs and no elevator. You'd be trapped. I…"

"Then carry me out in a coffin!"

The line went dead. After not crying for longer than she could remember, she had tears streaming down her cheeks for the second time in one evening.

Marcel made a move towards her, arms outstretched. She palmed him off. "I'm sorry," she said. "I just can't."

Each Sunday morning during lockdown, Eszter and Ferenc ran together to the top of Castle Hill. This morning they loped along the riverbank on the Buda side, traversing up the steep, winding Hunyadi János Street. The security barrier came into view and it was raised. A car in low gear overtook them, belching diesel fumes from its exhaust.

"Too much traffic along here today," said Ferenc. "Let's take the steps. Race you to the top." He grinned, sweat streaming down his forehead.

Yesterday had been spent painting their new apartment. This morning she would have preferred breakfast in bed. Instead, she had pulled on her running gear, stepped into her trainers and scraped back her blonde hair into a ponytail. For several seconds she watched him climb the worn stone steps like a mountain goat in Lycra. She gritted her teeth and set off. On and on they went: another ten, another twenty, another hundred steps. Despite the head start she had given him, she was within touching distance by the time they emerged into Holy Trinity Square.

He bent over, hands on his knees, gasping to fill his lungs with air. She slapped him on the backside. She was panting too, although she was fitter than him and her recovery time would be shorter.

Across the square, the brilliant blue sky framed the imposing white structure of Budapest's finest church. Its doors had been closed to parishioners and tourists for over two months. Eszter had become accustomed to the place being quiet. Today, however, there was a different vibe, and it was bustling once again. Even though the visitor ticket kiosks remained shuttered and closed, the square was busy and a long, socially distanced queue— most wearing facemasks — had formed outside the grand entrance to the Mátyás church.

"Looks like Sunday masses are back on," she said.

But his attention was elsewhere. They were standing close to a news kiosk at the edge of the square. He was staring at the billboard on the pavement.

"You guys made the front page," he said.

"Holy shit!" she replied. "Kelemen will blow her top."

CHAPTER SIX

At the front of the media room was a small raised platform, with a table covered by a white cloth. Levente placed name cards on the table: one for Senior Detective Erika Kelemen, one for himself. He had dressed for the occasion, in a navy blue suit, white shirt and a quirky purple tie. Ordinarily he would not sit at the speakers' table, but putting Kelemen there all alone would have been harsh.

After their meeting on Friday, he had prepared an invitation to a media conference, which would begin at nine-thirty on Monday morning. He emailed the usual list of press, TV and radio hacks. Initially, responses had been few in number, but after their story hit the front page of the local Sunday newspaper his inbox had been inundated. This was perfect from his perspective. The more attendees and the more airtime minutes, the better it would be. The more column inches, the better chance they had of finding leads that could point them towards the killer. Also, he would look better in the eyes of his boss.

Levente checked the time. It was already 8:50. He had done everything possible. Now it was up to Kelemen to show up on time and perform well.

"Commander Rácz will see you now," said Dora, smiling and welcoming as always.

Erika marched in, closing his door firmly. After being ambushed by Kudár, she had spent the weekend thinking about her next move. The shock of seeing her own photograph on the front page of a newspaper, not to mention the prospect of facing the media this morning, had kept her awake all night. She was like the proverbial cat on a hot tin roof, and in no mood for small talk. She cut straight to the chase.

"Someone who claims to be a friend of yours hijacked me on Friday evening."

"I have many friends," said Rácz, swinging around in his chair to face her.

"This one knew about the investigation. He also knew far too much about my personal life. He told me to keep my nose out of things that don't concern me."

Rácz maintained his poker face.

"Rudolf Kudár. Ring any bells?" she blurted out.

Rácz smirked. "Kudár? Where the hell did you bump into him?"

She had not expected empathy and therefore wasn't disappointed by the lack of it. "He intercepted me outside my apartment. On Friday afternoon, I had an AVH crash course from Professor Turay, curator of the House of Terror museum. I think their torture techniques inspired the killer's MO. The professor explained that the Ministry of Interior holds personnel records for some former AVH employees. So, Szabó and I went…"

Rácz laughed out loud. "You went to the ministry? Let me guess. They kept you cooling your heels in a waiting room. You talked to Szabó about this and that. Am I getting warm?"

Erika felt like a complete idiot. The waiting room was bugged, of course. That was where Kudár got his inside knowledge from. He must have had access to her own file, too. Now it all made sense. Well, some of it did. What she really wanted to know now was why Kudár was warning her off.

Dora knocked and entered. "Your 9.15 is here, Commander."

Erika had wanted to spend an hour with Levente, running through potential questions and answers. Instead, she arrived at the Media Centre sweating, with just five minutes to spare. She was wearing a conservative charcoal-grey trouser suit, with a white, open-necked blouse. She had considered wearing her scarlet Jimmy Choo heels, but in the end chose a pair of conservative black pumps.

She found a sign outside which said, in both Hungarian and English: *Sajtótájékoztató/ Press Conference*. Inside, it was busy with technicians, TV crew, journalists and photographers. At least half of the seats were occupied, with others blocked off for social distancing purposes. Erika spotted Levente heading her way at speed. He smiled and led her back into the corridor by the elbow.

"I've loaded your presentation, and we're all ready to go." His voice sounded calm.

She felt perspiration on her forehead. "You may be ready, but I hadn't expected so many people."

"Neither had I," he said, grinning. He held up a copy of the now-infamous article from yesterday's paper. "But this did the trick."

Her lip curled down. *Police Search for Budapest Butcher – Two Seniors Murdered at Home in 48 Hours.* Below the headline was that unflattering photograph of her, taken while escaping the unwanted attention of Viktoria Gindl outside the apartment in Hős Street. Further down the page, there was a photograph of the House of Terror on Andrássy Street. Underneath was the caption, 'Did the victim work here?'

Levente said, "Be grateful. Without that, we wouldn't have this turn out. With the publicity we should get from this, there should be plenty of calls from the public. Now remember, you'll look more trustworthy if you keep your head up. Look to the back of the room, not down at your papers. Present your slides from the lectern. You can either operate them from there, or give me a nod, and I'll control them from my laptop. Once you've finished, return to the table to take questions. Make a note of the question, and only try to answer it, if you are free to do so. Are you ready? Okay, let's go."

Erika sat nervously at the table, surveying the scene, facing the audience. Approximately thirty pairs of hostile eyes glared back at her. Her heart was pounding, and her throat felt parched. She reached for the glass of water and took a sip. This was her very first media conference. She glanced at Levente and was grateful at least one of them appeared calm. He leaned forward, tapped his microphone, and spoke with confidence.

"Good morning, ladies and gentlemen. Thank you all for coming. My name is Levente Barna. This is Senior Detective Erika Kelemen, the senior investigating officer, currently working on two cases we want to share with you this morning. She will explain the details. Our aim today, is to work with you, our media partners, to raise awareness of these crimes. Hopefully, members of the public will provide information to assist us with our enquiries. Detective Kelemen will make a brief presentation. She will then be pleased to take your questions."

Erika stood and made her way forward. Being the centre of attention made her feel physically sick. She stumbled, but steadied herself on the lectern. Standing behind it, she gripped it so tightly with both hands her knuckles turned white. She stared into the crowd and tried to breathe normally. The large screen displayed her opening slide. It showed their logo: a blue shield, overlaid with the horizontal tricolour of the Hungarian flag, red, white and green, the scales of justice and the words *RENDŐRSÉG* and *POLICE*. Alongside it were her name and rank.

She cleared her throat.

"Good morning, ladies and gentlemen. I have the unfortunate task of presenting, not one, but two murder cases. These cases may be connected, although we don't yet know that for certain. We hope members of the public who witnessed anything, or have information concerning either of these cases, will come forward. I will include our hotline number at the end of my presentation."

She felt her nerves getting the better of her and completely forgot how to control the slides herself. She nodded towards Levente for the next one.

A smiling photograph of a kindly face flashed onto the screen. It was Erika's cue to continue.

"This was Klára Menges, eighty-eight years old, murdered in her home in Bertalan Lajos Street. We believe this crime took place between the hours of five and seven p.m., on Tuesday the nineteenth of May. We want to speak with any member of the public who saw or heard anything suspicious." She nodded at Levente.

The next slide showed the only photograph of Ervin Nagy they had found. He was seen leaning on a wooden gate. It was a rural setting, with horses in a field behind him.

She continued, "This is Ervin Nagy, aged eighty-seven, murdered in his apartment in Hős Street, at around midday on

Thursday the twenty-first of May. Did a neighbour or passer-by notice anything suspicious? Both victims were in their eighties, both lived alone, and neither apartment showed signs of forced entry, which indicates they may have known the killer. Perhaps friends or relatives of the victims, those we could not contact yet, could come forward and provide useful background information? At this stage, I cannot divulge details concerning the way the victims died, but I can confirm there were similarities. Our forensic evidence and forensic pathology teams continue their work on the clues left behind by the killer, or killers. Ladies and gentlemen, that's the end of this brief presentation. I will now be happy to take your questions."

With that last sentence, Erika knew she would certainly fail a lie detector test. She resumed her seat at the table.

Levente covered his microphone and whispered, "Well done. That was perfect. I'll chair the Q&A. Take your time and say only what you're comfortable releasing to the public."

Over a dozen hands shot up. Levente pointed to a journalist in the front row.

"Lili Oláh from *Lokál*. Does the fact you are making this appeal so soon after these crimes were committed suggest that you currently have no suspects?"

Erika jotted, 'Lili, no suspects?' on her pad.

"Thank you, Lili. We are already following several lines of enquiry. However, members of the public may have important information which could help us bring the guilty parties to justice. We feel the sooner we can tap into additional intelligence the better."

Levente scanned the room and pointed to another extended hand.

"Ervin Lakatos, *Világgazdaság*. I understand they drafted you in from the Financial Crime Investigation Division to conduct this investigation. Does that show these crimes have a financial motive?"

That was an easier one to field, although she wondered whether she had previously come across this journalist. She wrote, 'Ervin, FCI?'

"The National Bureau of Investigation is flexible in its use of resources. It's good to be back in homicide after a five-year gap." She clenched her jaw, forcing a smile.

Levente moved on, pointing at another raised hand.

"Jazmin Németh, *Pesti Bulvár*. Is there really a serial killer on the loose in Budapest? The Sunday press labelled the perpetrator as *The Budapest Butcher*. How worried should our senior citizens be?"

Erika sipped water, buying her a vital couple of seconds to gather her thoughts. On her pad, she noted, 'Jazmin, How worried?'

"Thank you for your question, Jazmin. There might be a link between the cases, but it's too early to say this is the work of a serial killer. Our senior citizens should not be unduly worried, but they should be cautious about allowing people into their property, when alone at home. What's important is we apprehend those responsible as swiftly as possible. That's why we are calling on anyone with relevant information to contact our hotline."

"We have time for one last question," said Levente. His hand hovered until he pointed at the female reporter at the end of the second row.

When Erika saw who Lev had called upon to speak, her hackles rose. She instantly made a note, 'Gindl!'

"Viktoria Gindl, M1 TV. Detective Kelemen. Our sources say the first victim, Klára Menges, was a former employee of the AVH, and it was her association with that organisation that ultimately led to her brutal killing last week. Could you confirm that?"

Erika gripped the edge of the table but tried to keep her tension from showing. She had always disliked Gindl's aggressive style on television. Their meeting outside Nagy's apartment on Thursday had reinforced those feelings. Now she liked her even less. *Sources? Who had Gindl spoken with concerning Klára's AVH days? Whoever it was, they had hit the nail on the head.* There seemed no point in denying what she herself believed to be true, especially when confirming it may even trigger a helpful lead. She wrote the initials AVH next to Gindl's name, underlining it three times.

She said, "It's important to work with evidence and not supposition, but we are still investigating Klára Menges' background. We have some information that suggests she once worked for the AVH. Her precise role there is not yet clear, nor is its relevance to her murder. We also have information to suggest she later continued her career working for the government. So, if anyone can assist us in building up a profile of the victim, or knows anything that may lead to us apprehending the killer, please call our hotline number."

Levente took the hint. He finished by highlighting the hotline number when it appeared on the screen and promptly drew the session to a close.

Erika breathed a sigh of relief, but tried not to let it show.

Levente checked their mics were off and smiled reassuringly at her. Shielding his mouth with his hand, he gave her the positive feedback she craved.

"That went well. I'll call you later to debrief. If you need to go now, I'll make sure they pick up their media packs. I'll push them for coverage in today's news cycle. Is your hotline ready for action?"

"Don't worry," she said. "It will be."

There was a copy of the Sunday newspaper containing *that article* spread out on the table when Erika returned to the Incident Room. She knew someone had been enjoying a laugh at her expense and was fairly certain who had been laughing the loudest.

The door opened, and in sauntered Rigo, with Márkos and Dolman trailing behind. Their laddish, unprofessional attitude was wearing extremely thin. Eszter arrived shortly after the men and sat behind them.

Erika cleared her throat. "There have been some developments since our last briefing. On Friday afternoon, Detective Szabó and I visited the House of Terror museum, and met with the curator. He showed us the basement cells where the AVH tortured their prisoners. The torture methods included the use of hatpins, particularly by the female guards, and forcing male prisoners to stand for hours at a time, with a pencil pressed between their forehead and the wall. Anyone dropping their pencil got beaten badly. It's possible that our killer is imitating true life. Anyone who has taken a tour of the museum could have seen sufficient evidence of inhumane behaviour to fill their heads with many ideas."

Rigo sneered. "Are you saying these were some kind of revenge killings?"

"I'm saying the killer is using the AVH torture playbook. We know from Lotti Menges that Klára was deeply associated with the organisation, but we shouldn't jump to conclusions about Ervin Nagy's involvement. What we do know, from their respective phone call records, is an unidentified caller using burner phones was in touch with each victim in the days leading up to their death. Yet, even if Klára and Ervin were both ex-

AVH, how would the caller or callers know where to find them? I doubt either of them advertised the fact that they were formerly in the business of torturing their neighbours."

"Perhaps one of their surviving victims is a neighbour," said Dolman.

"Good point. But Menges and Nagy were not exactly neighbours of each other, and as far as we know, had no contact with one another."

"Maybe the killer knew both victims, and their backgrounds," said Márkos.

"That has to be a possibility. I've just come from doing a press conference downstairs, to launch a public appeal for information. Let's hope someone out there knows something useful."

"You didn't tell the media about the killer's MO, did you?" said Rigo.

She raised her eyebrow. *What did he take her for?* She grabbed hold of the newspaper from the table and waved it at him. "The story is already out there. It makes sense to provide the basic facts, and encourage the public to come forward, if they know anything that can make our job easier. I've issued a hotline number, active from eleven a.m. today. The good news is, you four are manning the phones. This is top priority. We'll review the calls later and go from there. Any questions?"

Her eyes bored into the belligerent gaze of Péter Rigo, challenging him to respond.

Rigo muttered something under his breath, then turned his head away.

She dropped a sheaf of pre-printed forms onto the table.

"Use these to record the calls. I'll be back later. I'm picking someone up at the railway station."

When the eleven-thirty-nine from Esztergom pulled into Nyugati Station, Erika was waiting on the platform. Passengers streamed past her, until eventually she spotted Lotti Menges slowly making her way towards the ticket barrier. Lotti wore a stylish cotton summer dress with a yellow leather clutch bag. She looked more like a lady who lunched, rather than a grieving sister in her mid-eighties. She was evidently still mobile under her own steam, albeit moving slower than she must have done in her prime.

Erika welcomed her. "Thank you for coming."

"I can't say it's a pleasure. I rarely travel to Budapest."

Erika's car was parked in Nyugati Square in a space reserved for police vehicles. Their eight-minute journey along Váci Street was uneventful, and the conversation comprised only small talk.

When they reached the main entrance to the Honvéd kórház, Erika explained that Klára's body was downstairs in the autopsy suite.

The pathologist's assistant was waiting for them. He had prepared the body and, on Erika's signal, pulled back the sheet to reveal Klára's face.

Lotti nodded solemnly. "That's her. My sister, Klára." Her wrinkled brow furrowed but her voice remained steady.

Erika's eyes were fixed on Lotti's face. She had been surprised by her lack of emotional reaction when they had first met, in her apartment in Esztergom. Yet she would have bet a month's salary on the sight of her Klára's corpse producing more than a flicker of emotion in her sister. *Even if they were estranged, what kind of person could see their closest living relative looking like that, and shows nothing at all?*

"Don't you want to know how she died?" Erika said.

Lotti waved a hand dismissively. "She's gone. That's all that matters."

"Someone poisoned her with cyanide. Then, the killer did this to her." She signalled for the assistant to remove the sheet. The waxy, white corpse lay bare on the trolley, revealing the hundreds of tiny stab wounds that had been so carefully inflicted.

"Raise the right arm," said Erika to the assistant.

He did as he was bade. The initials *AVH* were still clearly visible.

Erika continued to scrutinise Lotti's facial expression and body language, looking for a reaction. "Do you have any idea who could have done this?"

Lotti shrugged. "I can think of many who would have liked to; but no, I don't know who did it." She chuckled. "It's rather artistic, don't you think?"

One of the phones in the Incident Room rang. Nobody else seemed in a rush to answer it, so Eszter picked up a set of headphones and took the call. "Detective Szabó, Homicide Department. Who's calling?"

The others were chattering in the background, and for several seconds she strained to hear the caller whose quiet voice barely rose to more than a whisper.

"My name is Oliver Sorvány. I read the Sunday newspaper article about two old people murdered. I need to speak with someone. Your switchboard put me through. Have I come to the right department?"

She grabbed a chair and pulled out her notebook and pen, jotting down the incoming number from the display. "I am a detective working on the case. You can speak to me, Mr Sorvány."

"I don't want to get into trouble."

Eszter strained to hear the caller speak above the office noise. "Don't worry. Just tell me what you know."

"We have strict rules about patient confidentiality here, but I thought I should tell someone about him. I mean, there's no point finding out when it's too late."

She tapped her pen repeatedly on the desk, beating out a rhythm. "Where you are calling from?"

"I work at the Forensic Observation and Psychiatric Institution. If they find out I've told you anything…"

"Mr Sorvány, I don't believe you would have called the police unless there was something serious on your mind."

She listened for his voice, but heard only his breathing, which sounded heavy and laboured.

"We will treat anything you tell me in confidence."

With only the sound of heavy breathing on the line, she wondered about his true motives. "I'm going to hang up, if you've got nothing to tell me. Do you understand?"

The beat of her pen speeded up. *Ten seconds, I'll give him ten seconds, then I'm hanging up.* She reached eight when she heard him cough.

"What do you know about the Institution?"

"Very little," she replied honestly.

"It's a top security psychiatric establishment. Sometimes, low-risk patients are released on adaptive leave under the supervision of a caregiver, to prepare them for reintegration into society. I've been a nurse here for ten years, and could count on two hands the number released."

She scratched her head. *What was he driving at?* "Are you saying one of your patients, is currently out on adaptive leave?"

"Yes, you have it."

She leaned back in her chair, rubbing her chin between a thumb and forefinger. "What is your concern? I mean, if the experts decide to help a patient reintegrate back into society, what's the big deal?"

"They made the wrong decision."

Nurse or not, he seemed to have a high opinion of himself. "I don't doubt your knowledge, but surely many sets of eyes are better than one?"

"The AVH connection, reported in the newspaper, it just fits."

Her ears pricked up. "What do you mean, the AVH connection?"

"I can't say more now."

Now he had her full attention. She leaned forward, elbows on the desk. "I need details, Mr Sorvány. When was this patient released on his adaptive leave?"

"On the fifteenth of May."

Eszter was scribbling everything down. "I need a name. What is the name of the patient?"

The line fell silent once again.

"Mr Sorvány?"

The line crackled, "Varga, his name is Zoltán Varga."

"What can you tell me about…"

The call was over, even before she could finish the sentence.

After dropping Lotti off at the railway station, Erika mulled over the woman's callous indifference to her sister's brutal murder.

Another call interrupted her train of thought, and she listened on hands-free to Eszter's explanation about her conversation with a psychiatric nurse.

"You say this nurse called in because of the article in the Sunday papers?" she said.

"That's what he said, boss. You want me to keep this on file?"

Erika wondered whether the adage 'There is no such thing as bad publicity' was actually true. However, the idea of a psychiatric patient committing murders, while under the supervision of a caregiver, sounded far-fetched. Still, they were hardly inundated with leads, which meant this one may as well be followed up.

She said, "No, I want you to dig deeper. Leave the others to take care of the hotline and let me know what else you find out."

Eszter sent a text message to Oliver Sorvány, asking him to contact her as soon as possible. She was pessimistic about him responding, so was pleasantly surprised when he called within thirty minutes. He agreed to meet her after his shift finished, and even described himself as mid-thirties, of medium height with black hair, wearing black trousers and a pale blue t-shirt. His choice of venue seemed strange, but he told her the Dragon Centre on Gyömrői Street was on his way home. She knew the place, having previously eaten an excellent Chinese meal there.

Despite the easing of the lockdown the place looked a shadow of its former self. Shutters were down on most of the buildings, and there were few people out on the streets. By three thirty she was growing impatient, until a man corresponding to Sorvány's self-description approached on foot.

She showed her ID, introduced herself and thanked him for coming.

"I'm parched. Let's get a drink," he said.

One of the few open stalls was selling chilled water at one hundred forint a bottle. He paid for two and handed her one.

They sat in the shade, facing one another on plastic chairs. He looked on edge, his eyes darting nervously from side to side.

Concerned that he may leave at any moment, Eszter wasted no time.

"Mr Sorvány, what more can you tell me about the patient?"

He sipped his water. "You understand, I'm not a clinician. I'm a nurse. We do the dirty work and have no access to the patient's files. You should talk to the director, if you want to know more about his background."

She made a note. "Just tell me what you know."

He took another sip. "We treat patients who have committed violent crimes. Varga arrived in early 2019."

Surely a violent criminal would not be released on adaptive leave, would he? She nodded, encouraging him to continue.

"He's strong. Not tall, but thick-set and in his mid-twenties. It always took two or more of us, to give him enforced medication. We used meds to keep him calm, most of the time."

A picture was building in her mind of a person she'd rather not meet alone. "Why did he need calming?"

"It's the doctors' job to find that out. Nurses just do as we're told. Varga often had night terrors. Normally, sedation was the only thing that worked."

"So, what made you connect him with the cases we are investigating?"

"60 Andrássy Street," he said.

"You mean, the House of Terror?"

"There was a photograph of the place, in that Sunday newspaper article. Varga spoke about it too. You ever been there?"

She nodded. As expected, mention of the House of Terror would attract all kinds of interest, but nothing he had told her linked Varga to their investigation. "Did you ever hear him mention the names of any individuals, or threaten to harm anyone?"

"No names, but when I read the victims may have been former AVH, I remembered his words as if it was only yesterday. He told me, 'AVH torturers should all go to hell.' That's what he said."

She studied Sorvány's face. He seemed genuine enough. Yet all he seemed to offer were the ramblings of a disturbed criminal with a mental disorder. The defence lawyers would say Varga had been drugged up to his eyeballs. It was not testimony that would stand up in court.

She needed more from him. "Are you certain you never heard him make any threats to do actual harm to anyone?"

"Not in front of me. Maybe the other nurses or medics heard different?" He glanced at his wristwatch and stood up. "I need to be going."

She thanked him. "Call me again, if something else comes to mind. You have my number in the SMS."

He plunged his hands deep into his the trouser pockets and rocked on the balls of his feet. He seemed to be weighing her up and looked like he had more to tell her. Instead, he turned his back and walked away. He called out over his shoulder, "I told you everything I know. Leave me out of it from now on."

Erika was working on a mountain of paperwork when there was a rap on the door of her office.

Eszter peered in. "I can come back later, if you're busy."

Any distraction from administrative work was welcome, and she was eager to hear the latest news. "Did you meet the nurse?"

"I did. He seems genuine, but he may have read more into a situation than there really is. Zoltán Varga is the name of the patient they released into the community. He's mid-twenties, and has been an inmate for eighteen months. He has some kind of personality disorder." She referred to her notebook and continued.

"Sorvány claims he heard Varga say, 'AVH torturers should all go to hell.' Yet he heard no specific threats made to individuals. It seems Varga spent a lot of time on medication and sedation."

"What was he admitted for?"

"He didn't seem to know that. He said, if we wanted to know more about the patient, we'd have to speak with the director. I've found his name and number."

"Did you already call him?"

Eszter shook her head. "Not yet."

"Then what are you waiting for? Let's do it now."

Rigo assumed the role of hotline supervisor, but refused to deal with even a single call himself. That left Márkos and Dolman to answer the phones and fill in the paperwork.

He prowled around the perimeter of the Incident Room, casting an eye over each completed form, then adding his own written comments. At four thirty in the afternoon, he had not deemed even one call worthy of a follow up but pontificated to the others. "Cranks, conspiracy theorists and bull-shitters, that's all we've had so far. If that bloody woman had any sense, she'd know this was a complete waste of police time."

At the entrance of the Budapest Penitentiary and Prison complex in Kozma Street is a small car park, set in a landscaped garden. Eszter parked in the shade of a large beech tree. The entrance itself is under an austere, grey stone archway, and Erika and Eszter presented themselves at the sliding window of the gatehouse.

Erika showed her ID. "We're here to see Director Tár, of the Forensic Observation and Psychiatric Institution."

The guard flexed his muscles and the fabric of his prison service uniform stretched almost to breaking point. His eyes barely moved from the array of CCTV monitors.

"You have an appointment?"

"Yes, at 17:00," she said.

Even the sight of two well dressed, professional women failed to excite the guard's interest. He yawned. "Sign the book."

They signed as visitors and found shade outside the gatehouse, where they stood trying to keep cool.

Ten minutes later, a middle-aged man wearing a pale grey suit with a white, open-necked shirt appeared. He had thinning brown hair and a paunch. Erika made the introductions.

He said, "I am Doctor Oláh. Please follow me. Our facility is on the other side of the complex."

They walked alongside him as he led the way around the perimeter path.

After a minute of awkward silence, Eszter enquired about how long the institution had been based there.

"Since 1896, and we are the only top security psychiatric institution in Hungary. We deal with those requiring forensic compulsory treatment."

"What's that?" she said.

"The treatment of those who have committed violent crimes, especially when there is a risk they may commit similar in the future. We also receive prisoners from other penitential establishments. Some are referred here with suspected personality disorders."

Erika wondered which category Zoltán Varga fell into, but saved that question for the director. Instead, she asked him whether the institution was a hospital or a prison.

"It's part of the prison service, although supervising the treatment of patients comes under the Ministry of Health. Most of our patients receive involuntary treatment, because of their indictments for murder or manslaughter."

That comment weighed on her. As their walk took them around an empty exercise yard, she said, "How many staff work at the Institution?"

"There are currently one hundred and seventy staff, including ninety-five nurses, but only fifteen of us are physicians. Many of our psychiatrists were brought out of retirement to work here."

The doctor seemed keen to talk, so she fed him another question.

"Looking after how many patients?"

"Around three hundred. Mainly men, but also a couple of dozen women and a handful of foreigners."

Eventually they arrived at the southern tip of the site and stood facing an ugly low-rise concrete building, which stood in front of an even uglier five-storey block. He guided them through the double entrance doors and into a small reception area. He knocked on a door, then led them into a deliciously cool, air-conditioned office. Behind a desk sat a man with swarthy skin, dyed black hair and a thick moustache.

Oláh said, "Director Tár, this is Senior Detective Kelemen and Detective Szabó, from the homicide department."

Erika estimated the director to be in his sixties. He gestured to two chairs on the other side of his desk. When he spoke, she had to strain to hear what he was saying.

"That will be all, doctor," he mumbled.

They took their seats, and Erika said. "Thank you for your time. We are currently investigating two cases of elderly victims, found brutally murdered in their apartments. You may have seen or heard media reports."

The director sat with arms folded, shook his head and said blankly, "No."

"In that case, you will not have heard our public appeal for any information that could help us with our enquiries. The fact is, we received a call from someone who read in the press that one of the victims worked for the State Security Authority. For him, this raised his concerns about one of your patients."

Tár raised an eyebrow. "Is this a joke? Whatever crimes they may have committed in the past, our patients are securely incarcerated here."

"But that's the point. The caller told us that one of your patients is currently out on a period of adaptive leave. I believe the patient's name is Zoltán Varga."

Tár tossed his head backwards and laughed. "So that's it? Some do-gooder, who discovered we occasionally allow low-risk patients to spend supervised time in the community, as part of their rehabilitation back into society."

"Actually, no. This information comes from a source within your organisation. Anonymous, but credible, that's all I can tell you."

His frown line knotted.

"What else has this *source* of yours told you?" He almost spat out the words in disdain.

Ignoring his question, Erika said, "What can you tell us about the patient?"

"I can tell you he is not a person you need to concern yourselves with. He has no record of violence, except towards himself."

"So what was he doing here?" asked Erika.

"Varga was imprisoned for a minor misdemeanour. His prison psychiatrist identified he was suffering from BPD, borderline personality disorder. A penal institution was the wrong environment for him, so they referred him here. He arrived on the fifth of January 2019."

"What are his symptoms?" she said.

He paused for a beat, perhaps wondering how much to divulge. "For him, they fall into three major areas. First, effective dysregulation – or emotional instability. Second, disturbed patterns of thinking or perception, so cognitive or perceptual distortions. And finally, intense but unstable relationships with others. These symptoms range in patients from mild to severe, and usually emerge in adolescence, persisting into adulthood."

Erika checked Eszter was taking notes and said, "Do you have any idea what the root cause was in his case?"

Tár cleared his throat. "We have only known him as a man in his mid-twenties. My diagnosis can be only indicative and not conclusive. As with most conditions, BPD appears to result from a combination of genetic and environmental factors. We associate traumatic events that occur during childhood or earlier life with the development of BPD. Many people with the disorder will have experienced parental neglect or physical, sexual or emotional abuse during their childhood."

"And for him?" she said.

The director scowled. "All we know is his family circumstances were complicated."

You can't fob me off so easily. "How so?" she asked.

"We understand his parents were not around for most of his childhood. His grandparents brought him up."

Erika plunged in. "Director Tár, why did you decide to release Varga back into the community?"

He leant forward, fingers interlaced, elbows on the desk. His voice was low and barely coherent. "It was not the kind of decision we take lightly. The Chief Physician and I may only release patients based on the recommendations of the Adaption

Committee. In addition to myself and the Chief Physician, the committee comprises the Medical Director, head physicians of the departments, the head of the clinical psychology department and the heads of other non-medical departments. Furthermore, a respected member of the community signs to say he, or she, will supervise the care of the patient."

"Who is Mr Varga's supervisor?"

Tár mumbled, something about that being confidential information.

Erika was firm. "I'm sure it's a matter of public record, and may I remind you, this is a murder investigation."

A bead of sweat ran down the side of Tár's prominent nose, and his eyes flashed. There was a manila folder on his desk. He skipped several pages before pointing halfway up a page. "The caregiver is Father Jakob."

"A priest?"

Tár gave an almost imperceptible nod of his head.

She said, "Thank you. Where could we find him?"

"He is chaplain of the Order of Malta, on Fortuna Street."

"Do you have his contact number?"

Tár turned another page in his file and read out the number aloud.

She sensed he was still withholding information. "What about Mr Varga? If we could also trouble you for his contact details."

He shuffled awkwardly. "I believe Varga is staying at a hostel in Csepel. Father Jakob will have his number. Beyond that, I cannot help you."

She placed one of her business cards on his desk.

"Please call me, if you think of anything else that could help our investigation."

There was a knock on the door and Doctor Oláh re-entered.

Tár stood. He was easily two metres tall and towered over everyone else in the room. He mumbled something incomprehensible, and Oláh showed them out.

Tár slumped back into his chair and wiped the sweat from his face with a handkerchief. He had never shirked from doing the bidding of the brotherhood. He recalled how the priest had lobbied for Varga's transfer from prison and, more recently, had made the case for his release into the community. He supported whenever he could, but insisted on staying out of the limelight. Now, because of some loose-lipped whistle-blower, the police had come knocking.

He told himself he had nothing to be afraid of, except the possibility this would reflect badly on him. He turned the detective's card over and over, contemplating his next move.

Forewarned is forearmed. Better the explanation came from his lips than from someone else's. He picked up his phone and made the call.

He explained what had transpired, then added. "They were well informed, but would not divulge the name of their informer. Assume they are on their way, brother. If we are careful, they will prove nothing."

Erika spotted a white stucco-clad building with the number 10 mounted on the door.

"This it is," she said.

Eszter parked next to the pavement, and Erika got out. At one end of Fortuna Street stood the Hilton Budapest, and behind it, prominent against the clear, blue sky, the bell tower of the Mátyás Church. Directly above her, a red and white flag bearing the Maltese Cross fluttered in the breeze.

Erika gestured towards the discreet sign on the wall. "The Embassy of the Sovereign Military Order of Malta. I never heard of this place. Is it new?"

Eszter consulted Google and read from her phone, "Not exactly. It says here, they founded the Order over nine-hundred years ago. To the outside world, it highlights its work as a charitable organisation; yet it also acts like a country — the 'smallest sovereign state in the world' – with diplomatic relations with one hundred and ten countries, including Hungary. Even though it's a Catholic religious order, for centuries it acted independently of, and was therefore constantly in conflict with, the Vatican. But it seems like the balance of power has recently shifted. Pope Francis asked for and received the resignation of the Order's Grand Master in 2017, and they appointed a new Grand Master in 2018."

Before they reached the intercom button on the wall, the large double doors at the entrance of the embassy opened automatically. They looked at one another with raised eyebrows.

Erika nodded towards the CCTV camera. "Looks like someone is expecting us."

She led the way into a small foyer, up a spiral staircase with a wrought-iron balustrade The white walls of the staircase were adorned with dozens of heraldic emblems, each presented on a gold-coloured plate.

Waiting for them in the reception area at the top of the stairs was a man who looked to be in his forties, dressed in the attire of a Catholic priest. Behind him, there was a mural, with the words Hungarian Charity Service Founded in 1989, *'Tuitio Fidel et Obsequium Pauperum,' – 'Nurturing, Witnessing and Protecting the faith, Serving the Poor and the Sick.'*

"Detectives Kelemen and Szabó. Welcome to our newly renovated home. I am Father Jakob, chaplain of the Order of Malta in Budapest."

Erika produced her ID, made her introductions and said, "You appear to be well informed. If you were expecting us, you will be aware of our interest in speaking with Zoltán Varga. I understand you are his supervisor."

He said, "That's not strictly true. I am his legal caregiver, but his day-to-day supervision is taken care of by one of our retired priests, Father Laszló."

Eszter produced her notepad and pen.

Erika was becoming exasperated at the complexity and looseness of the arrangement.

"And where could we find Father Laszló?"

"He could be in any number of places. Helping the homeless, visiting the sick and the infirm, delivering the sacraments, or handing out food parcels. Tell me, detective, why is the homicide department showing such an interest in an unfortunate young man?"

"Some information has come to our attention concerning a patient at the psychiatric institution. We would like to ask Mr Varga some questions, as part of our routine enquiries. Do you have his address?"

He produced his phone. "Here is Father Laszló's number. He will know how to contact Varga."

Erika saved the number to her own phone and handed him a business card. "Please call, if you have any information that could help our investigation."

He nodded and smiled benignly. "And may God go with you."

Back in the car, Erika peered at herself in the vanity mirror. There was an unhealthy-looking greyness to her complexion. She leant forward, supporting her forehead on the dashboard.

Eszter sounded concerned. "Are you alright, boss? You don't look well."

"I'll be fine. Just give me a minute. I don't know what's come over me. Think I've got a migraine coming on. Do you have some water?"

Eszter reached into the driver's door pocket and handed over an unopened bottle.

Erika rummaged until she found some painkillers in her handbag. She swallowed them and sipped the water. For several seconds she sat, eyes closed, trying to push the past to the back of her mind, willing herself to focus on the present. She still needed to contact Varga's supervisor. Her call went straight to voicemail.

She left a message. "Father László, this is Detective Kelemen from the Budapest Homicide Department. Please call me as soon as you pick this up. My number is 06 55 741 298."

She hung up. Frankly, she was relieved he hadn't answered. The bass drum in her head was pounding away. It was almost seven o'clock, and this seemed like a good opportunity to call time for the day. The thought of Marcel preparing dinner was comforting. He was next on her call list.

Ever since Friday night's failed attempt to celebrate Erika's birthday, Marcel had been trying to get his head straight. Despite the weekend's record temperatures, he'd taken himself off on some long runs. The solitude and sweaty, physical effort had been cathartic, helping him apply perspective to a relationship that was unfortunately on the verge of turning sour. His attraction to her was as strong as ever. Yet, he had learned the hard way that she was difficult to live with. Her capacity to surprise him was never in doubt, and her call this evening was a prime example of that.

"I'm on my way home. What's for dinner?" was how she had opened the conversation.

A call as early as seven o'clock had been surprise enough. However, it had been the tone of her next question which rankled the most.

"Where are you?" She sounded suspicious and demanding of an explanation.

And, when he had said, "I'm out," she had sounded annoyed by the realisation he was absent without leave. She clearly expected him to be home, preparing dinner for her like some obedient house-elf, in the way he had done on so many occasions since moving in. Familiarity breeds contempt, he thought.

It had given him pleasure to say, "Catch you later. Don't wait up."

CHAPTER SEVEN

E arly next morning, Erika reached for her phone. There were no messages, and she tossed it onto Marcel's unoccupied side of the bed. Despite her earliest night in months, her sleep had been restless and fitful. She had been waiting for him to stagger home drunk; bracing herself for a fight. But neither he nor the row had materialised. Now she felt wretched. Exhausted before the day had even begun. She hauled herself up and dragged herself through the bathroom, grimacing in the mirror at the deep crevasses and puffiness around her eyes. At her dressing table, she layered-on more foundation and eye make-up than usual. It was seven-thirty when she set off for the office, and no sooner had she pulled out of the car park than her phone rang on hands-free.

The caller sounded breathless, even agitated. "Detective Kelemen? Turay here."

She had not expected to hear from him. Surely he was travelling. "What's up, professor?"

"During our meeting, you enquired about the records of former AVH employees. I believe you wanted to know whether your victims' names appeared in the files. Even though the chances of a match seems unlikely, I made an official request to the ministry for the release of certain government employee records. I know some such records exist, because I discovered them myself at the end of the Cold War, and personally ensured they were secured in the archive. The chief archivist at the Ministry once worked for me; I called in a favour to get a fast response. Now I'm dismayed to inform you; someone has removed the files."

The white van she had been following slammed on its brakes and Erika followed suit. She gesticulated at the driver and cursed under her breath while continuing the conversation. "You mean to say, someone has borrowed them?"

"I mean to say, Detective, there is no record of the files being borrowed. Someone has stolen the files; from a secure ministry archive few have access to."

"Professor Turay, does the chief archivist have any idea who has recently entered the archives? Perhaps they were captured on CCTV?"

"I'll make enquiries and get back to you."

She thanked him and manoeuvred around the stationary white van, shaking her fist at the driver.

As she sped away, she wondered whether the ministry was as efficient at guarding its archives as it was at spying on its visitors.

Eszter was attempting to read through her notes from the meeting with Daniel Tár, but was distracted by the din emanating from the other side of the Incident Room. She looked up and saw that Rigo, Dolman and Márkos had found something amusing in yet another newspaper.

But it was the sudden arrival of Commander Rácz that caught everyone's attention and caused all of them to stand.

"Has anyone seen Kelemen?" he said.

Rigo's nasal monotone was the first voice to respond. "No sign of her yet. She's running late this morning."

Rácz scowled. "Dora's been calling her, but keeps getting voicemail."

It was less than a week since they had seconded Eszter to the murder squad. During that time, Eszter had seen Commander Rácz only once. On that occasion, he had looked calm and in control. Today he appeared rattled.

Rigo spoke up again. "Could you spare a moment for me and the lads, sir?"

Rácz appeared irritated. "You've got one minute. What is it?"

Rigo briefly glanced in Eszter's direction and lowered his voice. But not so low that she couldn't hear him.

"The thing is, sir, we're not happy with the way things are being run on this investigation. We're being given the women's work to do. As you know, we've got a lot of experience between us, and we're stuck in the office answering phones while the *girls* are off doing all the detective work."

Eszter believed she had heard most of what was being said, even if she found it hard to comprehend. She didn't have to strain to hear Rácz's response, which carried around the room.

"We've got another victim, and it could be the handiwork of our serial killer. It's all hands-on-deck. Don't let your prejudices stand in the way of catching this murderer. The new Deputy High Commissioner won't stand for it, and neither will I. Do you understand?"

Rigo's face looked like someone had let the air out of it.

Erika pulled over and parked outside the Raiffeisen Bank on Váci Street.

At the newsstand, the proprietor greeted her with his usual smile, and a cheerful, "How are you this fine morning, my dear?"

She summoned up a polite smile. "I'd be feeling better, if the press were giving my investigation some coverage."

She scoured the headlines of the publications on display, searching for signs that her painful ordeal at the press conference had not been in vain.

He handed her a copy of *Lokál* and said, "They have it in here, on page seventeen."

She scowled, "Page seventeen! Is that the best they can do?"

He also gave her a copy of the business daily, *Világgazdaság,* which showed a photograph of the financier Ambrus Sipos on its front page, together with the headline, *Sipos Invests In Hungarian Green Energy Sector.*

"You get a mention in here, too. In the local news section."

It was better than nothing. She thanked him and paid for both.

Back in the car, she tossed the folded newspapers onto the passenger seat. Her phone chirped and a text message from Eszter said, "URGENT. Rácz came looking for you. Another body found. We should talk before you see him."

When Erika arrived on the tenth floor, Eszter was waiting inside her office. Ferenc from the IT department was there too. They were both deeply engaged in conversation.

She bustled past them and sank into the creaky revolving chair behind her untidy desk. "What's going on? Keep it brief."

Ferenc was the first to speak up. "Detective Szabó asked me to look at the activity of the two burner phones found with Klára Menges and Ervin Nagy. I've run a search with the telecoms provider." He pulled out an A4 map, lay it on her desk, and tapped with his index finger. He was pointing to the Visivaros district, directly across the river from the parliament building.

"They made the calls with the two victims from within this highlighted area. Here in Bathyány Square, and the blocks either side."

Erika smiled. "Good work! I'll take this. Eszter, you keep hold of this guy. We may soon have more work for him." She folded and slipped the map into her jacket pocket.

"Another thing, boss…" Eszter briefly recanted the conversation between Rigo and Rácz.

Erika needed no further proof that Rigo was a scumbag. If she had her way, he'd be out on his ear. At least Rácz hadn't succumbed to the lobbying, and perhaps his opinion of Rigo had shifted over the years. She sighed. Dealing with internal politics was so energy-sapping. All she was really interested in was finding the killer.

Dora waved Erika straight through. She found Rácz sitting at his desk, his head buried in his hands. He seemed not to notice her arrival.

She coughed. "You were looking for me?"

He looked distracted, but gestured her to take a seat. When she was seated, his brown eyes hardened and locked onto hers. "This investigation has grown in scope. A third body has been discovered, and it looks like the handiwork of the same killer. The new Deputy High Commissioner wants to know what's going on. Wants to know where our suspects are, and wants me to bring in reinforcements."

She leaned back in her chair; arms folded. "Then do me a favour and make sure the reinforcements are better than Rigo and his merry men."

He leaned back in his chair and tugged at his beard.

"The thing is, I'm thinking of putting someone else in charge. Someone with more recent experience of complex homicide cases."

She could hardly believe her own ears. For the second time in five years, he was going to screw her over. My God, she'd only been on the investigation since last Thursday. This was only her fourth working day, and she was making progress. It took every ounce of effort to keep her self-control. "I can see you have a lot on your plate. It makes no sense for you to stress over this, especially as we seem to have a breakthrough."

"What sort of breakthrough?"

He was hooked. She laid Ferenc's map on his desk. "The call records of our two victims show recent incoming and outgoing contact with burner phones. We tracked down the calls made by the burners, to a three-block location in the Bathyány Square neighbourhood. You say there's a possible third victim. Let me assess the situation at the crime scene. If it's true that it's the work of the same killer, he may also have used a burner phone to contact this victim. What's more, we had a lead yesterday, regarding a possible suspect. We're making progress. By the time you get someone else up to speed, we may have a suspect in the frame and a link to the burner phones. What do you say?"

He leaned back again, his large hands behind his head, sweat-stained armpits on display. "You have forty-eight hours. Then I'll review the situation again. This is the address for the latest murder scene. Get over there, and see what you think. Don't let me down, or we'll both be in the firing line."

He handed her a piece of paper, on which was written: *Apartment 31. Top floor, Corner of Nefeléjcs Street and Thököly Way, Above the fast food.*

On her way out, Erika stopped at Dora's desk. "What's going on?" she whispered.

Dora tapped the side of her nose with her right index finger and said quietly, "Not every problem is work-related."

The carpet inside Apartment 31 was sodden. Despite Erika's plastic overshoes, cold water squelched between her feet and the insteps of her new shoes. Other than the water damage, the living room looked intact. The bathroom was where the grizzly action had taken place. The bathtub was full to the rim, and through the crimson waterline protruded the battered head and shoulders of an old man. A white shirt and blue tie were visible too, and his thinning grey hair was matted with blood. His smashed skull was cracked open like an eggshell, exposing his brain matter to the outside world. This extreme violence was shocking, even to someone with her years of experience in homicide.

Standing alongside her, Eszter's knees suddenly buckled. It was all Erika could do to prevent the poor girl from collapsing into the bath and landing on top of the victim.

Professor Baldi, who had been extracting blood from the victim's arm, also stopped what he was doing. His tone was less acerbic than usual.

"Steady as you go, dear," he said.

Erika put her arm around Eszter's shoulder and led her out of the apartment, telling her to wait outside, and asking the uniformed police officer on duty to keep an eye on her.

Once she had returned to the bathroom, she asked the pathologist what kind of weapon had been used.

"It looks like the work of a hammer. Perhaps a length of heavy steel pipe. From the odour on his lips, I'd say this is another example of our cyanide poisoner at work. This sample will confirm, one way or another and, if my hypothesis is true, our serial killer has showed yet another way to mutilate a victim, post-mortem. I suspect the poison was administered in the living room, perhaps at around six p.m. He was then dragged in here, dumped into the bathtub and beaten to a pulp. The bath may have been filled while the beating took place. Whatever happened, the taps were on when the killer left here."

"He left the taps turned on?"

"Apparently so. Local police broke in, after a neighbour called the emergency services at two a.m., and reported flooding through his ceiling."

Erika made notes in her pocketbook and pondered the sequence of events. "What kind of torture scenario was being played out here? Perhaps he was interrupted and left the water running unintentionally? Or perhaps he wanted the body discovered?"

Eszter reappeared. The colour was returning to her cheeks, and she was carrying several evidence bags. "One of the SOCO guys just handed me these. They found his wallet, passport, and a phone. The ID shows the victim was named Zsigmond Horvát, and he was aged eighty-six."

With the victim identified and his personal belongings in their possession, Erika was impatient to unlock his phone records. She issued her instructions to Eszter. "Take them to HQ and book them in. Get Ferenc to work on the phone. I want to know whether any burner phones were used to contact Horvát. I'll make my own way back when I've finished here."

Erika wanted some time on her own. Time to think things through before her next conversation with Rácz. With the coffee shops still closed for business, she found a vendor who had created a mini street-café by placing half a dozen folding chairs at a socially distanced radius around his stall. She bought a black Americano and took a seat in the shade across the road from Keleti railway station.

On a page in her pocket notepad, she sketched out a vertical timeline and added the key events, dates, times and locations:

-Tuesday 19 May, 5.00 p.m. – Klára Menges, Bertalan Lajos Street

-Thursday 21 May, Midday – Ervin Nagy, Hős Street

-Monday 25 May, 6.00 p.m. – Zsigmond Horvát, Nefeléjcs Street

There had been three premeditated murders, each in different parts of the city, all in the space of one week. In each case, the killer had been meticulous in terms of planning and execution, leaving no obvious clues regarding his own identity.

But what was the motive? And why these victims? Random selection seemed implausible, so how were they connected? With three *successes* under his belt, the killer was on a roll. Where and when would he, or she, strike next? The only connection found so far between the first two victims was they had both received calls from someone using a burner phone. Erika sipped her coffee. If Zsigmond Horvát's call records showed he had also revealed similar calls, it would come as no surprise.

The initials the killer had tattooed under Klára's arm had clearly been a deliberate attempt to point the police towards the AVH. Yet, there was no evidence to suggest either Nagy or Horvát had been former members of the Secret Police. What if the killer had used the AVH connection to send the investigators up a blind alley? She urgently needed a connection, a motive, a suspect. And she needed it before Rácz reassigned the investigation elsewhere.

Her thoughts went round in circles, and with every revolution she felt less certain about the direction she should follow. She drained her cup and aimed it towards the refuse bin. It fell woefully short, spinning off into the gutter.

"Just about sums things up," she said aloud, before stepping forward, picking up the cup and placing it into its intended target.

She strolled with no destination in mind, crossing the street and passing under the vast stone and glass archway, into the cavernous concourse of Keleti station. On her last visit there, a sea of humanity had flowed and shifted in every direction: commuters, students, shoppers, refugees; men, women and children; all ages, all shapes and sizes. Today the scene was starkly different: it was sterile and, except for the muffled announcements on the PA system, eerily quiet. Perhaps two dozen people traversed the plaza. Uniformed police officers easily outnumbered them, each with weapons hung around their necks, looking bored out of their minds.

A newspaper headline caught her eye on a stand outside a bookstore.

Budapest Butcher Targets Elderly.

Stark and brutal as the message was, the clamour for action would be far greater when the media picked up on the third murder. At least the news had migrated onto the front page of the latest edition. If that didn't alert the public and draw out a useful lead or two, nothing would.

Her phone rang. The withheld number aroused her suspicion.

"Detective Kelemen?" said a male voice she did not recognise. "My name is Father Laszló. I am returning your call from yesterday. I've been rather busy. How may I help you?"

"Forgive me, father," Erika said instinctively, almost lapsing into confession-speak, before hauling herself back from that particular brink. "I understand you are acting as the supervisor for a patient of the IMEI."

"You mean Zoltán? He's a fine, young man. Truly making himself so helpful within the community. How can I help you?"

"We are making some routine enquires, as part of an investigation we are following. I'd like to meet, ask him a few questions. Do you have his address and a contact number where we could reach him?"

"He is staying in a hostel for the homeless. My next check-in meeting with him will take place this afternoon. He's a shy boy. Perhaps I can help?"

"I would appreciate that."

"There is a park in Csepel, on the corner of Károli Gáspár Street and Popleluszko Street. Meet us there at 12:30. It shouldn't be difficult to find us."

The priest seemed helpful. She agreed to his proposal, thanked him and hung up. Her next call was to Eszter.

"Did you hand over that phone to Ferenc?" she asked.

"Yes, I'm with him now."

"Good. Let him get on with his work and pick me up outside Keleti in fifteen minutes."

The park in Csepel turned out to be a well groomed garden, with a few benches and a children's play area. They circled the block in their unmarked black Audi and saw two men seated by the swings. Eszter parked opposite some factory gates, behind which was an industrial unit with a tall chimney belching out smoke.

Erika led the way. As they approached the bench, both men stood. The priest was barely taller than herself. Wiry with thinning grey hair, he carried a walking stick in his left hand. Unsurprisingly, he wore a black suit and a black shirt with a clerical collar. More unusual, particularly in such warm weather, was the black glove he wore on his right hand.

Standing alongside him, the other man looked to be in his mid-twenties, of medium height and with a heavy build. He had gold-rimmed glasses, short black hair, and was unshaven. He wore a red t-shirt, black jeans and black shoes.

The priest smiled. "Welcome. I am Father Laszló and this is Zoltán Varga. I won't shake your hands. At my age, they still mean for us to be shielded from the virus." He sounded affable. There was even a twinkle of humour in his eye.

They both held out their ID, and Erika made the introductions. "Thank you both for coming. Like I explained on the phone, we are here to ask Mr Varga some questions, concerning a matter we are currently investigating."

The priest gestured towards the empty bench on the opposite side of the footpath.

"Please, take a seat. I prefer to be outdoors. Zoltán's accommodation is nearby, but there is no privacy. It is a hostel run by the Hungarian Inter-church Aid Foundation. At least I know he has a safe place to stay while he is here. We meet every few days. I like to check things are as they should be. The devil makes work for idle hands. I make sure the boy is never idle."

There was nobody else nearby. Erika focused her attention on Varga. His expression looked strangely blank. She wondered whether he may have physical and neurological problems.

Eszter was ready to take notes.

Erika said, "Mr Varga, or may I call you Zoltán?"

He seemed to stare at her feet, his brow covered in perspiration. He peered over his glasses and nodded in silent agreement.

"Zoltán, what can you tell us about the Secret Police, the AVH?"

"He's a little young for such ancient history, don't you think?" said the priest.

"Exactly," replied Erika. She nudged Eszter. "What was it, they heard him say at the IMEI?"

Eszter read from her notebook, "AVH torturers should all go to hell."

Varga shrugged. His expression remained blank.

"Detective, are you aware of the treatment regime for psychiatric patients? During his stay, Zoltán was on medication. He also conversed with other patients. Some of whom will have said things he could repeat. If someone attributed that statement to him, I suggest you check your source."

Erika said, "Thank you, Father, but please let him answer the questions for himself. If he can't do that here, we may have to take him to the station. Zoltán, who told you about the AVH?"

"Dunno," he said.

She changed tack. "According to our information, they released you from the IMEI on Friday, the fifteenth of May. Is that correct?"

The corners of Varga's mouth turned down. Behind his glasses, his eyes were shut tight.

"Your information is correct," said the priest.

Erika replied, "Take your time, Zoltán. At this stage in our investigation, we are attempting to eliminate people from our enquiries. I'm going to ask you some questions about your movements over the last week. Please think carefully before giving us your answers."

Varga's mouth twitched involuntarily. Father Laszló laid a hand on his shoulder. It seemed to have a calming effect.

Erika checked her pocketbook and read from her notes. "Zoltán, where were you on the evening of Tuesday the nineteenth of May, between four p.m. and seven p.m.?"

Varga avoided eye contact and squirmed a little.

Father Laszló used his left hand to remove a notebook from his jacket pocket. He flicked through the pages until he settled on one.

"This is my diary, detective. The evening of the nineteenth was when we delivered food parcels to the homeless refugees. We began at five and finished around nine. Life for refugees in Hungary was very hard before the lockdown. But, since the virus enveloped our nation, it's been almost impossible for them to survive on the streets."

"Yes, thank you, Father. I'm well aware of the plight of the homeless. So, are you saying both of you were delivering food parcels that evening? Could anyone else confirm that?"

The priest sat back. "The recipients of our aid are transient. They spend their time underneath the arches, finding new shelter whenever your colleagues move them on."

Erika's jaw clenched. She continued, "There must be someone who could verify your movements. Where did you collect the food parcels from?"

"From the hostel kitchen," the priest said.

Erika tried again to engage Varga in the interview. "Zoltán, what were you doing around midday on Thursday 21 May?"

The twitch around Varga's mouth became even more pronounced.

Meanwhile, Father László once again turned the pages of his diary. "Midday, last Thursday? Hmm, Zoltán met with me, at the Order of Malta in Fortuna Street. Do you know it?"

Erika wondered whether this double act was ad hoc, or part of a predetermined strategy. "We know the place well. Detective Szabó, please make a note to check the footage of their CCTV. Now Zoltán, here's an easy one for you. I want you to answer for yourself, without help. Is that clear?"

Varga looked at the ground and nodded sheepishly.

"Yesterday evening, where were you, from five p.m. onwards?"

"At church," he mumbled.

"Which church?" said Erika.

His reply was barely audible. "St. F-Francis' Wounds."

"The one on Fő Street?" said Eszter.

Father László turned to another page in his diary. "That's the one. The first post-lockdown mass is due to take place there next Sunday. The parish priest is a good friend of mine. He asked for support in the preparations, and I was happy to agree. Unfortunately, this old body of mine is not as strong as it used to be. So, I drafted Zoltán in, to do some fetching and carrying."

Eszter said, "Was the parish priest there with you? Could he vouch for your presence in the church?"

Father László shook his head. "He wasn't, I'm afraid. But one of the flower arrangers was there for a while."

Eszter made a note.

It all seemed too convenient.

"So, are you telling us, Father, on all three occasions in question, Mr Varga was in your company and you can vouch for his whereabouts?"

"I am indeed, Detective Kelemen. Like I said, the devil makes work for idle hands, and when I agreed to become Zoltán's caregiver, I pledged to commit as much time as necessary to keep him occupied and in my orbit. He's not much of a conversationalist, but he's been very helpful to me, haven't you, boy?" He placed his left hand on Varga's knee and squeezed it. "You must be hungry, my son. It's lunchtime. You should go back to the hostel for your lunch. Unless the detectives have more questions for you?" His pale blue eyes sought confirmation from Erika.

Was there any point in questioning Varga further at this stage? The chance of him being the one responsible for three sophisticated and brutal murders seemed remote. Erika gave a nod of approval.

The priest nudged Varga, who picked himself up and exited without another word. He walked with a slow, shuffling gait.

Once he was out of earshot, Father Laszló leaned on his walking stick and sighed. "Now we're alone, ladies, let me tell you who and what you're dealing with here."

Chapter Eight

When Axel Rácz returned after lunch, there was no sign of Dora. He scowled and grumbled to himself, because he urgently needed her to fetch some files. Pouring himself some coffee from her cafetière, he carried it through to his office.

There he did a double take; for sitting behind the desk, and reading the papers that lay upon it was a most unwelcome presence. He could hardly believe the audacity of the man. He closed the door and said, "What the hell do you think you're doing in here, Kudár?"

"You really ought to improve your security. Your door was unlocked, and there's all this confidential information on display."

That conversation with Dora would come later. But for now, he braced himself. *Whatever Rudolf Kudár had to say, he knew his former colleague would not be the bearer of glad tidings.*

Until the formation of the TEK, he and Kudár had worked together, both of them on the fast-track through the National Police Force. Then in 2010, the Prime Minister had given the TEK responsibilities for protecting him and the nation against national and international terrorism. Kudár had been transferred into the counter terrorism agency, and once there had made his way up the TEK's greasy career pole. For the last decade, there had been no love lost between them.

Rácz jerked his thumb to one side. "You've made your point, now get the hell out of my chair."

Kudár swung himself round. "I can see the attractions of a comfortable office job." He rose and meandered towards the panoramic windows. His tall, lean frame silhouetted against the skyline, impeccably dressed in a well-cut black suit. "The thing is, Axel, some of the cases your department is currently investigating are politically sensitive."

Rácz was none the wiser. "Such as?"

"Such as the cases being handled by Erika Kelemen."

Rácz threw back his head and laughed out loud. "You mean Klára Menges and Ervin Nagy?"

"Not to mention the latest victim, Zsigmond Horvát. There's been a security breach, at the Ministry of Interior. A dossier has been mislaid. The dossier contains the identity of some former government agents. We need to prevent further embarrassment. This is a job requiring urgency and expertise. Kelemen is lightweight. You need to hand over the files. We will take it from here."

Rácz wondered how Kudár had already heard of the Horvát killing, and was concerned where the leak had come from. Right now, he felt like throwing the arrogant bastard out of his office window. But Kudár was like a multi-headed Hydra, and there was no way he was acting without the approval of others higher-up. Nevertheless, he refused to take this lying down. "Well, pardon me for your embarrassment. We have a sadistic serial killer on the loose, and my department is best placed to find and prosecute the perpetrator. Kelemen is interviewing a potential suspect as we speak. There's no way I'm taking her off the investigation, and even less chance of me handing the files over to you."

A smirk spread slowly across Kudár's face. "The stopwatch is running, Axel. Within forty-eight hours , I'll ensure this request becomes an order. So, do me favour. Make certain the case files are up to date. There's a good boy."

Erika ignored the vibration of her phone. She and Eszter were still in conversation with Father Laszló, who was proving to be an engaging speaker. His career as a parish priest in Budapest spanned more than six decades, although some of his time had been spent abroad, working in the African missions. He had known the Varga family for many years.

"Please, go on," she said.

He frowned. "With a drug addict for a mother, and a father in prison for murdering a man with a hammer, the boy had a terrible start in life. From the age of seven, his grandparents were his guardians. Fortunately, his grandmother was a devout Catholic, and he received an excellent education. I've known Zoltán, ever since he attended our primary school."

Erika took note of the hammer murder and said, "Director Tár at the IMEI described Zoltán as having borderline personality disorder. Apparently, he has emotional instability, disturbed patterns of thinking or perception, and intense, unstable relationships with others."

"It sounds like a fair diagnosis. He also has learning difficulties, but we should not give up on him. Since his temporary release, he has adapted well. He helps in any way he can. My aim is to support him and eventually see his permanent release back into society. Later this month, I shall submit my report to the IMEI committee. I may even ask you ladies for character references for the boy." The priest smiled kindly. His wrinkled face looked worldly-wise and full of compassion.

"You've seen for yourself, he's docile and certainly not the sharpest knife in the box. I see him as no more of a threat to society than you or I. Now, unless you have more questions…"

For several minutes Erika sat quietly in the passenger seat, reflecting on their interview. Varga was a troubled individual with a difficult past. Although the alibis the priest had provided seemed too convenient and needed verification, she could not imagine the young man being capable of such organised and sadistic deeds. Eventually, she broke the silence.

"We need to widen the net. Any ideas?"

Eszter seemed totally focused on the road ahead when her phone rang. The caller display on the dashboard of the Audi showed it was Ferenc.

Through the hands-free speaker he said, "We've examined your third victim's phone records. Looks like a third burner phone was used to contact him. Whoever it was, they've used a different burner for each victim, but all the calls have come from the same area of the city."

Erika was already straining against the seat belt. "We're on our way. See you in the Incident Room in half an hour. Detective Szabó is about to put her foot down, and I'm about to call a meeting."

A raucous conversation was taking place in the Incident Room between Rigo, Márkos and Dolman. It was loud enough to be heard in the general office. Yet as soon as Erika and Eszter entered, a tense silence descended.

Erika strode to the front of the room and faced them. "Since yesterday's public appeal, there have been several significant developments."

Rigo sneered and said, "Your publicity stunt brought us nothing but time-wasters."

Erika glared back at him. There was no way she would allow him to hijack another meeting with his negativity. She bit her tongue.

Dolman chipped in and said to Eszter, "You picked up the first lead. How did that one go?"

She replied, "Certainly not a time-waster. But the lead isn't as promising as first thought."

Erika was determined to regain the initiative from Rigo. "Our killer has now struck for a third time. We need to decide on an action plan. Let's recap on what we know so far."

She picked up a marker pen and wrote the name of Zsigmond Horvát on one of the whiteboards. "This is his latest victim, aged eighty-six. Found by local police, in his bath at two a.m. this morning, after his neighbour had complained of flooding from the apartment above. The preliminary pathology report suggests death by potassium cyanide poisoning, the signature MO of our killer. After poisoning Horvát, the killer dragged him from the living room and dumped him, fully clothed, into a bath, then beat his head to a pulp, with an iron bar or similar. The bath was filled to overflowing, possibly after the beating took place."

Turning to face another of the whiteboards, Erika drew out a timeline, then marked out the key dates and names of all three victims. "Tuesday the nineteenth, Klára Menges; Thursday the twenty-first, Ervin Nagy; and yesterday, Monday the twenty-fifth, Zsigmond Horvát. Each victim in their eighties; each living alone; each poisoned with cyanide, then tortured and mutilated uniquely."

Márkos chipped in, "Could the killer be poisoning them first, simply to subdue the victims?"

Erika nodded. "That would make sense. The delivery of the torture being the primary aim. The poisoning simply being the means of suppressing them."

"And the poison, administered in a way that aroused no suspicion for the victim," said Eszter.

"Hidden in a glass of wine, in Klára's case," said Dolman.

The door swung open.

Erika said, "For those who don't already know, This is Ferenc from the IT department. I asked him to join us. He has been supporting us with the phone tracing. I want him to present what he's found so far."

All eyes switched to the newcomer, who walked towards the large screen, picked up the remote control and said, "I've been looking at the phone records of the three victims. In each case, a different, unidentified number was in contact with the victim several times, in the days leading up to their death. Each unidentified number traced back to a burner phone."

"You got any more information? To help us narrow it down a bit," Rigo said, sniggering to himself. No one else joined in.

Ferenc used the remote. On the screen he showed them a map of downtown Budapest, on which he'd highlighted several blocks in the Viziváros district, on the Buda side, opposite the parliament building. He pointed with a laser pen and spoke confidently. "The Telecom company has run a search of the calls from each burner phone and they triangulate here, between the Bem Rakpart and Fő Street, with Batthyány Square to the north and the Calvanist Church to the south."

Dolman scratched his chin. "Why would someone make calls from different burner phones, then make all the calls from the same location?"

"Perhaps he's not as smart as he thinks he is," said Márkos.

This engagement, by the younger members of the team, pleased Erika. It was their first promising group discussion since her appointment five days ago, and she was keen to maintain the momentum.

She said, "Whatever the reason, the burner phones are our common denominators. Find the phones and we're in business. We now have three crime scenes to mine for information. Forensics have yet to come up with anything significant to help identify the killer. That means he's been very careful with the planning and execution. But he's no ghost. Someone out there saw him arrive or leave, possibly both. We're going to visit each crime scene with a fresh pair of eyes and interview anyone and everyone who may have seen something. Dolman, you take Klára's apartment. Records from the initial door-to-door enquiries show many of the residents were not at home when our officers called. I want you to try those addresses again. Márkos, you do the same in Hős Street; someone must have seen the killer come or go at Nagy's apartment. You just need to find that one person. Szabó, I want you to follow up those alibis for our friend Zoltán Varga. After you've done that, interview Zsigmond Horvát's neighbours."

Finally, she switched her attention to Rigo, and gave him a long, hard stare. "You work with Ferenc. Try the retailers around the location the burner calls were made from. Perhaps he lives in that neighbourhood, and perhaps our killer bought the phones locally?"

Rigo looked sullen but remained silent.

Erika clapped her hands. "People, we need to step up the pace. At the rate the murderer is working, he or she could strike again any minute. Each of you reports to me directly. I'll be here, to take your calls. In the meantime, I'll take another look at everything in the property store and go through the forensics reports one more time. Okay, let's get moving."

After the others had gone, Erika grabbed a coffee from the vending machine and headed back to her office. She felt energised, even though she had her doubts over whether Dolman and Márkos were doing more than paying her lip-service, and knowing for certain she would never win over Rigo. At least, by splitting them up and keeping them busy, they were less likely to have time to plot against her.

Her desk was heaving under the weight of box files, folders, and paperwork. On top of the pile was a yellow post-it note, with a handwritten message from Dora informing her that Commander Rácz needed to see her urgently. She checked her phone. There were five missed calls from him. What did he expect? Didn't he understand she was running a triple-murder investigation. There were not enough hours in the day to be updating him every five minutes. It was time to give him a piece of her mind.

There was clearly something amiss with Dora, and Erika asked if she was alright.

Dora averted her gaze towards her computer screen and silently waved her through to the commander's office.

She found Rácz standing with his arms folded, staring out of the window. She cleared her throat.

He turned, frowned and rubbed his bearded chin. Taking his usual seat at the end of the conference table, he interlaced his fingers and said, "Rudolf Kudár came to see me."

The hairs on Kelemen's neck rose, like they had done when Kudár had cornered her in the garage of her apartment building.

"The TEK want your investigation handing over to them. Kudár says it's politically sensitive. Your three victims' names came from a file stolen from the Ministry of Interior."

A light went on inside her head. "Professor Turay, the curator at the House of Terror, was right! When he made his own enquiries, he discovered some records of former AVH employees had been removed from the Ministry archives."

Rácz threw his hands back. "Why didn't you tell me this?"

"I was still looking into it, and you're already overloaded. Anyway, what's that got to do with Kudár?"

"He says your victims were all former government agents. The file apparently contains other names too. He didn't say whose. They want to find the killer before he strikes again."

"For Christ-sakes, isn't that what I'm trying to do? In the last half-hour we learned Horvát was the third victim to be contacted by a burner phone. I'm sure these phones were used by the killer; used to build trust and gain entry into the victim's homes. We're covering the ground at all three crime scenes, going door-to-door, looking for witnesses who saw the killer come or go. Rigo is on his way to Viziváros. Maybe the killer lives there, or bought the burner phones locally?"

Rácz nodded slowly.

Was she getting through to him? "You can't take me off this investigation. Remember, you asked me to do this. I'm sure we're onto something, but I need more time."

His elbows were on the table, and his chin was leaning on his huge fists. He sighed. "I'll try holding Kudár at bay for another day or two, but that's all. You need an arrest by tomorrow night."

It was the most preposterous thing she had ever heard. "You must be joking."

Rácz's eyes narrowed. "Do I look like I'm joking?"

At four-thirty p.m., Marcel was still nursing the worst hangover he'd had in years. Yesterday's impromptu invitation from an old friend for a post-lockdown drink had become an all-nighter of stupendous proportions, featuring several bottles of premium

Russian vodka. In the end, Marcel had crashed out on Viktor's bachelor-pad sofa. Neither of them had risen before midday.

Marcel had arrived back at Erika's apartment just after one p.m., and dozed on their bed. Now, he peered at himself in the bathroom mirror, his eyes bloodshot and surrounded by puffy, grey bags. His head was pounding too, while the inside of his mouth tasted like the bottom of a birdcage.

Last night, he and Viktor had sat together, putting the world to rights. They saw many things similarly, including the complexities of the female gender. Viktor's divorce had come through two years ago, and he lived alone in a small, rented apartment. The lockdown had stymied Viktor's efforts to date other women, though he'd been happy to discuss his near misses. From Marcel's perspective, he had enjoyed the male conversation and sharing his own ups-and-downs. Also, Viktor was the first person with whom he had discussed the full tale of his arrest and incarceration by the TEK Counter Terrorism Unit. It had felt good to have male company once again.

Should he have messaged Erika to let her know he was safe? Probably. Although he was more convinced than ever, she had been taking him for granted for weeks. She was a strong, independent woman, working in a rough, male-dominated environment. Still, that didn't give her the right to treat him as her lackey.

He sighed. At some stage in last night's proceedings, he had resolved to bring things between himself and Erika to a head. It would surely be easier to start this process another day, but the sudden recollection brought matters to the fore. It felt like an itch that needed scratching.

Back in the bedroom he found his phone and tapped out a WhatsApp message. After several edits, he was left with only six words.

"Is there a future for us?"

It was a simple enough question. Before giving himself time to reconsider, he pressed *Send*.

CHAPTER NINE

L ajos Dolman had done his homework. After this afternoon's briefing with Kelemen, he had spent half an hour reading through the Klára Menges case notes. There were statements in the file taken from her nearby neighbours — none of whom seemed to have ever seen anyone visit her apartment. He analysed the forms completed during the first round of house-to-house enquiries, noting the addresses where the occupants had been out. He read the report from Kelemen, written following a visit she and Szabó had made to Esztergom to meet the victim's sister, Lotti. The report included Lotti's statement that Klára had once worked for the AVH at their House of Terror headquarters. A further file note from Kelemen described Lotti's identification of her sister's body at the mortuary, where she had described the multiple stab wounds on her sister's body as 'rather artistic.' It was a weird and callous comment. Finally, there was the pathologist's report, confirming that the murder had taken place between five and seven p.m., on Tuesday the nineteenth of May.

Dolman looked at his watch. It was five-thirty-five. At precisely this time one week ago, the killer must have been in Klára's apartment, plying her with cyanide-tainted wine before torturing her and disfiguring her body with a sharp instrument like a nail or pin. Seated alone in his car, parked outside Klára's apartment block, the hairs on the back of his neck bristled.

Where to begin? If, as the reports said, the neighbours who had been found had already given their statements, he needed a new line of enquiry.

He gazed through the windscreen and drummed his fingers against the steering wheel, looking for inspiration. Most of the small street-level shops on Bertalan Lajos Street had not yet reopened since the authorities eased the lockdown. For those back in business, they appeared to be already closed for the day. He glanced in his rear-view mirror. Across the street, an old man with a bald head emerged from an entrance door. The man turned to lock the door behind him. *Could he be someone who knew the area and its residents well?* Dolman stepped out of his car and called across the narrow street. "Excuse me, sir. Do you have a minute?"

The man turned to face him. The sign on the shop said Odysseus Hungarian Language School.

Dolman crossed the road and held up his ID. "Detective Dolman from Budapest Homicide."

"I was wondering when the police would finally show up." The voice of the man was deep and melodious.

"Do you work here?"

"I am the founder, of the best Hungarian language school in Budapest, but right now we're low on foreign students. Agostin Lakatos, at your service."

Dolman held up a copy of a photograph taken from the victim's belongings. "Do you know this woman?"

"That's Klára. God rest her soul. May she rest in peace. I also know her sister. Lotti and I go way back."

Dolman produced his pocketbook and pen and made a note. "When was the last time you saw them?"

"Klára, not since the start of the lockdown. Like many people in their eighties, she appears to have taken the shielding advice seriously. In her case, it didn't do her much good in the end."

"What about Lotti?"

"I had not seen her for years until I saw her walk past the shop last Tuesday afternoon."

"Tuesday the 19th?"

"That is correct."

That was the day of Klára's murder. "Are you certain it was Lotti?" he said.

Mr Lakatos nodded. "We were lovers a very long time ago. For me, she's hardly changed. I'd recognise her anywhere."

Gábor Márkos dodged his way past a group of youths who were kicking a plastic football around, near to the entrance of the grim tenement block on Hős Street. The ball struck him on the back of the head. The blow didn't hurt, but it did shock him. He instinctively reached inside his jacket. The boys instantly scattered.

Márkos went straight to the apartment to meet Tibor, a crime scene officer he had known for years. Tibor had already opened up. It was clear, as soon as Márkos entered, that the place had yet to be re-assembled.

"We've finished in here, and changed the lock. You can take the spare."

Márkos thanked him and pocketed the key.

After Tibor had departed, Márkos pulled on a pair of latex gloves. He left the front door slightly ajar to get some fresh air circulating around the place. The SOCO team had stripped the place as bare as a vulture-picked carcass. While Márkos rummaged around the tiny bedroom, he heard footsteps behind him in the living room, then a crash followed by a high-pitched shriek. He pulled out his weapon and flicked off the safety catch, carefully stepped around the door, holding it level in the firing position. The front door was wide open, and he saw the backs of two youngsters running for it. Both wore blue jeans and t-shirts, one red, the other grey. On the floor of the living room was a broken table lamp and next to it an overturned side-table.

He shouted after them but harboured zero expectations they would comply. Re-holstering his gun, he scrambled across the debris to the door, and looked along the corridor in both directions. There were no signs of the juvenile intruders. Márkos had seen enough. He used the key to deadlock the door from the outside. It was time to interrogate the neighbours, and it would be a bonus if he came across the two intruders along the way.

By six forty-five p.m., Eszter's attempts to check out Zoltán Varga's alibis by phone had so far proved fruitless. There was little chance of tracking down any of the homeless refugees, who had apparently been the recipients of food parcels distributed by Varga and Father Laszló on the nineteenth of May. That left her two other possibilities to pursue.

She re-read her own notes. According to the priest, he and Varga had also met on the twenty-first of May, at the Order of Malta. She looked up the number, called it and listened to a recorded, out-of-hours message. There was a second telephone number listed at the same address in Fortuna Street, this one for the Diplomatic Mission of the Sovereign Order of Malta, Hungary. She tried that one too and listened to a second, similar, pre-recorded message before hanging up.

That left her pondering the events of the twenty-fifth of May, the date when Varga and his guardian angel priest had once again claimed to have been together. This time, apparently preparing a local church for the resumption of Sunday masses. She searched on Google for the Church of St. Francis' Wounds on Fő Street. There was a telephone number listed, which she called. Here, there was not even a recorded message to listen to. After several rings, a continuous tone signalled the end of the unanswered call.

She was certain Father László was covering something up for Varga. She needed information and evidence, and it looked like she would have to wait until tomorrow before resuming the exercise.

Then an idea came to her. She had nothing to lose, so drove to Buda Castle and parked on Fortuna Street. She pressed the intercom button on the wall on number ten and waited for several seconds. Holding her ID towards the CCTV camera, she spoke in a loud, clear voice.

"Detective Szabó from the Homicide Department. I'm here to see Father Jakob."

If no one responded, she was not sure what her next move would be. But while she pondered, the automatically controlled door swung slowly open.

Inside stood a black-suited, bald-headed gorilla of a man who resembled a bouncer at a nightclub. He folded his arms across his barrelled chest and grunted. "Can I help you?"

She stood her ground and presented her ID. "I am here to see the chaplain, Father Jakob. My colleague and I met with him yesterday."

"The offices are closed. Come back tomorrow," he growled.

"I need to see him now. I have some further questions to ask him."

The gorilla's expression changed quite suddenly. He held a finger to his ear-bud. His tone quickly changed too. "Follow me."

She needed no further invitation and tagged along behind him, inhaling his personal cocktail of body odour and cologne. In the reception area at the top of the stairs she was met by Father Jakob.

"Good evening, Detective Szabó. You are becoming quite the regular visitor to our humble abode. To what do we owe this latest pleasure?"

"Thank you for seeing me. Detective Kelemen and I met with Father Laszló and Zoltán Varga earlier today." She took out her notebook and referred to her notes. "Father Laszló told us he held a meeting here with Zoltán Varga. We need to check all alibis, as a matter of routine. I'd like to examine your CCTV footage."

His response sounded matter-of-fact. "You think their meeting here connects Varga with your investigation?"

"Everyone is presumed innocent until proven guilty. I need to know if he was here, around midday on the 21st of May."

Father Jakob gestured with a nod. The bouncer brushed past Szabó and made his way into an office behind the reception desk.

"Please follow Vlad," said the chaplain "We shall soon see."

The office was small and thankfully air-conditioned, filled with IT servers and communications hardware. Eszter stood behind the bouncer while he tapped his podgy fingers on the keyboard of a laptop. She watched the screen as images of various people came and went through the main entrance between the period of eleven-thirty a.m. and twelve-thirty p.m. The viewing continued mostly in silence for around thirty minutes, with no sign of the arrival or departure of either Zoltán Varga or Father Laszló.

Father Jakob waited with them and watched closely. "Perhaps there is a discrepancy in the timing?" he said.

"I need a copy of that file, from nine a.m. to five p.m. We'll examine it ourselves," she replied.

The chaplain nodded. Five minutes later, Eszter pocketed the pen drive.

"I'm sorry you didn't find what you were looking for," said Father Jakob.

She had drawn a blank and would feed her findings back to Kelemen as soon as she left. As things stood, none of the alibis offered by Varga and Father Laszló were verifiable.

"On the contrary, Father. This has been very useful. Thank you once again for your time."

Back in the car, Eszter immediately called Kelemen but heard only the busy signal. She decided not to leave a voicemail.

The last three months had been the hardest in the professional life of Greta Madár. On the positive side, the procedures she had implemented at the Daybreak Nursing Home protected and saved lives. Only two of the patients who had passed away in her care since March had shown COVID-19 symptoms. Greta believed underlying illnesses had contributed to the deaths of both patients. The General Physician who attended both cases had drawn the same conclusions. Neither of their death certificates had mentioned the virus, nor would the mortalities have appeared in the government's statistics.

The situation that had developed over the last twenty-four hours was different. Other than Nora Kelemen's dementia, there had been little wrong with the seventy-five-year-old until the persistent cough had developed yesterday. By this morning her temperature was soaring and throughout the day, under the watchful eye of her carers, Nora had become delirious. Greta had put in several calls to the off-site medical team. If a doctor didn't arrive soon, she would be forced to call an ambulance.

In normal times, Greta would have already called a family member and provided them with a heads-up of the situation. She already knew Nora's next of kin was her daughter, Erika, who worked for the police. It had been Erika who had initially contacted them, and it had been Erika who had moved Nora and her belongings into the home. Until the beginning of the lockdown, Erika had been a frequent visitor at Daybreak. Nora's son, David — whose contact details were also in the file — had never once been to visit his mother.

Despite the prevailing rules concerning 'no family visitors to the home,' it just seemed so wrong to Greta that the family should remain in the dark when a loved one became so ill. Finally, Greta took Nora's file from the cabinet in her office and called Erika's number. After two rings, the voicemail clicked in. She left a message.

"Hello, Erika. This is Greta at the Daybreak Nursing Home. I'm calling about your mother. She's not well at the moment. I thought you would want to know. The doctor is on his way. Please call me, either on the main line or on my mobile. I know you already have both numbers. Ciao."

Leaving a message was all she could do for now. She glanced at her watch. It was seven-fifteen, time to do her last round of the evening before finishing her shift.

Erika Kelemen's phone was red hot. In the rare moments between calls, she had been adding fresh information to the whiteboards in the Incident Room: one for Klára Menges, the second for Ervin Nagy, and the latest one for Zsigmond Horvát. Each board had photographs of the victims found in their respective apartments. Contrasting those smiling faces, she rearranged some awful images taken at the crime scenes and during the autopsies.

At just after six-thirty, Professor Baldi had called to say that, as he had predicted, Zsigmond Horvát's blood tests showed traces of potassium cyanide. Baldi also announced he and his staff would work overtime this evening to carry out the autopsy on Horvát. Erika changed the note on the whiteboard, from suspected to confirmed cyanide poisoning. These latest test results merely proved what they already knew to be true. Horvát was indeed the third victim of the multiple assassin.

Ten minutes later, Márkos called her from Hős Street, although so far he had discovered nothing new from any of the neighbours of Ervin Nagy.

Moments later came much more significant news from Dolman. He had found a witness who claimed to have seen Lotti Menges outside her sister's apartment on the day of Klára's murder. If that was true, she could charge Lotti with obstructing a murder investigation and even perverting the course of justice. It still seemed implausible that she had murdered her own sister, even less likely that she had murdered Nagy and Horvát. Yet Lotti knew more than she was telling, and she had some serious explaining to do.

Erika repeatedly called Lotti. Finally she called the local police in Esztergom and requested uniformed officers go round to her apartment, with instructions to detain her until one of the Budapest team arrived. She cursed her own laxness and for not getting the truth out of Lotti first time around.

"No mistakes next time," she told herself.

David Kelemen was still at work. It had been another late night alone in the office. Another attempt to rescue his business from the consequences of the lockdown. The call from the nursing home manager had broken his concentration. At first, he had found the information hard to comprehend.

His mother was apparently at death's door, probably because of the virus, and he should come immediately. The manager, Greta Madár, said she had tried his sister, Erika, and left a message, but there had been no response.

Well, there's a fucking surprise. He had wanted to say that out loud, but held himself back.

"I'm on my way," he said. "Give me the address."

From the hands-free in the car, he called Erika. Her phone was engaged. He tried again and again, before finally leaving a voicemail.

"Erika, please answer your fucking phone. Mum is seriously ill. They think it's COVID-19. I'm on the way to the home. Call me when you get this."

The door to the Incident Room swung open. Eszter poked her head in and said, "I've been trying to get hold of you, boss. Your phone has been permanently engaged."

Erika turned away from the whiteboards and faced her younger colleague. "I know. It's been crazy here. What have you got for me?"

"I checked out Zoltán Varga's alibis."

Erika took a seat. "What did you find out?"

"When we questioned Varga, the priest said they had been together at the Order of Malta, at around midday on the twenty-first. I figured the CCTV on the front door might confirm that. When I called, I got the out-of-hours voicemail. Then I thought, what harm could it do if I showed up and asked to speak to Father Jakob? It wasn't far out of my way and the worst that could happen…"

Erika rubbed her eyes and slid down in her seat. "Cut to the chase. You wouldn't be here, if you didn't have something for me."

Eszter produced the pen drive from her pocket and handed it over. "Father Jakob was very accommodating."

"What does it show?" Erika snapped.

"There's no sign of either Varga nor of Father László on the CCTV, at least not between eleven-thirty and twelve-thirty. Footage for the entire day is on here. Ferenc will look through it in the morning. I didn't get anywhere with the other alibis either. It is possible they *were* delivering food parcels to the homeless, but Father László needs to provide us with further information. Also, there was no reply from the Church of St. Francis' Wounds, where he said they were helping out on the 25th."

Erika stood and turned away. She had heard enough. "I don't believe we can rely on Father László's version of events. We need to track Varga's movements, starting tonight. I want you and Márkos to carry out surveillance on him. I'll organise relief, before dawn."

Eszter's shoulders slumped and her eyes looked up to the ceiling, but Erika ignored the body language of her younger colleague. They were all exhausted, that much was clear, but there would be plenty of time for rest later.

In the doorway of the small grocery store, on the corner of Fő Street and Batthyány Square, Péter Rigo lit up a cigarette. For the last two hours, he'd covered every inch of the patch, looking for the proverbial needle in the haystack. His feet were sore, and he was ready to knock off for the evening and head to the pub. He cursed when the call came from Kelemen. *Checking up on him, was she?*

"Péter…"

"Before you ask. No, I haven't found the place where the, as yet, unidentified suspect potentially bought several burner phones on an, as yet, unknown date."

"Don't worry about that now. I knew it was a long shot. Something more urgent has cropped up. Dolman found a witness who claims to have seen Klára Menges' sister, Lotti, near Klára's apartment on the day of her murder. That totally contradicts what Lotti told us. I've sent a uniform round to her place to keep her there. I want you and Dolman to bring her in for a formal interview. This time we're going to get the truth out of her."

Rigo tossed his cigarette stub onto the pavement and ground it with his heel. "Doesn't she live in Esztergom?"

"That's right," said Kelemen. "I've spoken to Dolman. He's got Lotti's address. Pick him up at Teve Street. If you get your skates on, you'll be in Esztergom by ten-thirty. Sorry, I've got to go. There's another call waiting."

The line went dead.

"That's not possible," he said. "I've got other plans. We'll go in the morning. Okay?"

Rigo didn't think Kelemen had heard his response, and frankly, he didn't care. There was no way he was going all the way to Esztergom to arrest an old woman and to bring her in for questioning at this time of the day. He spat on the pavement.

"Who the fuck does she think she is?" he hissed.

Erika ended her conversation with Rigo and answered the next incoming call. It was Professor Baldi.

"Good evening, Professor. What news?"

"The beating of Zsigmond Horvát is at the extreme end of the violence scale. I'm no psychiatrist, but would venture we are dealing with extreme psychopathic tendencies here. I believe you are looking for a hammer as your weapon. We found evidence of steel fragments embedded in multiple open wounds to the head, face and neck. However, I repeat, the beating took place after Horvát ingested the potassium cyanide. There are no signs that the victim's hands were tied. Nor that he attempted to use his hands and arms to shield himself from the beating. In beating the victim in the bathroom, the killer's clothes must have become heavily bloodied. He may have disposed of them, of course, but that's not my department. Horvát was eighty-five kilos. It must have taken considerable strength to haul him from one room to another and lift him into the bath. I'll send my report over as soon as its ready. I wish you God's speed in finding this killer, ideally before he strikes again."

Erika's phone cooled off after nine-thirty and she spent the next half-hour updating the whiteboards. The profiles of the victims were becoming ever clearer, yet the killer remained as elusive as ever. There were currently two lines of enquiry on her radar: Zoltán Varga and Lotti Menges, but with no evidence to link either to the murders, she couldn't even call them suspects.

Baldi's comments concerning the physical strength required to haul Horvát and lift him into the bath played on her mind. Varga undoubtedly possessed the physique, but lacked the mental capacity to have organised and executed three sophisticated poisonings. Lotti showed mental acuity but lacked the physical strength. If either Zoltán or Lotti were involved, it seemed logical to suppose each of them must have been working with an accomplice.

Then a thought struck her. What if Varga and Lotti were both involved? It was fanciful, blue-sky thinking, with not a shred of evidence to support it. Yet, like a tune that suddenly pops up and plays in the mind over and over, the notion of these two working together would not go away. Like all theories, it was there to be proven or disproven.

She deliberately focused on the counter-theory, because far more likely was the prospect that neither was involved in any of the three murders. If that was the reality of the situation, she was better off knowing sooner rather than later. Of course, that outcome would leave her back at square one, with the clock ticking remorselessly and Rudolf Kudár standing in the wings, waiting to pull the rug from under her feet.

Eszter parked her unmarked squad car close to the junction of Popieluszko Street and Árpád Street in District XXI, a suitable distance from the hostel. This was the first occasion in which she had spent any time alone with Gábor Márkos. After only one hour of surveillance duty, his laddish behaviour was already grating on her. She even wondered whether he was trying to come on to her. If he did, she'd rip his head off before the night was out.

"You ought to come out with me and the lads one night. We could have a few beers and a good laugh," he said.

She could tell he was being friendly, but her attention was elsewhere, her gaze fixed on the rear-view mirror. "Hold on," she snapped. The street lighting in this part of the city was poor, but Eszter watched a hooded figure on the other side of the street, walking towards the hostel. Initially, it was the person's gait which looked familiar. Almost certainly male, wearing dark clothes, including a hoodie, and carrying a holdall. A car approached, and the headlights illuminated the figure, but the face remained hidden.

"I'm sure it's him," she whispered, reaching for her phone.

They both watched the figure reach the entrance of the hostel. From this distance, it looked like he used a key before going inside.

Eszter tried Kelemen's number and was pleasantly surprised to get through straight away.

"Varga's just arrived at the hostel, boss. I couldn't see his face, but I'd recognise that slow shuffle anywhere. He was alone, and carrying a holdall."

Kelemen replied, "Hold your position. I want to know what's in that bag. I'll take care of the paperwork. In the meantime, if he reappears, follow him. From now on, anywhere he goes, we go."

After organising the warrant, Erika returned to the tenth floor. She gazed across the sea of idle computer screens in the almost deserted open-plan office. The wall clock told her it was ten forty-five. She stopped at the vending machine in need of caffeine, made her selection, and the machine whirred into action.

Once again, her phone rang. Wearily retrieving the phone from her trouser pocket, she looked at the display. The name of the caller seemed incongruous. She couldn't recall the last time her brother had called her at work.

"David. What's up?"

"Are you sitting down?"

She took her cup from the vending machine. "Why are you calling me? Are you in trouble? Is it about the business?"

"Erika. Shut up and listen. I've been trying to call you and I'm not the only one. You'd know that, if you ever listened to your bloody voicemails. I'm at the Daybreak."

David at the Daybreak Nursing Home? Wonders would never cease. "What are you doing there, especially at this time of the day? Mum's been lobbying me to get her out of there. She's done the same to you too, hasn't she? The trouble is, David, I don't have space to look after her, and I can't see Marcel entertaining her while I'm at work every day. So, unless you're offering to take her in?"

"She's dead, Erika. Mum's dead."

Boom! The words set off a tsunami inside her brain. She dropped the plastic cup and stood open-mouthed as hot coffee spilled over her shoes and made a pool at her feet. Her voice croaked. "Are you sure?"

"Of course, I'm sure. Do you think this is a hoax? Greta Madár called me at twenty past seven. She said Mum may have caught the virus, but they weren't certain because they didn't test her. Before Greta got through to me, she tried to call you. I tried too, but you didn't answer. Anyway, I got here as fast as I could. The doctor was here when I arrived. They wouldn't let me in to see her; not until it was all over. They recorded her official time of death as 21:57. The doctor wrote 'death by natural causes' on the certificate, but I'm not convinced that's the full story. While I was waiting, I spoke with a carer. She told me Mum had a cough, a fever and had been delirious. They laid her out, in the Daybreak Chapel of Rest. They wouldn't let me get close to her, just in case. The funeral director is on his way."

A large salty tear ran down Erika's cheek. "I don't know what to say, David. I still can't believe it."

"What time will you get here?"

Erika's mind raced, weighing up her options. She wanted to see her mum one last time, to throw her arms around her and hug her. She wanted to say she was sorry for not being there in the end. Even now, she knew the guilt of being absent was something she would carry around for the rest of her life. But arriving at the home, at this time of night would achieve nothing. If they hadn't allowed David to get close, they were hardly likely to treat her any different.

She felt the urge to explain. "We're in the middle of a surveillance, about to make an arrest. I'll go to the funeral directors in the morning."

"Christ, Erika! Our mother just died. When did you stop being a human being and turn into Robo-Cop?"

This was too much, coming from the man wedded to his business; the man who had previously never set a foot inside the nursing home. Erika yelled down the phone, "How dare you! I'm the one who's been in contact with her every day. I got her a place in the nursing home. Without that, she'd be—"

David cut across her. "For all the good that did her, Erika! You get back to your surveillance. Make your fucking arrest."

The line went dead.

Shaking with anger, shock, and grief, Erika punched four digits into her keypad and listened to her voicemails. The first few were from members of her team, asking her to call them. These she deleted.

Finally, she came to a message received at 7.15 p.m. It was the familiar voice of Greta Madár saying, *"Hello, Erika. This is Greta at the Daybreak Nursing Home. I'm calling about your mother. She's not well at the moment. I thought you would want to know. The doctor is on his way. Please call me, either on the main line or on my mobile. I know you already have both numbers. Ciao."*

Why hadn't she received this earlier? She saved it, then waited for the next message to play. It was from David, timed at 7:47. *"Erika, please answer your fucking phone. Mum is seriously ill.*

They think it's COVID-19. I'm on the way to the home. Call me when you get this." This she saved, too, although his words were already seared into her consciousness.

She felt numb, but the enormity of the situation was beginning to dawn on her. The ever-present rock in her life was no more. The mother who had picked her up when she fell - not only as an infant, but throughout her adult life too — had passed, leaving an unimaginably large void in her heart. She had never, not in her entire life, felt more alone. Losing her father to lung cancer had been devastating. Losing her mother meant, at fifty, she was an orphan. Now her world felt empty. Totally devoid of love, affection, and support.

"Are you alright, dear? Spilt your drink, I see. Never mind, I'll soon get that cleaned up for you. Here's a tissue. You wipe those eyes of yours."

Erika lifted her chin off her chest and saw a cleaner, but not one she recognised. The woman was around her own age. She wore a blue overall and carried a bucket with a mop. She looked sympathetic. Erika took the tissue from her outstretched hand and wiped her eyes. Mascara smeared the tissue.

"Thanks," she said before blowing her nose loudly into the same tissue. "I must look a mess."

The cleaner placed down her mop and bucket. "Don't worry about that. You'll soon fix your looks. I don't know what bad news you've just had; that's none of my business. Just remember, things happen that none of us can control. Just try to be kind to yourself."

The kindness of a stranger suddenly meant more than words could express. She took the woman's hand in her own and squeezed it warmly, trying to conjure up a smile.

"Thank you. I'll be fine. I'd better clean up. There's a search warrant on its way over."

Marcel had waited at the apartment all evening, watching TV, brooding about the situation he had found himself in. It was now six hours since he had sent his WhatsApp message to Erika, asking whether they had a future together. In his mind, the absence of her response spoke volumes. No matter how busy she was, in six hours she could have found time to reply. He was growing ever more impatient as the evening wore on. Naively, he had expected her to breeze in, disappear into the shower and emerge fresh, expecting another meal on the table. He intended to have it out with her, once and for all. Yet she had neither shown up nor messaged. *How do you fight with an opponent who doesn't bother to show up?*

He glared down at his phone and drained the dregs of the Merlot bottle into his empty glass. The solution to his predicament seemed as elusive as ever. He noticed a subtle change in the messaging app. The two ticks had turned blue, meaning Erika had finally read his message. It called for decisiveness. Carpe diem.

When she answered his call after only one ring, Marcel was both surprised and flustered. "Erika! Hello."

"Marcel. Will it wait? I'm still at work. I saw your message, but can't talk now."

Once again, she was fobbing him off. He tried to gather his intoxicated thoughts and form an articulate sentence. "You didn't answer my message. Should I therefore assume we have no future together?"

"I really can't discuss this now," she replied.

Without another word, he tapped *End Call*.

Marcel retrieved his suitcases from under the bed and began to pack them. He prided himself that he was not the kind of man to outstay his welcome.

CHAPTER TEN

After the suspected sighting of Zoltán Varga returning to the hostel, the next two hours of surveillance had been tedious. In this quiet backwater, under an inky-black, leaden sky, Eszter struggled to stay awake. If it had not been for the constant and mostly banal chatter of Gábor Márkos, she most certainly would have nodded off.

Just after midnight things suddenly livened up, when a call from Kelemen informed them she was on her way over with the search warrant.

Kelemen signed off with the ominous words, "He'd better be there when I arrive."

Eszter sat up straight and said to Márkos, "I hope for your sake he hasn't escaped out the back. She's a monster when she's angry."

Erika's journey to the southern edge of the city was as quiet and uneventful as any she could recall, but playing inside her head on a continuous loop were the frustration, anger, and guilt associated with her mother's death. To make things worse, she had an uneasy feeling she may have upset Marcel; although there would be time to make things up with him later. For now, there were more urgent things to attend to, such as apprehending a triple-murderer before the investigation was taken off her.

Kelemen crossed onto Csepel Island via Kvassay Bridge and made her way along Weiss Manfréd Street before turning left. Two minutes later, she spotted the number plate of Szabó's squad car, parked behind it and switched off her engine. She got out of her car and looked up and down the deserted street. The street lamps were off, and every building had its shutters down. The only sounds were of dogs barking somewhere in the distance. Moments later, she was joined by Szabó and Márkos.

Erika peered into the gloom. "Which one is the hostel?"

Márkos pointed it out. "There's been no movement, in or out, for the last hour. The residents seem to have their own keys. What do you want us to do?"

"You go round the back, and make sure Varga doesn't do a runner. We'll take the front. Come on, Szabó. It's time to wake them up."

Their movement triggered a security light above the front door. Erika shone the light from her phone on the doorbell. Seeing *Hostel Warden* on the label, she pressed it repeatedly. Meanwhile, Eszter thumped on the door with the edge of her fist. After several minutes, a light went on inside. A rotund man in his fifties appeared and shouted angrily at them through the glazed panel at the side of the door. He wore pyjama bottoms and a stained white t-shirt.

"What the hell do you think you're doing? It's after midnight. Get lost, or I'll call the police."

"We are the police," said Erika, presenting her ID. "Open up."

Once inside the building, she inhaled the pungent smell of dampness and stale cigarette smoke. Her nose twitched. The interior was grubby, with chipped plasterwork and cardboard boxes piled high. The man led them to a cramped office next to the lobby. Inside, there was a battered wooden desk and two wooden chairs. On the wall was a crucifix. He slumped into the chair behind the desk and rubbed his tired eyes. The two detectives remained standing.

Erika held up her credentials once again. "Senior Detective Kelemen and Detective Szabó, from the Budapest Homicide Department. I take it you're the warden."

"Yeah. What do you want?"

"Tell me about this place."

He rubbed his eyes and scratched his stubble. "We've got sixteen bedsit-type rooms over four floors. We only accommodate men — mainly homeless, alcoholics, drug abusers. There's a shared kitchen and a common room on this floor. I live here too, for my sins. It's funded by a Catholic charity. You looking for anyone in particular?"

Erika said, "You have a resident by the name of Zoltán Varga?"

"Sure. He's in room twelve. He says little. Bit of an oddball, if you ask me."

"How long has he been a resident here?" asked Eszter.

The warden opened a ledger and ran his podgy finger down a page. "Checked in on the fifteenth of May. Someone pulled a favour to get him a room at short notice. I had to kick the previous occupant out, to free up a place for him. Seems like Varga has friends."

Erika tilted her head slightly to one side. "Friends?"

"A priest has been here. Making sure he's well looked after."

Bullseye, we're at the right place, thought Erika. "An old priest called Father Laszló?"

"That's the one."

Erika pulled out the search warrant and slapped it onto the warden's desk. "We have a warrant to search Varga's room. Lead the way and bring a spare key with you."

Room twelve was on the third floor. Erika stood away from the door while Eszter beat loudly upon it.

"Mr Varga. It's Detective Kelemen, with Detective Szabó. Let us in."

They could hear the voices of other disgruntled residents calling out from rooms along the corridor, impolitely urging those making the racket to quieten down, or else.

Erika nodded to the warden, who duly obliged by unlocking the door and standing back. Eszter kicked it wide open. The room was in darkness until Erika found the light switch by the door. A single, low wattage bulb hung from a ceiling rosette, making the sparsely furnished room look dingy. The once-white blockwork walls were stained brown. Behind the door stood a battered wooden wardrobe. Against the opposite wall was a metal-framed single bed and a cheap bedside cabinet. Fluttering in the breeze next to an open window were a pair of curtains made from a gaudy red and orange fabric. There was also a strong smell of stale alcohol and nicotine. The obvious thing missing from the scene was the man they wanted to question.

Erika stepped across to the window and looked out. It was a sheer drop to the rear of the building. Down below, she could see Márkos. She called out to him, "Did you see anyone come out of this window?"

"No one," he shouted back.

"Wait there and keep your eyes open." She turned to the warden and ordered him to check the communal bathroom, kitchen and common room.

He scuttled away.

Left alone, Erika turned on Eszter. "Where the fuck is he, Szabó? I put you in charge. Why the hell didn't you send Márkos round to watch the rear exit? Too busy gossiping, were you?"

Eszter said nothing. She looked at her shoes, her cheeks crimson.

It was during that moment of silence that a sound, perhaps the rattling of coat hangers, caught their attention. Erika gestured with a nod. Eszter quietly closed the door, blocking the exit.

With a firm, confident voice, Erika issued an order. "Mr Varga, come out of the wardrobe. Now!"

The wardrobe door creaked and opened partially. A face peered out at them, wild-eyed. From a crouching position, Varga tumbled out and landed on the floor in a heap, completely naked.

Erika picked up a pair of jeans from the pile of dirty clothes on the floor. She tossed them over.

"Here, get dressed," she said.

While Varga foraged in the pile for a pair of underpants, Erika called to Márkos down below, "We've found him. Get yourself up here."

There was a knock on the bedroom door. Eszter opened it and let the warden in.

Erika said to him, "Mr Varga was hiding in the wardrobe. Another detective is outside. Let him in and bring him straight up here."

The warden didn't need telling twice.

Erika turned her attention back to Varga. "Why were you hiding?"

Varga's face flushed pink. He turned his back on them, fastened his jeans and pulled on a crumpled navy blue t-shirt. When he spoke, his voice was tremulous. His was the voice of a frightened child, in the body of a man. "Don't want to be sent back. Not to that place."

Erika tried to engage him eye-to-eye, but Varga shied away from her. She tried a softer approach. "Nobody is talking about sending you anywhere, Zoltán. You remember, we spoke with you and Father Laszló yesterday at lunchtime. We just need to ask you some more questions." She thought that if the tall, imposing figure of Eszter had not been blocking the doorway, Varga might have made a run for it.

Instead, he shoved his hands deep into the front pockets of his jeans and seemed to fix his eyes on the threadbare carpet, twitching nervously and looking like he might burst into tears.

Erika maintained a calm, even tone. "You returned to the hostel at just after ten. Where were you this evening?"

Varga shuffled from side to side. "With a friend."

"Which friend?" Erika's steely gaze was fixed on him.

"Can't say."

"Where did you go with your friend?"

He wrung his hands together. "Can't say."

There was a knock. Gábor Márkos peered around the door.

Erika signalled for him to join them.

"Zoltán," she continued, "If you refuse to answer our questions here, I will have no choice other than to take you into custody."

Varga was avoiding eye contact with any of them. Enough was enough. Erika needed to get the truth out of him. "Okay. Have it your way. Zoltán Varga, I am arresting you in connection with the murders of Klára Menges, Ervin Nagy and Zsigmond Horvát. You do not have to say anything, but it may harm your defence if you do not mention when questioned something which you later rely on in court. Anything you say may be given in evidence."

Varga gave a sharp intake of breath, but maintained a sullen silence.

Erika then waved the warrant under his nose. "This is a search warrant, authorising me to search this room. Is there anything you want to tell me about first?"

He shook his head.

Erika took a pair of latex gloves from her pocket and pulled them on before peering under the bed. She used the light from her phone, placed her hand on an object and slid it out. Hauling herself back up to her feet, she brushed the dust from her trousers. The brown canvas holdall she had found was placed carefully onto the bed.

"What's in here, Zoltán?"

Varga twitched. Sweat was running down his forehead onto his nose. "D-d-dirty c-clothes," he stammered.

Erika unzipped the holdall. The rancid smell of stale sweat that greeted her nostrils made her shudder.

"You're right about one thing. There *are* dirty clothes in here." She rummaged around and found some heavy items wrapped in cloth. Removing the first and carefully placing it on the bed, she unwrapped the cloth covering and unveiled a pair of bolt-cutters.

"Why would you have a pair of bolt-cutters in your room?"

Varga hung his head.

She delved back into the bag and retrieved another cloth covered item. When she removed the covering, she discovered an electric power drill. The dusty drill bit was still in the chuck. She rummaged again, until this time she came across a lump-hammer.

"You're quite the handyman, aren't you? Forensics will soon tell us what you've really been up to with these tools. You two, take him away and book him in. I'll call SOCO and stay until they arrive. I'll see you back at HQ later."

Eszter pulled Varga's hands behind his back and Márkos slapped on a pair of handcuffs.

As they led Varga away, Erika could hear several voices in the corridor. She stood at the doorway and saw the warden talking with three other men. Each of them was in various stages of undress. She assumed they were residents, woken by the noise.

"This is now a crime scene, and there will be more police officers here shortly. They will go over the place with a fine-tooth comb. If any of you have anything to say, wait here, and I'll take your statements."

The group quickly dispersed, leaving Erika alone to call the SOCO duty officer.

Alone in Varga's room, she paced up and down and processed what she had just witnessed. Those tools had not been used for DIY. Nevertheless, she had strong doubts concerning Varga's capability to be the principle suspect in their triple-murder investigation. He was hiding something, and she urgently needed to find out what that something was.

Laszló rubbed his eyes and groped in the darkness for his spectacles. The phone on his bedside cabinet shone brightly, and its bell tower ringtone stunned his brain into action. His throat felt parched.

He pulled on his spectacles and croaked into the phone. "Whoever is calling, do you know what time it is?"

"Father, it's the warden. The police came. They arrested Zoltán and have taken him to Police Palace. A woman, Detective Kelemen, declared his room a crime scene. She said more police are on their way."

Even though his mind was racing, Laszló needed to stay calm.

"God bless you, my son. I'll take it from here."

He sat up, switched on his bedside lamp, then scrolled through the contacts on his telephone until finally he found the one he was looking for.

It took four rings before the person answered the call.

"This is Father Laszló. I need you to do something for me. Right away."

Erika took the lift to the tenth floor, where for several minutes she stood alone in the anteroom next to Interview Room 10-A. On the desktop monitor were live CCTV images from the interview room. In the top-left-hand corner of the screen, the clock said 02:35:48. Varga was seated, attached by handcuffs to the interview table. He appeared perfectly still, except for his facial twitch which seemed more pronounced than earlier. She could see Gábor Márkos, standing sentry by the door. She turned up the loudspeaker volume, but there was no conversation taking place in the room.

Eszter entered the anteroom. She handed Erika a business card. "There's a lawyer downstairs at the desk. He insists he needs time with his client, before we interview him."

Erika sighed and examined the card. It read, *dr. Bálint Damiani, Criminal Lawyer.* She had crossed swords with him in the past. Somebody with power and money had pulled strings to get a lawyer of his calibre to turn up in the middle of the night.

"Show him up. We'll give him fifteen minutes. Then, I swear, I'm going to get Varga to talk."

The Digital Interview Recorder was switched on, and Erika spoke slowly and deliberately.

"This is a recorded interview. I am Senior Detective Erika Kelemen. Also present are: Mr Zoltán Varga, Detective Eszter Szabó, Detective Gábor Márkos and Mr Bálint Damiani, Criminal Defence Attorney. We are in room 10-A, at Police Headquarters on Teve Street. The date is Wednesday, the twenty-seventh of May, twenty-twenty. The time is three a.m. Mr Varga, please state your full name, current address and date of birth."

Damiani, who wore a dark-grey suit and an open-necked white shirt, sat alongside Varga. He waved a finger disapprovingly and interjected. "Not so fast. My client has not been charged with any offences. I insist you release him from the handcuffs before we begin this interview. This situation is already stressful enough for him."

Erika nodded, and Márkos stepped forward with a key.

Once freed, Varga rubbed his left wrist, which looked red and sore.

Erika said, "Once again, please state your full name, current address and date of birth."

Varga slumped even lower in his seat, eyes down, hands fidgeting on his lap.

"Z-Zoltán Varga. Árpád Street Hostel. 14th April, nineteen ninety-f-four."

"It is my duty to remind you, you have already been formally cautioned and anything you say may be given in evidence. You refused to answer our questions at the hostel and have been arrested to enable us to question you further, specifically in relation to an ongoing murder investigation. Do you understand?"

Varga's gaze remained fixed firmly on the table top.

"It wasn't me," he whispered.

Erika continued, "You are currently enjoying a thirty-day period of adaptive leave from the Forensic Observation and Psychiatric Institution and have been resident at the hostel since the 15th of May. Is that correct?"

He gave a sullen nod.

"You need to speak, Mr Varga, for the recording."

"Yes."

Erika referred to her notes.

"While you were in the Institution's care, a member of staff heard you say, and I quote, 'AVH torturers should all go to hell.' Mr Varga, the AVH has not existed since the 1950s. Who put that notion in your head?"

"Other p-patients."

Erika sighed. "Here's the thing: three murders have taken place since your release on the fifteenth of May, and we confirm at least one victim to be a former employee of the AVH. What do you say about that?"

"Not me."

"During your period of adaptive leave, you have been under the legal charge of a caregiver. Father Laszló Rákoczy is the name of your caregiver. Is that correct?"

Varga twitched. "Y-yes."

"You recall that Detective Szabó and I met with you and your caregiver yesterday lunchtime. During that informal interview, you and he told us of your supposed whereabouts on the three dates that particularly interest our investigation. Remind us, where were you at around five p.m. on Tuesday, the 19th of May?"

Beads of sweat formed on Varga's brow. "Tuesday evening? W-we delivered food parcels."

"Can you provide any evidence of that, Mr Varga? Who prepared the parcels? How many parcels were there? Where did you deliver them to?"

"The hostel kitchen. W-was my first time. F-father Laszló knew what to do."

"What about two days later? Where were you at midday on Thursday the 21st?"

Varga paused and looked up at his lawyer. Damiani nodded reassuringly at his client.

"F-father Laszló told you. We met at the place on Fortuna Street."

Eszter said, "We checked the CCTV footage at the Order of Malta, from nine a.m. until six p.m. Neither of you showed up."

Erika's tone hardened and she glared at him. "You're lying to us, Mr Varga. You were not there. So, where were you? And why did Father László cover up for you? Isn't it the truth that you were actually in Hős Street, at the apartment of Ervin Nagy, where you poisoned and then brutally tortured him? You used your power drill on his skull."

Damiani scoffed at the questions. "Really, detective. Do you have any proof? You are throwing wild accusations at my client, based purely on speculation. Perhaps he is confused, or mistaken regarding the date of his visit. Perhaps the CCTV is faulty. I need more time to explore that with him. Without proof, you have no grounds to detain him further. You must stick with evidence-based facts."

Erika was highly sceptical of Varga's response. Yet without being able to produce solid evidence, she knew Damiani would continue to rebuff her arguments. The same was true of Varga's alibi for Monday 25th of May - the date of Zsigmond Horvát's murder. In that case, she knew they had so far been unable to contact anyone at the Church of St. Francis' Wounds on Fő Street, in order to verify Varga's whereabouts. That was an important loose-end they needed to close. Now it was her move, and she needed to make it a good one.

"When you entered the hostel at ten p.m., you were carrying a holdall. When we searched your room, that holdall was under your bed. Inside it were a pair of bolt-cutters, a power drill and a hammer. Those tools are being analysed by forensics as we speak. It would be better for you to come clean now, and tell us what you were doing with them."

"Was helpin' a f-friend."

Erika leaned forward. "Helping a friend to do what?"

Varga slid even lower in his chair. Any further and he would be under the table. "Gardening work."

"What was his name, this friend of yours?"

"Damari F-Farkas."

"And where was this garden?"

Varga continued to stare at the tabletop. "He picked me up and drove me there. Don't know the address. He brought me back later and dropped me off."

"We only saw you, alone, walking back to the hostel," said Eszter.

Varga shook his head, but with little conviction. "He d-dropped me off. I walked from the bridge."

Erika leaned forward on her elbows. "None of this is true, is it, Mr Varga? *If* you have contact details for this character, Damari Farkas, I suggest you tell us now, so we can bring him here to corroborate your story."

The lawyer interjected. "Could we take a time-out here? There are matters I need to discuss in greater detail with my client."

Erika nodded. *A delay now would be good. It would provide her with more time to receive the forensics report. It might also give the lawyer chance to talk some sense into his client who, by the sound of it, was digging a bigger and bigger hole for himself.* She leaned back in her chair.

"Interview suspended at three-twenty a.m. How long do you need, Mr Damiani?"

"An hour."

"Agreed," said Erika. She exited the room.

Szabó and Márkos followed her and closed the door with a loud clunk, leaving Varga and his lawyer to confer.

In the corridor Erika said to the others. "Varga is laying traps for himself, and before too long, he's going to land in one he can't get out of. I'm going to freshen up and get ready for round two."

A twenty-one hour working day had taken its toll. Erika peered disparagingly at herself in the washroom mirror. Her eyes looked bloodshot, and the bags under them were heavy. She repaired what she could with foundation, reapplied eye-liner and lipstick, then brushed her hair.

Perched next to the wash-basin, her phone vibrated. Surprised to see the name of Axel Rácz on the screen, she answered it.

"It's an early start for you."

"Another body has been found. Male, in his eighties and living alone. I need you there, right now. I'll forward you the address." He sounded even grumpier than usual.

"But I'm in the middle of interviewing Zoltán Varga at HQ. We found bolt-cutters, a power drill and a hammer in his room. Forensics are running the tests right now. Varga's got a lawyer with him."

"Leave him and his lawyer to stew for a while. You need to go the crime scene straight away. I'll see you when you get back."

"Okay. I'm on my way," she said, rubbing her tired eyes.

The commander's SMS arrived, and she checked the location in her navigation app. For a moment she allowed herself to imagine her hunch to search Varga's place would prove decisive and would lead to his conviction. She snapped herself out of the daydream. In her experience, things rarely turned out the way you expected. She would have her work cut out, but at least there was now a direction of travel. The investigation was going somewhere at last.

En route to the interview room, Erika found Eszter and Márkos. She explained to them what Commander Rácz had just told her. She gave her instructions to Márkos, clearly and deliberately. "Transfer Varga to a custody cell. His lawyer can stay with him. Order them some breakfast. Tell Damiani there have been developments in our investigation that need urgent attention. For now, he can have as much time as he wants with his client."

Eszter stifled a yawn. The poor girl looked dead on her feet.

In different circumstances Erika would have told her to get some rest, but right now she needed someone to accompany her to the latest crime scene. "Go splash some water on your face. I can't have you falling asleep behind the wheel. We have work to do."

CHAPTER ELEVEN

T he first rays of sunlight were peeking over the horizon, bathing the city in foggy, golden light. When they arrived in District XIX, the front gate of the small, detached, two-storey house in Dobos Street was cordoned off. Eszter raised the tape while Erika ducked underneath. After identifying themselves to the two uniformed officers who were guarding the scene, Erika asked who had first raised the alarm.

"Apparently it was the barking dog that roused the neighbours," said the first officer.

The second read from his notes. "The victim's name is Támas Németh. Seems he lives here alone. It was his next-door neighbour, Mr Gogan, who found the body and called 107. He met us when we arrived, and said the dog was not normally a nuisance, but after midnight it began whining and wouldn't stop. He said it was keeping him and his wife awake. When he got here, he knocked and rang the doorbell, then went round the back of the property, found the back door was open and went inside. He said, he thought Németh might have had a heart attack or something. That was until he found Németh's body in the living room."

Erika stepped inside, followed closely by Eszter and the two officers. All four sets of eyes stared down at the old man laid out on the floor. He was of medium build and dressed in what looked like his Sunday best. There was a pool of vomit on the sofa, but the body lay on the floor. Támas Németh's arms were crossed, with his hands placed upon his shoulders. Two fingers from each hand were missing, and blood from the wounds had soaked into the fabric of his white shirt and red tie.

The sight of the mutilated hands made Erika's stomach turn. "Have you found the fingers yet?"

"Not yet." The first police officer shook his head.

"We always had dogs in the house when I was growing up," Eszter said. "Dogs are sensitive to the health of their owners. Perhaps it knew its owner was injured and was sounding the alarm?"

From behind the group came a familiar voice. "And pathologists are sensitive to their lack of sleep." Professor Baldi bustled past them before peering down at the victim. He leaned forward and sniffed around the victim's open mouth. "Another case of the burned almonds. Sadly becoming all too common in this city."

Erika bristled. "We have a potential suspect in custody. We also found a pair of bolt-cutters in his belongings, together with a power drill and a hammer. Perhaps SOCO will find traces of blood or DNA on them. They are rushing their samples through the lab as we speak."

Baldi stifled a yawn. "And you want me to do likewise, to see if there's a match. In which case, detective, you had better get out of my way."

From the garden, they could hear barking.

The first police officer took a step towards the kitchen door. "I'll deal with it," he said menacingly.

"No. Let me," said Eszter, easing her way past him.

"Any signs of a forced entry?" Erika asked. She bent down and snapped some photographs of the victim's hands with her phone.

The second officer, the one with the notepad open, replied. "There are no signs of a forced entry through the front door, or through the ground floor windows. I checked them myself before you arrived. As the neighbour said, he found the back door open, but that may not have been the killer's entry point."

Eszter returned, holding a plastic dog bowl. She looked ashen-faced. She placed the bowl on the floor, enabling Erika, Baldi and the two uniformed officers to peer into it.

No words of explanation were necessary. The bowl contained all four of the severed fingers. If the killer had intended for the unsuspecting pet to feast on his owner's flesh, the dog clearly had other ideas.

Erika snapped a photograph of the bowl and its gruesome contents. She thought of Zoltán Varga waiting in the interview room. Was he really capable of talking his way into the home of Támas Németh, administering the deadly cyanide poison, cutting off four of his fingers, then feeding them to the dog before making a clean escape? It seemed highly unlikely, yet she knew over the next few hours it was her job to find out.

By the time they arrived back at Teve Street, Erika and Eszter had both been awake for over twenty-four hours. Once inside the lift, Erika punched the button for the tenth-floor and exhaled deeply. She gazed into the mirrored wall and surveyed the damage. Feeling and looking like she'd been dragged backwards through a hedge, she said wearily, "You freshen up. Get some breakfast from the canteen too."

"You not going to join me, boss?"

"I need to brief Rácz before Rudolf Kudár gets to him."

Eszter looked nonplussed. "Rudolf Kudár?"

"Kudár is with the TEK, and he wants our investigation handed over to them. He and Rácz go way back. I'm certain, if it hadn't been for my lobbying, you and I would already be back working on white-collar fraud cases."

If the prospect of an early return to the second floor was in any way appealing to Eszter, she hid her feelings well. Instead, she rubbed he hands together. "Do you want to get straight back in there with Varga?"

"I want the results from those labs tests first. If we can match any DNA from Varga's tools with the samples from Németh, or from any of the other three victims, then we've got him."

The elevator chimed their arrival and its doors slid open.

Erika glanced up at the digital wall clock. "7:54. You've got thirty minutes," she said as she strode off. Looking back over her shoulder she called out, "Bring me a coffee. And a croissant."

Rácz clasped his hands behind his back and made clockwise laps of his conference table, while Erika sat and recounted the gruesome scenes she had discovered at the home of the latest victim, Támas Németh. She showed him the photographs she had taken of the body, the disfigured hands, and the severed fingers in the dog bowl.

"It should be a simple enough task for you to nail this Varga bastard. Let me know if you need any help," he growled.

The last thing she wanted was for Rácz to take over the interview at the eleventh hour, and claim all the glory. "It's still all circumstantial. We've currently got no hard evidence to link Varga to Németh's murder, or any of the others for that matter. But I'm optimistic that forensics will come up with something."

Rácz loomed over her. "You've got a psychopath on release from a psychiatric hospital for violent criminals. You've got a toolkit which probably containing the weapons used in at least three murders, which he was hiding under his bed. You've got him missing from the hostel yesterday evening. What did Baldi give as the time of death?"

"Between seven and eight p.m."

He continued to pace around the table. "Does Varga have an alibi?"

"He claims he was helping a friend, Damari Farkas, with some gardening."

"It sounds like bullshit to me. Charge him, and do it before the media runs more scare stories. There was a piece yesterday, accusing us of doing nothing to stop *The Budapest Butcher*, while he was ripping through the elderly population, faster than an outbreak of COVID-19 in a nursing home."

Tears instantly welled up in Erika's eyes. *His comment had been crass and inappropriate. But he had no way of knowing how poor his timing was.* Instead of tearing a strip off him, she simply got up and walked out of his office, leaving him calling after her and shaking his head in bewilderment.

Back in the quiet solitude of the only ladies' washroom on the tenth floor, Erika glared at her bloodshot eyes in the mirror. Everything felt surreal.

'*She's dead, Erika. Mum's dead.*' David's words were seared into her memory, scorched like a fiery brand.

If only, if only, if only! Behind her, the door to the washroom swung open and in the mirror she saw the reflection of Dora's kind face and felt a gentle hand on her shoulder.

"Are you okay?" Dora said softly.

Erika plucked a tissue from the dispenser. Never one for bringing her personal life into work, she decided some sort of explanation was necessary.

"My mother died last night, in her nursing home. It was a shock."

"Oh, Erika, how awful! I don't want to pry, but if you need someone to talk to…"

Erika's pocket buzzed. She retrieved her phone and saw it was Professor Baldi. "I need to take this," she said.

Even over the telephone, the pathologist's excitement was palpable. "Stand by for some good news, Kelemen. There were traces of blood on the bolt-cutters. They are a match with Támas Németh. That was undoubtedly the tool used to sever his fingers. Also, we can confirm the cause of death for Németh as potassium cyanide. Furthermore, on the drill bit, we found traces of bone dust. The DNA sample is a match for Ervin Nagy. It's the same story with the hammer. SOCO found blood traces on the wooden handle. They match with Zsigmond Horvát. You've found your serial killer. I'll send you my preliminary report by email."

The adrenaline boost kicked-in. Zero to sixty in under a second. "That's splendid news, Professor. Thanks to you and the lab for such a quick turnaround. I'll be in touch."

A wide smile spread across Erika's face. Dora looked nonplussed but smiled back. For a few seconds, the two of them hugged. Dora left, leaving Erika to make herself presentable. She fixed her make-up and brushed her hair again. She gathered up her things and spoke resolutely to the mirror. "Showtime!"

Uniformed officers escorted Varga and his lawyer back to interview room 10-A, where they sat waiting in silence.

Erika sent Eszter and Márkos in first, while she stood outside a few seconds longer. She pulled back her shoulders and pushed out her chest before entering the room with as much gravitas as she could muster.

Damiani's face was like thunder. That was hardly surprising, since he and his client had been cooling their heels in a custody cell for the last seven hours.

Varga adopted his usual slumped posture.

The lawyer looked ready for confrontation. He stood and opened his mouth to speak.

But Erika pointed at his chair, gave him an evil look, and barked at him to sit down. She delivered the command with force, and it was no surprise to her when Damiani meekly complied. She took her own seat at the table, before speaking in a more business-like tone.

"For the DIR, interview resumed at ten-thirty-five a.m. on Wednesday, twenty-seventh of May. The same people are present in the room. Apologies for the delay, gentlemen. Like I told you, there have been developments in our investigations. Important developments."

She glared at Varga, who shuffled in his chair.

Damiani had regained his composure and said, "Is this pertinent to my client?"

Erika ignored him. "Mr Varga, detectives Szabó and Márkos saw you at ten p.m. yesterday, returning to your accommodation at the hostel in Csepel. Let me ask you again, where were you yesterday evening?"

Her eyes focused on the top of his head.

Varga's eyes meanwhile remained firmly focused on the table top.

"L-like I told you. With a friend, to help him out."

"Where exactly did this *helping-out* take place?"

"He p-picked me up in his car. D-don't know the address. Somewhere on the Wekerle Estate."

"How were the arrangements made?"

"He called me."

Eszter handed over an evidence bag to Kelemen, who placed it on the table, directly in Varga's line of sight.

"We found this next to your bed. Is this your phone?"

Varga shrugged.

Erika pressed. "For the DIR, please speak up. Is this your phone, Mr Varga?"

"L-looks like mine."

Erika nodded to Eszter, who produced a folder and opened it. Inside were several sheets of A4.

Eszter said, "For the DIR, I am handing over phone records for Mr Varga's phone. Which of these numbers belongs to Damari Farkas?"

Varga averted his gaze towards his lawyer and shook his head once.

Damiani intervened. "My client wishes to make no comment."

Erika's patience was already wearing thin. She pointed and said, "Can you see the calls we have highlighted, Mr Varga? They are the calls, to and from your phone. All link you to burner phone numbers we know were also in contact with at least three of the four murdered victims we are currently investigating."

Damiani's ears pricked up. "Four victims?"

"We found a fourth victim several hours ago; murdered by the same killer who took the lives of the other three."

Erika jabbed her finger at the highlighted phone numbers.

"Who do these phones belong to?"

Varga remained tight-lipped.

She tried a different tack. "What were you doing with a pair of bolt-cutters, power drill and hammer under your bed?"

"T-they belong to my f-friend. He asked me to look after them."

"Mr Varga, yesterday evening you were in Dobos Street in District Nineteen, where you committed the brutal murder of another man in his eighties?"

Varga's gaze remained fixed on the table top. His hands gripped the edge of the table, and he shook his head. "It wasn't me. I d-didn't kill him."

"The bolt-cutters had only one set of your fingerprints on them, Mr Varga. Yours! They also had blood on the blades. That blood belonged to the latest victim..." Erika paused, allowing time for the point to sink in. Once again she nodded to Eszter, who produced another folder, this time containing A4 sized prints of the photographs taken at the latest crime scene. Erika laid the photographs in front of Varga.

"Look at your handiwork. Another defenceless old person, murdered and tortured. Bloody hell! You cut off his fingers and fed them to his pet dog. That is the act of a monster. The blood samples taken from the victim's mutilated hands match that found on the blades of the bolt-cutters you stashed away under your bed. They also showed traces of cyanide, as did the other three victims."

In the pregnant pause that followed, the only sound came from the rattling floor-mounted fan in the corner.

Varga rocked backwards and forward in his chair. He finally cleared his throat. His words were almost inaudible. "I didn't kill him."

Damiani intervened. "I insist we halt proceedings while I confer with my client."

Erika wanted more, and had no intention of stopping until she had wrung a confession out of him.

"No, I'm afraid this won't wait. Ervin Nagy, poisoned with cyanide, his forehead drilled and a pencil inserted. The drill bit from your power drill kept traces of bone dust. We have been able to match the DNA. It belonged to Ervin Nagy. What do you have to say about that?"

Varga continued to rock. His knees were pulled to his chest, and he clamped his hands around them.

Erika wasn't done yet.

"Zsigmond Horvát: poisoned with cyanide, beaten with a hammer and water-tortured in his bathtub. Blood samples from the hammer shaft match with those of Zsigmond Horvát. It was you, wasn't it?"

Tears streamed down Varga's cheeks. He clasped his hands together in front of his face, as if he were praying.

"It's time to get it all off your chest, Zoltán." Erika whispered, barely loud enough for the DIR system to pick up.

"I didn't kill them. It wasn't me."

Her voice was louder and firmer once again. "You're lying. It's time to tell the truth."

Zoltán Varga put his head on the table and sobbed like a child. He shielded his face, clasping his left arm around his head.

Erika watched his dramatic performance for several seconds before turning her attention towards Damiani.

"You've got ten minutes. Interview suspended at ten fifty a.m."

Erika had a call to make. She told Eszter and Márkos to wait for her in the anteroom.

When she was alone, she fished for her phone, but paused when Rigo came around the corner. She had been so preoccupied with Varga's interrogation; she had completely forgotten about Lotti Menges, whom she assumed was in custody somewhere, awaiting her interview.

"How was Lotti, when you picked her up last night?"

Rigo shuffled his feet and looked away. "I had other commitments last night. I couldn't go. But I sent Dolman up to Esztergom to pick her up this morning."

"You mean, she's not here in custody?"

Rigo glared back at her in his usual arrogant manner.

She could hardly believe it. But then again, why not? He was worthless, and his attitude made her furious. She stepped forward and wagged her finger in front of his nose.

"You disobeyed an order from your SIO on this case. Don't you understand, Lotti is a key witness and one of the last people to see her sister alive. She may also have been involved in these murders. We need to question her again. Your colleagues didn't shirk their responsibilities. They worked all night long, while you had *other commitments*. What was it? A few hours in the pub? You make me sick, Rigo. You're off the case. I don't want to see you anywhere near this investigation again."

He made a move towards her and sneered. "Don't get your knickers in a twist, darling. You've got no authority in the Murder Squad. Rácz wants me to monitor you. He's playing the game, that's all. Making sure the new Deputy High Commissioner thinks there are equal opportunities on the tenth floor."

He pressed his face up close to hers.

His breath was appalling. Her blood chilled.

Then his hands grabbed at her breasts.

For a split second, she focused her eyes on his. Her body pressed towards him and she forced a smile.

"See, you know you want it. You've always wanted it," he said.

She placed her arms around his neck. As he moved his mouth towards hers, his eyes closed.

It had been many years since Erika had received self-defence training at the police academy. She remembered the instructor saying, 'If you strike an attacker, make sure they don't get up again.' In a heartbeat she brought her knee up with the maximum force she could muster. It found its soft, fleshy target with unerring accuracy.

Rigo screamed in agony and dropped like a stone.

With wild eyes, she glared at him. He writhed and wailed on the floor; hands clasped to his groin. Her heart beats per minute must have been off the scale and she panted heavily. For a nano-second she wanted to stamp on his face and grind her heel into his eye socket. Yet kicking a man when he was down was not her style; not even one as odious as Rigo. Instead, she straightened her clothes, turned on her heel and walked away, feeling a warm glow of satisfaction.

When Erika entered the anteroom Szabó and Márkos were jabbering away like a couple of excited schoolchildren, oblivious to what had just taken place in the corridor. She leant against a steel filing cabinet. Her head was pounding. She found paracetamol and an almost empty water bottle in her bag, and swallowed a couple of pills. She needed to focus on events in the interview room, and to put other matters to the back of her mind.

It had been a simple enough task to beat down Varga's ridiculous story with the aid of the forensic evidence. Yet he had persisted with his lies, despite clear evidence to incriminate him. He seemed to possess a child's intellect in the body of an adult. He appeared weak-minded, without the ability to think or plan strategically. Given that, she was certain he could not have planned and executed the killings by himself. There had to have been a leader of the operations. An orchestrator of the ritual murders of four people. That was her next task – to find the motive, and to discover who had been pulling Varga's strings.

The interview resumed at eleven a.m.

Erika wasted no time. "Zoltán, let's talk about your time at the Institution. While you were there, you were heard to say, 'All AVH torturers should go to hell.' You seem to know a great deal about events that took place long before you were born. Who taught you all that stuff?"

She waited for a reply, but there was none. So she tried again.

"Father Laszló told us you lived with your grandparents from an early age and he has known you since primary school."

Varga nodded. "I l-lived with my grandparents. The AVH jailed them both in the fifties, because they were Catholics." His sudden and unexpected verbosity seemed to quickly run out of steam. He crossed his arms across his chest and once again averted his gaze downwards.

Erika pressed on. "We believe victim number one, Klára Menges, was associated with the AVH, and she was murdered and brutally tortured, just days after your release from the institution."

Varga remained in his slumped position and shook his head.

"How did you discover Ervin Nagy, Zsigmond Horvát and Támas Németh were also members of the AVH?"

"Not just m-members, but jailors and torturers, terrorising innocent, God-fearing people."

She had finally latched onto something; a line of enquiry that was provoking him into action. "Now we're getting somewhere. Where and when did they carry out the torture you allege, Zoltán?"

"In the p-prison headquarters on Fő Street, in the prison camps like Recsk, and at the House of Terror."

Erika tried to push him further. "So, assuming our four victims were all former AVH torturers, like you say. Searching for them would be like searching for four old needles in a very large haystack. Most AVH members must already be dead by now. If anyone was so motivated to give them their due deserts, how would they have found them?"

"Names are in the d-dossier," said Varga.

"Where did the dossier come from?"

Erika studied his expression, but Varga looked blankly at her and said nothing. "Zoltán, we already have enough evidence to charge you with all four murders. Do you understand that?"

Varga averted his gaze.

Erika continued, "But I think you were not acting alone. It's in your best interests to tell me the truth. Who was with you? Was it your friend, Farkas?"

She ignored the vibration in her pocket. But when it occurred for the third time in quick succession, she checked to find two missed calls and a WhatsApp message from Axel Rácz. He was obviously watching the interview with interest.

His text message read, *'You've got your killer. Charge him.'*

Surely Rácz could see it was more complicated than that? Even though Varga was a party to these crimes, he had not acted alone. He was shielding someone, and she intended to discover the name of that person.

Damiani shuffled his papers but seemed a loss for words.

"So that's it, is it, Zoltán? All four targets in your dossier successfully taken care of. You can spend the rest of your life in jail contemplating a job well done."

Varga folded his arms tightly across his chest. His eyelids compressed together, and his frown lines deeply furrowed. He hissed as he formed his next words.

"Not all bad people are in the dossier. S-Sipos is next."

"Sipos is a common name. What else can you tell me?"

He said, "I spy with my little eye, something beginning with... A."

Varga was now playing games with her. A thought flashed across her mind. She held up her hands and made an announcement. "Interview suspended at eleven twenty-five. Don't move. I'll be back."

With a speed of movement that surprised even herself, Erika left the interview room. She ran across the open-plan space and was panting by the time she reached her own office. She tossed memos and overtime authorisations from her desk onto the floor until she came across what she was looking for: the copy of *Világgazdaság* she had bought yesterday morning.

There was the headline she remembered.

Sipos Invests In Hungarian Green Energy Sector.

Below the headline, the wizened face of the Monaco-based multi-millionaire beamed as he posed outside the entrance of the luxury hotel with its spectacular views of the Chain Bridge and Buda Castle. He was a socialite and a financier, renowned for staying in his suite at the Four Seasons Gresham Palace, whenever he was in town.

Clutching the newspaper, she sprinted back to the interview room. Slightly out of breath, she took her seat and signalled the interview was back underway. She spread the newspaper in front of Varga, pointed to the headline and said, "Are we getting warm?"

Varga looked up at her. There was something in his expression that was defiant, challenging, mocking. An altogether more Machiavellian character had replaced the persona of the shy child. It was possible that Varga read the newspaper article yesterday and was now simply regurgitating a snippet of useless information that would prove unreliable and distracting. Yet there may be substance behind his teasing.

Erika snapped her notebook shut. "Interview suspended at eleven twenty-eight. You'd better not be wasting police time, Varga."

The warning sounded hollow, even to her. It was a warning unlikely to hold much weight, with a man accused of committing four murders. She stood up and issued her orders. There was not a second to waste.

Chapter Twelve

Back in the anteroom, Erika wasted no time in calling the Four Seasons Gresham Palace Hotel. When she got through to reception she said, "This is Senior Detective Kelemen, Budapest homicide department speaking. I understand Ambrus Sipos is staying at your hotel."

A plummy voice responded. "That is public knowledge, so I may respond in the affirmative. I am the duty manager. How may I help you, Detective?"

"We believe Mr Sipos may be in danger. Did he leave the Gresham Palace this morning?" she said.

The duty manager sounded incredulous. "As far as I am aware, he is in his suite. We were told Mr Sipos would hold a series of meetings in there this morning. The last meeting over-ran. His latest *visitor* has only just gone up."

"Did you see the visitor?"

Three words into the duty manager's response, Erika cut him short.

"Call Mr Sipos immediately. Tell him the police are on their way, and not to allow anyone into his suite. Send your security to apprehend the visitor until we arrive. We'll be there in ten minutes."

Eszter sped up the ramp from the underground car park, tyres squealing. With blue lights flashing and their two-tone alarm in full flow, she sped along Váci Street. At Dráva Street she turned sharply right before racing along the riverside embankment. They passed the parliament building in a blur, braking only when they reached the Chain Bridge and approached István Square.

When the Audi screeched to a halt outside the hotel, Eszter looked smug. "Seven minutes, forty-three," she said.

When Erika released her grip on the dashboard, her knuckles were white. Easing herself out of the car gingerly, she regretted authorising Eszter's attendance on that advanced driving course at Mogyoród.

Waiting for them under the canopy outside the grand art nouveau main entrance was a dark-suited under-manager with slicked-back brown hair. They followed him at breakneck speed through the lobby, towards the great reception desk at the far end. Suddenly he veered to the right, where a similarly dark-suited woman - her grey hair in a tight bun - stood holding the lift doors open.

The lift ascended quickly to the top floor, where the duty manager and two uniformed security guards were standing. The manager hastily introduced himself. He wore a frown, together with the inevitable dark suit. When he spoke, he sounded flustered and a little less plummy than he had when Erika had called him. He said, "I telephoned the suite, but there was no response. There is also no sign of the visitor. I didn't know whether I should knock. Mr Sipos values his privacy."

Erika despaired at the man's ineptitude.

"I'm sure he also values his life," she said sharply. "You have the key?"

He looked sheepish and laid a gold-coloured plastic key card in her hand.

"Does this lead directly into the living room?" she asked.

"There's a hallway which leads to the drawing room."

She placed the key card on the sensor. The quiet buzz of the magnetic release was the signal for her to ease open the heavy mahogany door. She pulled her weapon from its shoulder holster, gripped it firmly with both hands, and peered around the gap between the door and its frame. The hallway was lit and about five metres long. The door at the far end was slightly ajar. Beyond it, she heard a voice that sounded familiar. She motioned for Eszter to step closer and follow her, but shooed the duty manager away

"Wait here," she mouthed to him and the security guards.

Eszter produced her own weapon. The pair entered the suite and moved stealthily until they were close enough to touch the door to the living room. Erika put a finger to her lips and leaned her ear towards the gap. From this position, she anticipated they would be able to hear everything. She wanted to listen to the ongoing conversation, before they made their move.

A raspy voice could be heard. Erika immediately recognised it as belonging to Ambrus Sipos, from the many times she had seen him on television.

The voice said, "I am ready, and time is short. My condition is known only by you, me and my personal physician. He calls it a glioblastoma multiforme. I call it the devil's vengeance. Either way, it is a tumour living inside my cerebral hemisphere; one that has already spread quickly into surrounding areas. Your call came at the perfect time. Although it is still a mystery to me how you got hold of my private number."

A second voice said, "God moves in mysterious ways, and I have many contacts. The good news is, I am here. So let us begin. You will soon be at peace. We start by wiping the slate clean with The Almighty. I have everything we need here. There's no need to kneel, not at our age. Let us sit. Here, take this card and read the words aloud."

There was a pause for several seconds. Then the raspy voice of Sipos said, "Bless me, for I have sinned. It's been seventy-five years since my first and last confession. Some would say, I have lived a life of sin. I honestly don't know where to begin."

"Do you recall the ten commandments: you shall not steal; you shall not kill; you shall not desire your neighbour's goods? Let them guide you."

There was a raucous, throaty laugh. "How much time do you have?"

"As long as it takes, but I suggest you begin with the sins that burden you the most."

Sipos said, "One thing leads to another. When I was eighteen years old, I informed one of the local communist party leaders that a boy in our group was a fascist. They arrested the boy and took him away. Is that a sin?"

"It was not a charitable act, but at those times quite commonplace. Is that the sin you wish to confess?"

"It's not even the warm-up act. As a reward, they gave me a job in the police force. Things were going well, but everything changed the following year. They sent me to work as a guard in the prison camp at Recsk. It was a disaster. Life there was almost as bad for us guards as it was for the prisoners."

"So what happened?"

"One day, the unthinkable occurred - a small group of prisoners escaped. They ordered us guards to round up two hundred and fifty random prisoners, and herd them into a special prison within the prison. For weeks we beat them and starved them. We punished them, over and over. Within two months, there was not one sane man left. When we threw them their meagre chunks of meat, we laughed while they fought and tore at one another. Every day a guard would announce over the loudspeaker, 'You are here because your friends escaped.' A few weeks later, they captured one of the escapees, as he was trying to flee across the border. They brought him back to Recsk, and we led him into the prison within a prison. Through the loudspeaker an officer announced, 'Here is one of the men whose escape caused you your misfortunes.' We stood back and watched, while they literally tore him to pieces."

The second voice responded. "It's a terrible tale, but it was a collective act. Did you commit any individual crimes while you were there?"

"I was the youngest guard, the lowest of the low. If I had not done what they expected, they would have thrown me in with the prisoners. I saw it happen to one guard. They killed him within hours."

"How long were you at the camp?"

"For thirteen months, until one day they called me into the commander's office. I shit myself, thinking one of the other guards had denounced me. Instead, the commander told me I would transfer back to Budapest, to work in Stalin Street."

"At the House of Terror?"

"Yes. That was where I worked until the uprising in fifty-six. By the end of October, I could see the way it was going, and decided to escape to the border. From there I fled into Austria, then to Canada. And it was in Toronto I founded the small business, which has today become the Sipos Group. I established the Sipos Foundation twenty years ago, to put something back into Hungarian society."

"And what do you seek from The Almighty today?"

"I seek peace and absolution."

"Do you promise not to offend God in the future?"

"I can count my future in a few days. I promise not to offend Him in the time I have left."

"I will grant you absolution, but first you should make a good Act of Contrition for your sins. If you need help, you'll find the words on the card in front of you."

Several seconds passed before Sipos spoke again. "Oh my God, with all my heart, I am sorry for my sins. In choosing to do wrong, and failing to do good, I have sinned against you, whom I should love above all things. I firmly intend, with your help, to do penance, to sin no more, and to avoid whatever leads me to sin. Our Saviour Jesus Christ suffered and died for us. In His name, my God, have mercy. Amen."

"Your penance is something we shall discuss later, after you have received the sacrament of Holy Communion. Give thanks to the Lord for He is good."

Sipos replied, "For His mercy endures forever."

"The Lord has freed you from your sins."

"Thanks be to God."

"Now, it is time to prepare you for the sacrament of Holy Communion."

In the hallway, Erika and Eszter listened to every word in silence. The visitor's strategy was crystal clear: to build up trust and offer hope of absolution. Knowing their days were numbered, each of the victims had been content to confess their sins. They had been happy to receive the sacrament of Holy Communion, to maximise their state of grace, not knowing it would the last conscious act they would ever take.

Erika had seen how this story played out on four previous occasions. She was not about to allow the murderer to strike again. On the silent count of three, Eszter booted open the door.

Erika rushed in, pointed her weapon, and shouted. "Don't move!"

Framed by one of the hotel's 'Danube View' windows, Ambrus Sipos sat on a sofa, hands clasped in the praying position.

Facing him was the stooped figure of a priest. The priest held a golden chalice in one hand, and a piece of the communion host in the other.

"The Body of Christ," he said solemnly, ignoring the intrusion.

Erika launched herself towards them, imagining the communion bread to be poisoned.

Before she could stop him, Sipos said, "Amen," and swallowed the host.

His Adam's apple bulged. Then, as if waking from a trance, he noticed the two intruders and looked at Erika in a state of confusion. "Who the hell are you?"

Erika stepped between Sipos and the priest. She holstered her pistol and held out her ID.

"Mr Sipos. I am Senior Detective Kelemen and this is Detective Szabó. Your life is in danger."

On the floor next to Sipos was a black pilot's case. In between the sofas was a coffee table. Upon the table stood a silver chalice containing communion wine. It was then she saw the face of Father Laszló Racokzy. Given the turn of events, he looked remarkably calm. She gently removed the golden communion chalice from his hands and placed it on the coffee table.

Leaning on the arm of a chair for support, Sipos hauled himself up and raised his raspy voice.

"My life in danger? You mean from an old priest, kind enough to offer me the blessed sacraments in the privacy of my suite?"

Erika said, "Don't let appearances deceive you. We believe this man has already murdered four people. He poisoned them with cyanide, before supervising their brutal torture and disfigurement."

"Are you telling me, *he* is The Budapest Butcher?"

"Yes, together with an accomplice," she replied. She produced a pair of latex gloves from her pocket and pulled them on. Next, she picked up the silver chalice and sniffed its contents.

"What is it?" Sipos demanded.

Erika had inhaled the scent of burned almonds all to often in the last week. "Cyanide," she said.

The priest offered no resistance as Szabó yanked his arms behind his back, slapped on a pair of handcuffs and pulled them tightly around his skinny, wrinkled wrists.

Sipos lunged at the priest.

"You murderer! I trusted you, and you try to kill me!"

Eszter stepped between them.

Father Laszló broke his silence.

"You call *me* a murderer? Look at yourself in the mirror. I was one of those, in the prison within a prison at Recsk. You may have forgotten my face, but I will never forget yours. Don't you remember your little game of the white mare?"

He turned to Erika and said, "For the uninitiated, 'white mare' is a sadistic game where they insert a broomstick under your knees then double you up into a tight ball, lashing your wrists to your ankles. Often, when we crouched on our knees in this position, the guards would beat us with rubber hoses. I was only eighteen when Sipos made a white mare of me, but still he beat me until I was numb all over. I rolled against a hot stove." He shuddered.

"With the loss of feeling in my hand, I pressed against the fire, fried two fingers and half my palm. I only knew what was happening when I smelt my own burning flesh. Of course, he already knew what was happening, but he and his friends were laughing."

Erika focused on the priest's right hand. His glove would be removed later for fingerprinting. She wondered what torture method had been in store as his retribution for Sipos. The lid to the pilot bag was open. She reached inside the bag and grasped the handle of an object, carefully lifting out a blowtorch.

"Standard equipment for administering the sacraments?" she said.

Receiving no response, she searched the bag's side-pockets. She held up a phone between her thumb and forefinger. It was an old-fashioned model, certainly not a smart phone. "Detective Szabó, what odds would you give me, on this being one of our missing burner phones?"

She had seen enough. SOCO would forensically examine the bag and the rest of the scene.

"Father László Rákoczy, I am arresting you for the murders of Klára Menges, Ervin Nagy, Zsigmond Horvát and Támas Németh, and for the attempted murder of Ambrus Sipos. You do not have to say anything, but it may harm your defence if you do not mention when questioned something which you later rely on in court. Anything you say may be given in evidence."

Eszter called for a custody wagon, and for the next fifteen minutes she watched over the handcuffed priest like a hawk.

Meanwhile, Erika sat with Sipos in the dining room of the suite, taking down all his contact details.

His voice wavered. "I still can't believe what just happened."

Erika was appalled by his self-confessed deeds at the Recsk camp, but said diplomatically, "I'm glad we got here in time. We will need your detailed statement. As the only survivor of his attacks, you are a key witness and your testimony will be crucial. Given your health, I'm sure we will require you to remain in Hungary for the foreseeable future."

Sipos was still shaking. The shock and the strain were clearly getting the better of him, and in the last five minutes he looked to have aged ten years.

Erika's work was far from over, but this arrest was a massive step forward. She felt she was once more back in the driving seat, even though she wondered for how long could she remain there.

By late afternoon, Erika's sleep deprivation was weighing heavily on her. She had been working almost continuously for the last thirty-six hours. Now, back at Teve Street, she could hardly stop yawning, and struggled to keep her eyes open. Yet she feared more than ever being booted off the investigation. There was simply no way she could afford to take her foot off the gas, at least not until she had charged both suspects. She stopped at the tenth-floor vending machine to top up her caffeine level with black coffee and an extra shot. Cup in hand, she strode into the Incident Room a little after five p.m., where she found the rest of the team in good spirits. She made her way to the front of the room.

"Listen up. We've got work to do. Do we have a home address for the priest?"

As usual, it had been a uniformed desk-sergeant who had taken Father Laszló's fingerprints and mugshots, completed the paperwork and supervised the change of clothes and collection of belongings. However, she had tasked Gábor Márkos with overseeing the booking-in process. He read from his notebook.

"Apparently there's accommodation for him and some other priests, provided gratis by the Order of Malta at nineteen Fortuna Street. We found these keys on him. He's in a holding cell right now, on continuous watch."

Erika was itching for the opportunity to go through the priest's accommodation with a fine toothcomb. She issued her instructions.

"Get a search warrant, and take a SOCO team. Let's see what he's got hidden away. Go on. What are you waiting for? Move!"

The moment Márkos was out of the door, Erika turned her attention towards Dolman.

"What news from Lotti Menges?"

Dolman checked the notes in his pocketbook.

"She's in room 10-E. I picked her up from her apartment at ten this morning. The local uniforms kept an eye on her apartment last night. She told me Klára begged her to come to Budapest. She says, Klára called and told her she'd found God at last, and had agreed to see a priest. According to Lotti, Klára wanted a reconciliation, before it was too late. Lotti said she was reluctant at first, but finally agreed to come. She says, they met up at Klára's apartment around lunchtime on Tuesday the 19th of May. Things didn't go well and Lotti said she left before two p.m., took a taxi to the station and caught the train back to Esztergom."

Erika looked askance. "Then why did she lie and tell us she hadn't seen Klára for years?"

"She said she didn't want to get involved and, after she heard news of the murder. She thought her presence at the scene may look suspicious."

"And lying to the police looks even more suspicious. Let's see whether our two suspects implicate her. In the meantime, she stays in custody, pending further investigations."

She turned to Eszter. "Come on, Szabó, we've got work to do."

Eszter's half-closed eyelids sprang wide open. "You going to interview Father Laszló next?" she asked.

"Not until we've checked his phone records and seen what he's got stashed away in his room. I want every piece of the jigsaw in place first."

Varga and his lawyer were escorted back into to room 10-A by uniformed officers, where Erika and Eszter sat waiting for them.

After the arrest of Father Laszló, Erika's intention was to charge Varga either with four counts of first degree murder, or with conspiracy to murder, depending on the outcome of this interview. The forensic evidence already clearly showed Varga's fingerprints on the weapons used in the murders of all four victims. At the forthcoming trial, his lawyers would surely parade a host of psychiatrists to argue the case for diminished responsibility. For now, that was not her concern. She need only worry about establishing the facts and making charges based on the evidence. She announced the interview had resumed, leant back in her chair, folded her arms and scrutinised Varga's demeanour.

He was clasping his hands, as if in prayer.

She said, "You were right, Zoltán. We were very warm. Warm enough to catch your accomplice red-handed. Unfortunately for him, his appointment was delayed. We arrived in time to overhear Ambrus Sipos make his Holy Confession. He admitted to doing some terrible things, but that doesn't mean you and your buddy get to act as judge, jury and executioners. All four of your victims were stalked, offered the chance of making their peace with God, then poisoned and tortured. The game is over, Zoltán. Father Laszló is going to spend the rest of his life inside prison. You will too, unless you plead guilty and tell us the whole truth."

Damiani whispered something into Varga's ear.

Erika continued, "You need to tell us everything, from the beginning. Father Laszló roped you into this, and I want to know why. For your own sake, you need to tell us everything."

Varga sighed and rubbed his bloodshot eyes with his fingertips. His mouth opened and closed several times like a goldfish.

"Come on, Zoltán. Spit it out."

There was no bravado or teasing manipulation left in him. Tears ran down Varga's cheeks. After a while, words formed. "I didn't kill them. I'll g-go to hell." He sobbed.

Someone had indoctrinated this young man, probably from a very early age. Erika pitied him, not for what he had done, but for how easily someone like him could be manipulated.

Eszter's phone vibrated. She scribbled something on her pad and slid it sideways.

Erika glanced at the note and nodded. "We'll pause here. Make no mistake, Zoltán. The next time we convene, we'll be bringing charges against you. What level of charges depends on what you can tell us. I suggest, Mr Damiani, for his own sake your client takes this opportunity to clear his mind and prepare to give us a full statement. Now is the time for him to come clean. Interview suspended at seven-fifteen p.m."

Waiting outside in the corridor for them was Ferenc. He was grinning from ear to ear, clearly excited and brandishing a plastic folder. "The records of the phone you found this afternoon show Father Laszló made calls to Ambrus Sipos, Zoltán Varga, and other numbers I haven't had time to identify yet."

Erika gave a half smile, then turned and hurried off.

Ferenc looked bewildered and unsure of what to do next.

Eszter gave him a peck on the cheek, then took the folder from him and ran after her boss.

"Well done," she called out to him.

It was almost eight-thirty when Márkos called from the priest's accommodation on Fortuna Street. He sounded jubilant as he listed the items they had discovered.

"We found potassium cyanide pills, several phones, and a dossier you'll be interested in."

Erika permitted herself a gratified smile. "Excellent work. Now get yourselves back here pronto."

Before long, Ferenc and his colleagues unlocked the four burner phones Márkos had found in Father Laszló's room. The resulting call records were pored over and soon the pattern of short introductory calls, followed by longer conversations with each of the victims, became all too clear.

Erika filled in the gaps in the timeline of each murder. Eszter ticked off the calls from the list, as slowly but surely the detailed picture of events that had taken place over the last two-and-a-half weeks emerged.

With Eszter by her side and Dolman and Márkos trailing behind, Erika strode along the corridor. She had instructed the two men to enter the room first, with Eszter one pace behind. All three remained standing with their backs to the wall while Erika entered and sat at the table opposite Father Laszló.

The priest was wearing a standard-issue custody suit. They had also removed his glove, and now both hands rested on the tabletop, left covering the right. He looked at her across the table. Given the circumstances, his heavily wrinkled face looked calm, and there was even a faint smile.

He said, "Good evening. I hope you don't mind me saying, you all look exhausted. You should get some rest."

Thanks for nothing, she thought.

"This is a recorded interview. I am Senior Detective Erika Kelemen. Also present are Detective Eszter Szabó, Detective

Gábor Márkos, and Detective Lajos Dolman. We are in room 10-C at Police Headquarters in Teve Street. The date is Wednesday, the twenty-seventh of May. The time is nine-thirty p.m."

She nodded to the priest. "Please state your full name, current address and date of birth."

He cleared his throat. "My name is Laszló Bence Rákoczy. I live at the priest house on Fortuna Street. Born on the 24th of February 1935."

"I understand you have declined legal representation for this interview. Is that correct?"

He looked steadfastly into her eyes. "That is correct."

"Do you understand why you were arrested?"

"I do."

"It's my duty to remind you, you have been formally cautioned and warn you that, anything you say may be used in evidence. We have arrested you on suspicion of the attempted murder of Ambrus Sipos and the premeditated murders of Klára Menges, Ervin Nagy, Zsigmond Horvát and Támas Németh. Do you understand?"

"I understand you are doing your job, Detective, but I am not guilty in the eyes of the Lord. Those people you named were once members of the hated and dreaded State Security Department. After the war, seventy percent of the Hungarian population was Roman Catholic, and the AVH persecuted and terrorised us. They closed our churches and schools, stole our property, jailed our priests, monks and nuns. They even jailed our leader, Cardinal Mindszenty. Their cruelty and brutality was boundless. The aim of the communists was to crush the spirit of the Catholic church. The AVH was the means they used to achieve that goal in Hungary."

Kelemen slid a manilla folder across the table. On its cover, in bold print, were the words:

TOP SECRET

PROPERTY OF THE MINISTRY OF INTERIOR

"We discovered this under your mattress. It contains the names, history and contact details of all your victims, and many more besides. How did it come into your possession?"

The priest nodded. "When members of the people's revolutionary forces broke into the House of Terror in October, fifty-six, they found the personnel records of those who worked there. Those records were taken and kept hidden for many years. For several weeks, the AVH was disbanded, but after the Russians destroyed the city in the Battle of Budapest, and the communists came back into power, many of the former AVH stalwarts reappeared. Thousands of them took prominent and well-paid roles under the communists. Of course, many of them have died since then. That dossier contains details of some who have survived until the present times. It is the result of decades of painstaking detective work, by people whose mission it is to track and trace the enemies of the Church."

"Are you saying the Order of Malta compiled this dossier?"

Father László smiled and shook his head. "Not at all. Those responsible, operate independently. They belong to an Order whose members operate in plain sight, within the Church. You may expect their work to continue, even when I am away from the front line. What you should focus on, detective, is that each of your so-called victims confessed to their crimes, and was relieved to do so. I offered them absolution before God. That was what they sought." There was an unruffled air of confidence about the priest.

"Your accomplice was Zoltán Varga. Are you saying others were also involved?"

"The Church has many enemies. We need an army to combat them. I am a mere foot soldier in this war."

"You groomed Varga. You used him as your muscle."

"He has always struggled to make sense of the world. I have shown him a clear path to redemption. For that, he will be eternally grateful. When the AVH scum are languishing in the fires of hell, Our Lady will hold Zoltán to her bosom, like the Lamb of God."

The interview was becoming surreal. Erika wondered whether the priest actually believed in his own fantastical narrative.

"Let's get back to basics. How did you get hold of the dossier?"

Father Laszló looked at her impassively. "The Brotherhood is sworn to secrecy. That is one secret I shall take to my grave."

Erika made a note. He did not deny his involvement, but nor had he yet confessed to any of the murders. It was time for her to check the facts.

"The phone we found in your case and the others we found in your room. Where did you get them from?"

"From a member of the Brotherhood. Technology is not my strong point. I understood the calls could not be traced."

Erika had wondered why the murderer had used multiple burner phones, but had not discarded them. Was this elementary mistake really down to an old man's techno-confusion? She produced the call log, which ran to many pages.

"Every call you made with those phones is here. Look for yourself."

Father Laszló maintained eye contact with her.

"There's no need, my child. I'm sure what you say is true."

She referred once again to her notes.

"At eleven-thirty-two a.m. on the tenth of May, you called Klára Menges. You introduced yourself and offered your services, as her bridge to God. You knew from her personnel records; she was originally from the Catholic faith. You offered to visit her apartment, to give her the blessed sacraments and absolve her from her sins, so she could face death in grace and peace. Klára found that a compelling offer. Over the following week you made several calls with her, building trust, planning for your house visit. She was so excited, she even called her estranged sister, Lotti, to tell her she had once again found God. She invited Lotti to her apartment. Was Lotti part of your deception?"

The priest looked nonplussed.

"Klára Menges said nothing to me of a sister."

Erika made a note and continued. "At approximately five p.m., on Tuesday, the 19th of May, you and Varga arrived at Klára's apartment. She invited you both into her home. You listened to her confession, then gave her Holy Communion. First you gave her the bread, followed by the communion wine - which you had laced with one of the potassium cyanide pills we found in your room. You and Varga watched her die. It took around twenty minutes of excruciating suffering before she lost blood pressure, ending with a cardiac arrest. All that time, the pair of you watched while she begged you for medical help, but you wanted her to die, slowly and painfully. At what stage did you produce the needle? It was the same tool she had used to torture prisoners in the basement of the House of Terror, wasn't it?"

The priest's pale blue eyes flashed, and his left hand slammed down on the table top.

"Her victims were conscious when she used her hat pin on them. She needed to understand the terror she had brought to them."

For the first time, Erika glimpsed his prosthetic right hand.

She said, "It took some time for you and Varga to inflict so many wounds, and tattoo her with the AVH initials. At some point she lost consciousness, too weak to struggle or shout out for help from her neighbours. You were thorough in your clean up. You left no fingerprints or useful clues behind. You were on your way by seven p.m., and Klára's body lay there, until discovered the following morning by her cleaner."

The priest closed his eyes and sighed. "I must commend you, Detective Kelemen. It's a fair summary of events. I am certain your analysis of the others is equally detailed. So, save your breath. I admit, I did all of them, Menges, Nagy, Horvát, Németh and, of course, you know about Sipos."

Erika did a double take; uncertain she had heard him correctly. The admission dumbfounded her, and the words stumbled out of her mouth. "You are still under caution. Could you say that again?"

No one else in the room moved or uttered a word.

"It was me. Zoltán was there, as my bag carrier – my chopper of wood and carrier of water – but actually he did little. My good hand did every poisoning and crafted every moment of torture. But understand this, detective. Those were evil people. I simply gave them the opportunity to confess their sins and beg for God's forgiveness."

"If only that were true, Father. Your motive was revenge, served cold after sixty-five years."

"I will not argue the point, but only God will be my judge."

It was all Erika could do to keep her emotions under control. Her principal suspect had just confessed to murdering all four victims. She knew, without her intervention, he would have made it five and would probably still be on the loose to kill others on his to-do list. With a sharp intake of breath, she sat up tall and placed her hands upon the table.

"Laszló Bence Rákoczy, I am charging you, with four counts of murder and one of attempted murder. Detective Dolman will arrange for you to be removed to a holding cell and held under continuous surveillance until you are transferred to prison, where you will be held on remand awaiting your trial. You may elect to have legal representation."

After Dolman and two uniformed officers had taken Father Laszló away, Erika fixed her gaze on Eszter and Márkos, both of whom were grinning from ear to ear.

"Wipe those stupid smiles off your faces," she said. "Márkos, you can release Lotti Menges. Be sure you get her to the station, in time for the last train back to Esztergom. Szabó, you come with me. We still have work to do."

She allowed both of them to leave the room ahead of her.

Behind their backs, she broke into a broad smile.

Erika and Eszter made the short walk to Room 10-A to resume the interview with Zoltán Varga.

Damiani, his shirt crumpled with sleeves rolled up to his elbows, said wearily. "My client maintains his innocence. He claims he was coerced and was following…"

By now Erika was in no mood for lengthy speeches.

"Don't waste your breath," she said. "Your client's supposed supervisor, Father Laszló, has confessed to all four murders and one count of attempted murder. According to him, your client was present during all four executions and assisted in the torture of the victims."

She allowed that bombshell to sink in for several seconds before leaning forward and continuing.

"Zoltán Varga, I believe you were part of the planning, and you assisted Father Laszló, knowing that he intended to murder and mutilate the bodies of the victims. He may have poisoned the victims, but your involvement was essential to his success. I am formally charging you with being an accessory to the murders of Klára Menges, Ervin Nagy, Zsigmond Horvát and Támas Németh. I have already cautioned you. We may use anything you say in evidence. Detective Szabó will organise your transfer to a holding cell. In the morning they will transfer you to prison, where you will await trail. Do you have anything more to say?"

Varga sobbed, "It wasn't me. I didn't do it."

He was a pitiful sight. Erika was certain there was a lot more he was not telling them. For now, that did not matter. *She* had caught, and *she* had charged the two men responsible for the murders of four people. She had also saved the life of Ambrus Sipos. There seemed little doubt that Sipos and perhaps all four of the deceased victims had committed heinous crimes on behalf of the dreaded AVH. Yet, where would the country be if victims and their associates could take the law into their own hands?

Two uniformed officers arrived, and she watched Eszter and the officers lead Varga away. Damiani followed in their wake, leaving Erika alone in the interview room. Suddenly, the intercom buzzed and startled her.

The voice of Axel Rácz boomed through a speaker.

"Outstanding work, Erika. Come to my office straight away. There's someone here who wants to see you. By the way, bring that dossier with you."

CHAPTER THIRTEEN

Despite the lateness of the hour, Dora was still at her station outside the commander's office.

"He's waiting to see you," she said with a broad grin.

Erika smiled. "Don't you ever go home?"

"Not while he needs me here." Then Dora winked conspiratorially. "He has company."

"I heard as much."

The door to the commander's office was slightly ajar and their chatter alerted him. "Dora, is that Kelemen? I called her ten minutes ago. Send her in."

Erika tilted her head to one side and placed a finger on her lips. "Oh, I wonder who's in there with him?" she said to Dora. Clutching the dossier in her hand, she pushed open the door and strode into the boss's office. There she found Axel Rácz seated at the conference table, his back to her. Opposite him sat Rudolf Kudár. A shiver ran up her spine.

Rácz craned his neck. "Hey, Erika, come on in. We watched your interviews with the two suspects. You did well to nail them."

Kudár seemed less interested with issuing congratulations and said, "You have something that belongs to the Ministry."

Erika clamped the dossier under her arm. "This is essential evidence in our investigation. We cannot release it until it's been thoroughly inspected and logged."

She needed support, but Rácz turned his back to her and mumbled. "You need to hand it over, Detective Kelemen. Now."

Erika considered her options, then made the only decision available to her. She tossed the dossier across the table. It slid effortlessly on the polished surface, landing in front of Kudár.

He placed his hand on top of the file. "I will return this to you, in due course, suitably redacted."

Erika was ready to explode. "You can't just—"

Rácz tried to calm her, "He can and he will. We have our confessions. Make them stick."

Was this the beginning of a cover-up? If Rácz was in on it too, she knew she had no chance of overturning the decision tonight. Anyway, she was mentally and physically drained and wanted to get out of there as quickly as possible.

She said, "If there's nothing else…" She stood to leave.

So did Rácz. He led her by the elbow to the door. He lowered his voice. "Péter Rigo came to see me."

She knew it would only be a matter of time until that slimeball put in a complaint about her. "And?"

"He says you assaulted him."

"Did he tell you why?"

"I'm sure you had your reasons. Anyway, I don't care. I want you back in the department permanently. The Deputy High Commissioner agrees. Rigo will be transferred. There's a job waiting for him in Debrecen. Just one more thing, Erika, be careful out there. Walls have eyes and ears."

She had many questions, but now was not the time. She thanked him and said she'd think about his offer.

On the way out, Dora asked how she was doing.

Erika honestly didn't know how to respond. She was doing her utmost to hold back tears of exhaustion, frustration, and grief. "I could be an hour late in the morning," she said lamely.

Dora needed no explanation. "Go home and get some rest."

The general office was deserted. On her way past the photocopier, Erika stopped and opened the storage cupboard. She reached inside, searching for the copied pages she had hidden there.

They had disappeared.

"Fuck them. Fuck all of them!" she hissed under her breath.

When Erika finally reached her apartment, she found it was in darkness. She pressed the light switch and gently placed her handbag on the sofa, concerned not to wake Marcel. The clock on the wall told her it was just after one a.m. By her reckoning, it was over forty hours since she had last slept. All she wanted was to slide into her bed, snuggle up behind Marcel's warm body and drift off into a dream world; a world without brutal murders and treachery.

She eased open the bedroom door. The shaft of light from the living room penetrated the room sufficiently to show the bed was empty once again. She kicked off her heels and switched on her bedside lamp. An envelope addressed to her in Marcel's handwriting leaned against the lamp. Only then did she remember his WhatsApp message.

Do we have a future?

It had seemed so bizarre at the time. Unworthy of an answer. She threw back her head and laughed out loud. It had to be better than crying, and she willed herself not to shed any more tears tonight.

Dressed only in her bathrobe, Erika sat at the dressing table and removed what remained of her make-up. She felt totally drained. His letter could wait until morning, because truthfully there was nothing she could do about it now.

She crawled into her empty bed, switched off the light and prayed for sleep to come quickly. It didn't.

Erika pulled up in the car park of the funeral home the next morning amidst a fleet of black hearses and limos. Marcel's letter sat unopened on the dashboard. She was just about to see her mother for the last time. She didn't need to read Marcel's bullshit to know he wasn't coming back. She tossed the envelope onto the passenger seat, checked her make-up in the driver's mirror, and reapplied her lipstick before getting out of the car.

At the entrance, she pressed the doorbell.

The intercom crackled. "Do you have an appointment?"

Something about the officiousness of the voice irked her. "Yes, I'm here to see Nora Kelemen at nine. They brought her here last night. I'm her daughter, Detective Erika Kelemen."

The door buzzed open, and Erika stepped inside the small, unstaffed reception area. A red, leather-bound photograph album lay forlornly on the simple coffee table between two wooden chairs. She averted her gaze. Decisions would have to be made. But for now, all she wanted was to see her mother, and to kiss her stone-cold forehead.

It had never crossed her mind that this simple wish would not be granted. Yet when the funeral director explained the rules concerning people who may have died because of COVID-19, it seemed so obvious. As a police officer, she already knew these rules. As a grieving daughter, they seemed so inhumane.

She was grasping at straws. "Couldn't I just see her, through a glass panel?"

"I'm sorry, Detective, but we didn't prepare your mother for a viewing. Anyway, it's really not allowed." His eyes seemed kind behind the face mask. "Are you ready to discuss the funeral arrangements?"

"I need to consult with my brother. Perhaps tomorrow?"

He nodded. "Of course. Make another appointment. We can discuss everything when you and your family are ready."

Back in the car, she felt stupid for having raised her own expectations. Covering her face with both hands, she wept like a baby. Huge, uncontrollable sobs engulfed her, and hot, salty tears coursed down her cheeks, until finally she could cry no more. She mopped up the mess with tissues, which she tossed onto the passenger seat on top of the envelope from Marcel.

Ah yes, the rest of the mess. Why not? Her hand snaked out in resignation. It was now or never.

She tore open the envelope. Inside was a single sheet of notepaper. Unfolding it, she gazed at Marcel's handwriting. She was shaking to the point it was impossible to read. Several times she inhaled through her nose and exhaled through her mouth. Eventually, she regained control and focused on the letter.

My darling Erika, she read, *I know you have been under the most intense pressure at work. Whereas I find myself with too much time on my hands — too much time to ponder. I had hoped our futures may have been together, however; I fear you may not share this vision. I am planning to spend a few days at Viktor's place. This will hopefully give you time and space to think. Let's meet and talk whenever suits you. I will understand, if you do not wish to see me again. Meanwhile, know that you are always in my thoughts and in my heart.*

It was signed simply, *Marcel*.

Erika felt both relief and shame. She was relieved that Marcel had called time-out and not totally given up on her. She was also ashamed she had failed to ever see things from his perspective. She checked the time. It was already nine-thirty. There were a million things to do at Teve Street this morning, and she was already later than she'd planned. She fastened her seatbelt and turned on the ignition, but her hand paused on the gearstick.

Would her relationship with Marcel turn to dust, just like all her previous ones had? She was fifty. All prospects of ever being a mother had passed her by, and she had never been keen on the idea of marriage. But the thought of ending up lonely and alone in her old age was far from attractive. There would be no children to call upon when she was in a nursing home, not even a thoughtless son like David. Marcel's letter was not at all what she had expected. Perhaps she had been taking him for granted. After all, she knew she was difficult to live with, particularly when she became so engrossed with a case – and this investigation had consumed her like no other.

She wondered what she would have done if the roles had been reversed. It was clear from his letter, the ball was now in her court, and there was nothing to be gained by further procrastination.

She took her phone in her hand. *"Where are you?"* she messaged.

Seconds later came his reply, *"Still at Viktor's"*

Surprised by the immediacy of his response, she typed, *"Fancy a coffee at the Café Madal?"*

"On Hollán Ernő Street? Sure. When?"

Erika knew that the moment she returned to Teve Street she would once again be swept along by the momentum of the investigation, and there really was no time like the present. She typed, *"That's the one. How about now?"* This time she waited for ten seconds for a response, then added, *"Unless you're busy..."*

"I'm on my way," he replied.

She glanced into her rear-view mirror. The ends of her lips curled upwards. Perhaps, after all, this one was a keeper.

Her phone rang. It was Eszter, presumably checking in. The temptation to engage, to get into the detail, to direct events was as strong as ever. This time, though, Erika's willpower to resist was even more powerful.

She accepted the call. "I've been to see the funeral director. I need some time to get my head straight. You know what to do. I'll see you around midday."

Eszter sounded matter-of-fact. "No problem, boss. See you later."

The priest doused Nora Kelemen's coffin with Holy Water and said his final blessing before the purple velvet curtains parted. Erika, dressed all in black, gasped when the coffin slid effortlessly forward, towards the eight-hundred degree heat of the chamber. Even though a week had passed since her mother's death, the grief she felt was still overwhelming. She knew her grief would eventually wane. She had no such expectations concerning the guilt of not being there at the end. That was something she knew she would carry forever.

She had attended many funerals, but today was a very different experience at the Fiumei Road Graveyard. Only five other socially distanced mourners were present, each wearing a black face mask. Hearing her gasp, Marcel instinctively held out his hand, reaching for hers. Yet the physical gap between them was too far to bridge. Her brother David, seated across the narrow aisle, bowed his head and made the sign of the cross.

Outside the crematorium the sky was leaden and the rain fell in sheets. Six umbrella carrying mourners emerged, and stood for several seconds in sombre silence.

Erika smiled ruefully. She thanked Greta Madár, the manager of the Daybreak Nursing Home for coming. She also thanked Dora who had taken a day's leave to attend. Eszter was there too. Erika gave her a thin smile. She desperately wanted to hug her colleague, but knew it was not allowed.

David approached from behind. He had left Erika to make the funeral arrangements, claiming pressure of work. It had suited her too, not to have him interfering.

"How are you feeling, sis?"

"Worse than ever," she replied. "I should have been there."

David stooped under her umbrella and put his arms around her. After so many years, it felt uncomfortable for her, and probably for him. His moist eyes peeped out over his mask and connected with her own.

He said, "You have nothing to feel guilty about. You've been there for her, ever since Father died. If anyone should feel guilty, it's me."

It was the first bit of empathy she could ever recall hearing from her brother.

She said, "We're not meant to hug, what with the virus."

He tried to pull away, but she held onto him for a few seconds longer.

On the way back to the parking-lot, Marcel produced a silver hip flask, unscrewed the lid and offered it to Erika.

"It will take the edge off. I'll drive."

Erika had booked the whole day off as compassionate leave. She took a long swig. The distinctive herbal taste of the Unicum spread from her throat to her chest and made her cheeks glow. Marcel put his arm around her shoulder and squeezed. She nuzzled in close and, in step with one another, they meandered slowly towards the car.

Zoltán Varga was lying on his bed, when his cell door crashed open and a warder barged in.

"On your feet and follow me. You've got a visitor."

Other than his lawyer, it was the first visitor he had received during the eight months he had been on remand. The warder led him into the prison chapel and handcuffed him to a table. Zoltán instantly recognised Father Jakob from the Order of Malta.

"Keep your distance from him, Father. I'll be waiting outside."

The priest nodded. "I know the drill, thank you."

When they were alone, the priest said, "How are you, my son? You've lost weight since we last met."

Zoltán said, "The f-food is bad."

"Father Laszló asked me to pay you a visit. He's worried for your well-being. We all are."

Zoltán paused, his head bowed. Unlike the dark anonymity of the confessional box, where the priest was hidden from view on the other side of the screen, here there was no hiding place. He felt Father Jakob's eyes boring into him. His bottom lip trembled. "Is he still in c-custody?"

"He is, my son."

"Grandma told me he was like a saint on earth. He looked after us. Even when he was tortured, he never betrayed his parishioners. She said, after he was sprung from the House of Terror, he was leading from the front. Fighting against the Russians."

"Quite the hero."

Zoltán swallowed, tears welling in his eyes. "She said I had to obey him at all times. He touched me sometimes, and told me I'd go to hell if I didn't do what he said."

Torrid memories came flooding back. Tears streamed down his cheeks, and he gulped.

"I was eight years old when it started."

"Have you ever spoken to anyone else about this?"

Zoltán shook his head. "Never."

"He's behind bars now, Zoltán. He can no longer hurt you. Nevertheless, it's important that you speak to no one else about this. Do you understand?"

"W-will the Order punish me?"

The priest looked sternly at him. "You surely don't mean the Order of Malta, do you?"

Zoltán shook his head.

"No!" he gulped. He had said too much. He was alone, without protection. Now, more than ever in his life, he feared the Order, even more than he feared the eternal flames and everlasting pain of hell.

Father Jakob stepped forward. He clasped hold of Zoltán's hands and slipped a set of rosary beads into them. "Pray to Our Lady. She will bring you comfort and support."

"I told you to stand well back, Father," called the warder who was standing in the open doorway, arms folded across his barrelled chest.

Father Jakob stepped back several paces. Cheeks burning, he turned and left in a hurry.

Chapter Fourteen

I t was late March when Father Laszló Rákoczy and Zoltán Varga were finally brought to the Budapest Regional Court to answer the charges against them.

For the last ten months Erika had eagerly anticipated this day, which, given the complexities of the trial and her previous experience of delays in the Hungarian criminal justice system, had come earlier than many had expected. As the senior investigating officer, she had devoted hundreds of hours to preparing the case, working with lawyers from the Chief Prosecutor's Office. It had been her full-time job, preventing her either from taking on further homicide cases, or from returning to her former role in Financial Crime Investigation.

Global media interest in the trial of the so-called *Budapest Butcher* - a label which Erika had always despised - had already reached fever pitch. While taking her own seat inside the courtroom, Erika spotted Joe Baker, the renowned international reporter, sitting next to the local TV journalist, Viktoria Gindl.

Baker leaned over to ask, "Where does the jury sit?"

In her usual loud, obnoxious manner, Gindl replied.

"There are no juries in Hungarian trials. Don't they teach you anything at CNN?"

When the two accused men arrived in the courtroom, there was a great commotion. They were surrounded by a dozen heavily armed counter terrorism officers, each wearing balaclavas to protect their identities. Father Laszló shuffled in. He had been given permission to wear his priestly garb for the trial: black suit and clerical collar. Varga's head was shaven and he had grown a beard. He wore a plain grey t-shirt and black jeans. Both were handcuffed, and several burly guards separated them.

Minutes later, everyone rose when the panel of three judges entered.

The Clerk of the Court promptly read out the charges.

"Laszló Bence Rákoczy, you stand before this court accused of four indictments of murder and one of attempted murder. That on the 19th of May, twenty-twenty, you did murder Klára Menges, contrary to common law…"

From across the steeply banked, semi-circular gallery, Erika observed that Lotti Menges' gaze was firmly fixed on the backs of the defendants. They had taken the life of her sister and tortured her hideously. Although the two sisters had been estranged, their meeting on the day of Klára's death had temporarily brought them back together again. In her witness statement, Lotti had expressed guilt at leaving her sister early on that fateful afternoon. "If only I had stayed longer, she may still be alive."

"… That on the 21st of May, twenty-twenty, you did murder Ervin Nagy…"

Two rows further back in the amphitheatre-shaped chamber, Mr and Mrs Juhász, the next door neighbours who had found the body of Ervin Nagy, craned their necks to see the action. During a second round of witness interviews and some prompting by Axel Rácz, Mr Juhász had finally recalled seeing a priest and another man leaving the vicinity of the crime scene at lunchtime on the twenty-first of May. He had subsequently picked out Father László in an identity parade and would be called as a witness during the trial.

"… That on the 25th of May, twenty-twenty, you murdered Zsigmond Horvát…"

Near the back of the gallery, József Urbányi looked on impassively at the naming of his former neighbour. He was the thirty-two-year-old manager of the burger bar below Horvát's top-floor apartment. He had alerted the local police when his own flat became flooded from above, after he could not rouse Horvát. Erika had been shocked but not entirely surprised to hear how trade at the burger bar had benefited from its macabre notoriety, when the location of the killing had become public knowledge in the media.

"… That on the 26th of May, twenty-twenty, you unlawfully took the life of Támas Németh…."

Mr Gogan, the neighbour who had heard Németh's dog barking in the night and come to investigate, sat pale-faced next to his wife. Being deeply religious and of the Catholic faith, they had expressed their disbelief to the police regarding the charges being made against a man of the cloth.

"And, that on the 27th of May, twenty-twenty, you attempted to murder Ambrus Sipos…"

Beatrice Sipos leaned forward on her elbows. Her father had died of a heart attack, barely a week after the attempt on his life, although his brain tumour may have played a significant part in his demise. Beatrice – the sole heir to his fortune and business interests – believed the priest had brought about her father's premature death. She had travelled from her home in Toronto in order to attend the trial and, as reported in social media, was determined to see the man responsible brought to justice.

Erika sat to one side of the courtroom from where she could watch the entire scene unfold. Her eyes turned towards the three judges – two men and one woman – and she studied their facial expressions. All three remained impassive.

"Laszló Bence Rákoczy, having heard the charges against you, how do you plead?"

Erika switched her gaze towards the priest, as did everyone in the courtroom. Father Laszló looked calm. He stared directly at the Clerk.

He said, "As God is my witness, only he will ever judge my sins." Then, in one seamless motion, he raised his handcuffed hands up towards his throat. It appeared at first as though he may offer a prayer, until he yanked at his clerical collar, stuffed it into his mouth and began to masticate voraciously.

Erika saw what was happening and screamed out a warning cry. "No!"

Leaping from her seat, she vaulted the barrier and took desperate strides in the priest's direction. Her arms flailed as she reached for him, only stopping short when she slammed into the butt of a semi-automatic rifle. The unyielding bulk of one of the armed guards wrestled her down to the floor.

"Stop him!" she yelled, her head twisting, desperate to keep the priest in view. He had collapsed. It was at floor level that her eyes met his. It was there she saw his features spasmed in pain.

The guards had already formed a circle around the priest, their backs towards him. They seemed more interested in keeping others away than in giving him the urgent medical attention he needed.

Above the pandemonium, Erika heard clearly the hysterical voice of Zoltán Varga, He was screaming something that sounded like "Abaddon."

Erika squirmed on the floor in pain, the knee of the guard pressing down on her neck.

"Let her up," said a voice she recognised.

Certain the voice belonged to Rudolf Kudár, Erika was determined to implore him to allow medical attention for the stricken priest. But by the time she scrambled to her feet, Kudár was gone.

The doors of the courtroom burst open dramatically and a team of paramedics rushed in, making a beeline for the prisoner who appeared to be having a fit on the floor.

Meanwhile, four guards bustled Zoltán Varga out of the dock, disappearing with him down the stone staircase, towards the cells.

"Clear the court. Clear the court!" shouted the head judge, frantically banging his gavel.

A team of security men did as they were bade until they restored relative calm.

Erika, who had waved her ID in the faces of the security guards, paced anxiously and insisted she remain in what was now a crime scene.

Several minutes later, her worst fears were confirmed. Father Laszló Rákoczy was pronounced dead at the scene by the chief paramedic.

A week after the courtroom debacle, and for the first time in her career, Erika was required to take the lift to the executive suite at Police Palace. In the pocket of her dress uniform was a letter, written on fancy notepaper and headed, 'From the office of Lena Petrus, Deputy High Commissioner of the Hungarian National Police.' It was an invitation to attend a ceremony of her own commendation at 11.00 a.m., on Tuesday, 6 April 2021, and she could not have been more surprised to receive it.

She straightened her hat in the mirror. When the lift doors opened on the top floor, Commander Rácz stood waiting for her.

He too was also wearing dress uniform. She had to admit to herself how impressive he looked. Tall, barrel-chested, buttons gleaming. What struck her most of all was he was clean-shaven. Beardless for the first time in the twelve years she had known him, and he looked ten years younger.

He looked her up and down. "Very presentable,"

"You scrub up well too, sir, if you don't mind me saying."

His cheeks flushed pink.

He said, "Before we go in, let me give you some advice. Only speak when you're spoken to and address the DHC as ma'am. Say nothing controversial. Just accept the commendation and leave when I give you the nod. Okay?"

Was this a serving police officer she was about to meet for the first time, or the Queen of England? She bit her tongue.

"Understood, sir."

The large, ornate double-door at the end of the lobby opened. A young blonde woman wearing a sharp navy blue trouser suit, white blouse, and navy heels beckoned them to enter. "The Deputy High Commissioner will see you now," she said with a warm smile.

Axel Rácz led the way, and Erika followed close behind. The soles of her shoes sank into deep-piled carpet. Her nose twitched as she picked up the earthy scent of leather, together with some sweet undertones of beeswax polish. Her eyes flicked from side to side, taking in the expensive teak furniture, plush upholstery, silver-framed photographs on the credenza, and certificates on the wall behind the executive desk.

The first face she recognised belonged to Levente Barna from the media department. He was standing by one of the floor-to-ceiling windows, and alongside him was an older man with an expensive-looking camera with a long lens, which was hanging around his neck. Erika exchanged nods with Levente and was about to say something when in walked an elegant woman with a silver-grey bob-cut, wearing a similarly styled uniform to Erika's. Their significant differences in rank were abundantly clear by what she carried on the epaulettes and collar of her immaculately pressed green jacket. Erika had read on her Wikipedia profile that Lena Petrus was sixty-two years old. Her youthful complexion made that difficult to believe.

"Detective Kelemen, what a pleasure it is finally to meet you. And Commander Rácz, it's good to see you again."

"Ma'am," said Rácz.

Erika echoed him.

"I believe you have already met Levente from the media department. I've asked him to make the most of today's little celebration." She moved gracefully to the far end of her spacious office and stood in the space between the Hungarian national flag and the flag of the National Police Force. She beckoned Erika to join her and said, "The two-metre rule is unhelpful for photo opportunities, but we should abide by it."

While the photographer organised his subjects, Lena Petrus turned to Erika and spoke loud enough for everyone in the room to hear.

"Detective Kelemen, your achievement in bringing the two murderers to court is worthy of recognition, even if one defendant took his own life to evade justice. Dates for the retrial of the second defendant will be set shortly, and justice will no doubt take its course. It is, therefore, my pleasure to mark your success by awarding you an official commendation. Your hard work and dedication will serve as an example to all detectives, including other women in the force who aspire to follow in your footsteps. Congratulations."

The photographer snapped away and Levente took notes. Commander Rácz caught Erika's eye, subtly gesturing towards the exit.

Perhaps sensing his eagerness to leave, Lena Petrus summoned the PA and instructed her to serve the champagne.

"You'll stay for a toast, won't you Axel? Birgit, a glass for the commander."

Before Rácz could utter a word, the Deputy High Commissioner turned to Erika.

"The view from up here is spectacular. Come and see for yourself, Detective."

Then, in one smooth but decisive movement, she guided Erika out onto the balcony.

High above the city, Erika's teeth chattered. But the view from the wrap-around balcony at the very top of the circular tower was truly magnificent. Beneath the clear blue sky, the Danube glistened like quicksilver, as it meandered north to south to the horizons and bisected hilly Buda to the west from flat Pest and the east.

"I admire your resilience, detective. We both know you've had to deal with the misogyny that is commonplace, but you've battled through, and I like that."

Erika felt dumbfounded by the woman's frankness, and did not know what was expected in return. The warning received from Axel Rácz to say nothing controversial rang like a siren in her head. For the moment, she held her tongue.

Petrus continued, "It was me who urged Commander Rácz to give you the opportunity to come back to homicide. And, although you may not thank me, it was me who told him to put Rigo on your team. I read your file, and I know about your unresolved complaint in 2015. I thought that by putting you in charge of Rigo, I would see what you are truly made of. So tell me, Detective, how are you feeling right now?"

How did she feel? For one thing, she felt confused. Petrus knew more about her than she ever dreamed of. But was the woman more intent on helping her career, or in playing her like a pawn?

Erika said, "How I feel is angry."

"Angry with my interference, or about Rigo?"

Erika laughed. "Idiots like Rigo don't bother me, ma'am. And you were doing your job, to fill gaps when the homicide team was under pressure."

Lena Petrus fixed Erika with a steely gaze.

"Then it's something else. Speak up. You wouldn't be here if I didn't want to hear the truth from you. From what I understand, your bluntness is one thing that sets you apart."

For one moment, she had the attention of the Deputy High Commissioner and was being pressed to speak her mind. This was an opportunity she could not pass by.

"Ma'am, the prosecutors have more than enough evidence with which to convict the second defendant, Zoltán Varga. But it was the priest, Father Laszló, who pulled his strings. I'm certain the priest was not working alone. Someone supplied him with that cyanide impregnated clerical collar. The prison governor confirmed Father Laszló received Holy Communion from a priest on the morning of his trial – from Father Jakob, the chaplain of the Order of Malta. Then, despite the high security measures in the courtroom, not one guard tried to intervene during the prisoner's very public suicide. Also, according to the priest, the production of the dossier we discovered in his accommodation, was the work of an underground organisation. It was stolen from the Ministry and used by Father Laszló to trace and contact the victims. The dossier was confiscated from us. It's vital evidence, and is essential for an ongoing investigation into who really is behind these murders. That's why I'm angry, ma'am."

Deputy High Commissioner Petrus gazed into the distance. After a while, she turned and spoke. "It looks like you have the balls to go further, Detective Kelemen. But my advice is to stay safe and remember, a dead detective achieves nothing. Now, let's go inside and try that champagne, shall we? Commander Rácz will wonder what's keeping us."

Back inside, Erika declined the offer of chilled champagne, but was pleased to receive a mug of hot coffee, to warm her hands on. While Lena Petrus conversed with Axel Rácz, Levente chatted with Erika about an article he intended to write and would place in the next edition of the police magazine.

"How does 'Women in the Modern Hungarian Police Force,' sound as a working title?" he said.

Erika bit her tongue. She had already been outspoken enough for one day.

ACKNOWLEDGEMENTS

I first visited Budapest in 2009, but the inspiration to write a novel set in in the city came in the autumn of 2016, during a dinner with friends and colleagues at the Four Seasons Gresham Palace Hotel. We normally dined in pubs and cafes, but on that occasion the boat was pushed out in style, to mark my forthcoming retirement from the multinational company we all worked for.

Several plots for a Budapest-based novel were tested and subsequently placed on the back burner, before a friend suggested that I should pay a visit to The House of Terror Museum on Andrássy Street. Commissioned in 2002, the House of Terror serves as a stark reminder of the forty-five years of totalitarian rule of Hungary, under both Nazi and Communist oppressors. I wasted no time and took the guided tour that same day, on the 16th of July, 2019. The brutality of the place and its exhibits was harsh, and it became easy to picture oneself being held captive and tortured alongside the many hundreds of named victims whose images adorn the walls of the museum.

My ideas continued to percolate, until I finally began to outline the plot and write *Confession* during the first Covid-19 lockdown in 2020.

Confession was a challenge to write. Among several themes that needed in-depth research was the mental condition and treatment of Zoltán Varga. My thanks go to the Mental Disability Advocacy Centre (MDAC) and the Hungarian Helsinki Committee (HHC) for their report entitled *Prisoners or Patients: Criminal Psychiatric Detention in Hungary,* published in Budapest on 9 August 2004. For background information concerning the October 1956 uprising and the hateful mentality of the AVH Secret Police, I was particularly inspired by James Michener's *The Bridge at Andau,* first published in 1957 by Random House. Although largely a work of historical fiction, *The Bridge at Andau* is based on Michener's interviews with many Hungarians who had lived through more than a decade of Soviet oppression, and survived the quelling of the October 1956 uprising.

For her first-hand knowledge of Hungary in general, and Budapest in the '50s, I am also eternally grateful to my friend, Julianna Lancaster. Julianna was ten years old, living in Buda, when she and her family were shot at from the balcony of the parliament building during the failed people's revolution. They managed to flee Hungary shortly after, and headed to England via Austria. Despite being stripped of her citizenship, Julianna successfully applied to regain her Hungarian passport after the collapse of the communist regime. She now owns homes in both London and Budapest and spends time in both cities.

Thanks also to my developmental and copy editor, Tiffany Shand. Thanks also to Phyllis Ngo and the team at 100 Covers for my cover design.

There has been an author's fire burning inside me for more than forty years, but this first novel would never have been written without the support of my close friends, my family, my Beta readers, coaches, mentors and trainers. Thank you to those special ones who gave me the confidence and motivation to write and publish.

ABOUT THE AUTHOR

Steve Dickinson was born in 1957 in Liverpool, England, and brought up in the Roman Catholic faith. After graduating with an engineering degree from the University of Liverpool, he spent a forty year career in the world of manufactured building products, travelling the globe for business. He says, "Communicating with people at all levels, and in many countries, has always been a key part of my role. Writing and presenting has been central to that. How could I not want to write?"

Now a recovering international businessman turned author, Steve says, "Ultimately, stories are the only way to change the world, which makes writers very powerful people."

He lives with his wife in the beautiful English county of North Yorkshire and is a proud father and grandfather.

Set in Budapest, Hungary, a city where he has worked and explored extensively, *Confession* is Steve's first novel.

He can be found at SteveDickinsonBooks.com

Free Bonus #1

I hope you enjoyed this book. Writing a novel is like making a movie: a lot of material gets left on the cutting room floor. I originally wrote a prologue to reveal how Erika came to be thrown out of the Budapest Murder Squad in 2015. It was edited out, but if you are curious you'll want to know more about "the whole sorry episode," and what really happened on that fateful day.

To discover what happened when Erika was thrown out of the Murder Squad, visit SteveDickinsonBooks.com and download your FREE BONUS CHAPTER

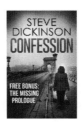

Free Bonus #2

T hank you for reading **Confession.** When the body count of tortured octogenarian victims rose, Erika discovered links to the Cold War era and deadly grudges that have their origins in Hungary's dark, post WW2 history. As a special bonus for my readers, you can download **House of Terror**, a short story set during those dark times in Budapest, containing crucial backstory to one of the characters in the book.

Visit SteveDickinsonBooks.com and download your FREE COPY OF *HOUSE OF TERROR.*